The

HIMALAYAN KINGDOMS

By

VISHAL SINGH

THE HIMALAYAN KINGDOMS

For My Father...

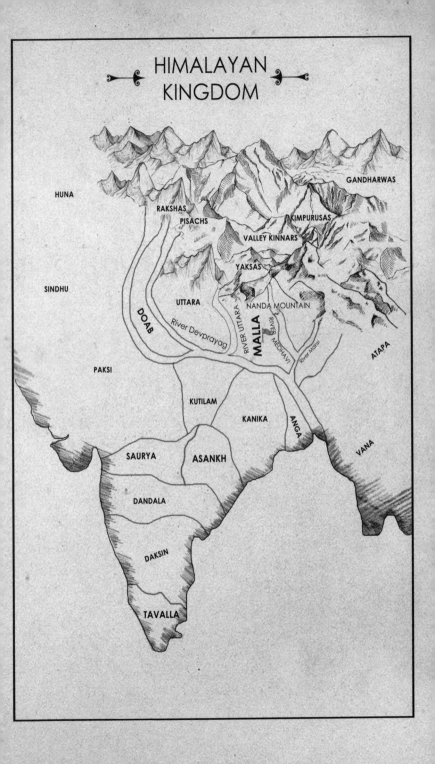

MALLA KINGDOM
OGANA

HIMALAYAN KINGDOMS

By

VISHAL SINGH

Vishal Singh

CHAPTER 1
The Sunrise

At the very first ray of sun, Om was standing outside Rishi's house. Eager to see his guru again, he slid down from his horse, grabbed his bag, and walked inside.

When he saw Rishi meditating, he thought he would come back later, so as to not disturb him. He had placed the offerings in a bag in a corner of Rishi's hut and turned to head back home when out of nowhere something caught his foot and he stumbled backwards.

"Meer," he muttered, regaining his balance before he noticed Meer's strange behavior. Meer pawed at the ground, snorting loudly, his bright eyes wild with panic.

Not able to control the horse, Om looked around to see what was wrong. Shocked, he saw a leopard sitting in the top of the tree below which Rishi was meditating. Om had seen the hunters of the forest before and knew they lurked in wait for their prey—stalking them from above

1

before dropping down and tearing them to pieces. The thought of the consequences made him tremble. A knot of panic rose in his chest.

With one fluid motion, he drew his bow and aimed an arrow at the leopard. The moment before releasing his positioned arrow, he heard a voice that sounded very much like Rishi's. "Stop, Om!"

Om was the favorite student of Guru Rig Muni, or "Rishi," as some people called him. Rishi not only taught Om about their religious scriptures, but he had also trained him to be a warrior of unprecedented power and strength.

The night before, Om's mother had instructed, "Don't forget to bring these offerings to Rishi" as she set aside a bag of food.

Om's big white horse, Meer, was waiting outside. He whistled, and Meer trotted over. He leapt up on him, and they made their way to the forest.

Om contemplated the rationing of the rest of his night. His favorite place was the forest. He liked hanging on trees and playing his flute. He relished the solitude of the wilderness and communing with nature. He could meditate there for hours, feeling in tune with every tree, bush, and blade of grass, sensing the slow fermentation of fallen leaves, and hearing every rustle of the wind.

Om had become tremendous at sitting still; even the birds didn't notice as he hid in plain sight. Wild animals often approached him, fearless and unafraid of the young man who sat in their midst, perfectly still except for his breathing. He liked the squirrels and birds best; their innocent curiosity charmed him.

Practicing archery right at dusk, he would take Meer for rides that lasted past sunset. Testing himself and reveling in his own strength, he liked climbing mountains and rocks—often trailed by animals and birds in the forest, whom he considered friends.

Om considered his evening and decided to practice training Meer. The horse was his best friend, and Meer seemed to enjoy testing himself as much as Om. Lurking in a tree, Om decided to startle Meer. He jumped down and landed on the horse's back. Meer whinnied in surprise, then nosed his friend.

After he spent some time clearing his mind and soaking in every detail of the vernal world around himself, Om and Meer rode to the hilltop.

His haven was on top of a banyan tree there. People said that it was a magical place—so beautiful that angels visited it at night.   Om knew the stories, and sometimes he would go there late at night to see if they would appear.

Still, he could never stay away all night; his mother would wait for his return. Om didn't want to distress her, so he decided it was time for him and Meer to return home.

Though Om had roamed much of the forest that night, he had no idea that the next morning would bring him before one of its greatest hunters.

Om paused as a voice like Rishi's told him to stop before he shot the leopard. Om turned around, but he saw no one. He aimed again and heard the same voice coming from behind.

"Leave the leopard be; it will do no harm to me."

When he looked back, he saw that Rishi had not moved his lips—not even stirred a hair.

"Who is that?" Om yelled, and started looking everywhere, his arrows still stretched and aimed.

The leopard, now on the ground, idly pawed at Rishi's feet and simply sat down. Om decided to stay with Rishi to ensure the leopard did him no harm. His concern subsided as the beast seemed to rest, not moving. Om sat very still, trying to accept the great hunter, but his heart still beat wildly.

After a few hours, the leopard ran into the forest.

At dusk, Rishi opened his eyes, saluted the sun, and said to Om, "Why don't you cook the rice you brought?"

"How did you know?" asked Om, confused. "You never saw me coming, and your hut isn't visible from the direction you were meditating. Even I didn't know what was in the offerings."

"Come see me before sunrise tomorrow, and I will tell you."

Om went home and couldn't sleep. The only thought in his mind was, *What will Rishi tell me?*

He spent the night looking restlessly at the bright stars.

At the very first ray of sun, Om, with Meer, was standing outside Rishi's house again.

"Good. Follow me." Rishi handed him a bag to carry.

Staggering for a moment under its weight, Om didn't ask what was inside the bag; instead, he asked, "Where are we heading?" He fastened the bag to Meer's saddle and took his reins, leading the horse next to him.

"You need only to trust me."

"Yes, Rishi."

They walked for a great time, and Om's curiosity rose again. "What are we heading towards?"

"The Northern Hills."

Om knew that the Northern Hills were a haunt of gurus and rishis, but he didn't know of another human who had ever visited them.

After walking for some time, Om asked, "How much further?"

Rishi said, "It's a long way. I have already informed your family of our journey."

They started passing through a dense forest. Each moment brought a new feeling for Om. Whenever they rested for water or food, Rishi taught Om something new.

"The first lesson is to control your senses," said Rishi.

They camped in the forest for a day while Rishi taught him the art of controlling his senses. Om tried and tried and felt nothing.

"It will come to you eventually. Listen, and follow my example. Controlling your senses is the first step towards full meditation. Whatever you did or knew before were droplets in an ocean," Rishi explained.

"But don't you want me to be a warrior?" asked Om. "I want to be a warrior, not a hermit!"

"Om, whatever I teach you during this journey will make you a better warrior—a warrior who will fight for justice and protect the truth; a warrior who will not fight for mere pleasure and games alone. I know that you have a lot of questions, and I intend to answer all those. You want to go to a land whose path only I know; you want to be a great warrior, the methods for which only I know. Have faith in me, and you will become what you are supposed to be."

The next morning, Om woke up early to prepare a meal before Rishi got up. He went to the nearby lake to fetch some water. There was fog all around them; the sunrise was still an hour away. As he entered the lake, he heard a voice.

He turned and saw nothing. After some time, he heard the same voice again. He turned, but still he saw nothing. Om got worried and tried to fill his pot as fast as he could, but in a rush, he dropped it in the lake. It immediately sank. He tried to reach for it, but he accidentally stepped on it and broke it.

He got out of the lake and started walking towards the camp to get another one.

At that moment, he heard another faint voice, which gently grew louder and sounded melodious. Thoughts of angels came to his mind, and he started walking towards the voice. Walking around the lake, he saw a hut in the distance.

He approached the hut, only to see a beautiful lady cooking something. He walked closer, and his movements alerted the lady. She turned, and Om could not take his eyes off her—such beauty, he had only heard of. *She is definitely an angel, such as those the people of my town talk about,* thought Om.

"Please, come. Sit…" the lady said before Om could open his mouth. She brought him some water and bread.

As she spoke about how peaceful life was in the forest, Om didn't realize that the sun had already risen and that Rishi would be waiting for him. He was lost in her enchanting voice.

"Why don't you rest, and I will bring some fresh fruit and water from the spring for you?" the lady said to Om.

Om happily lay down and fell asleep. In his dreams, he saw the same lady.

She was an angel who had come to destroy the meditation of a saint and, by mistake, had crossed paths with Om. As servants of the gods, both good and less benign, angels knew that some rishis were young, and even changed their appearances. She didn't want to take the risk and had decided to trick Om.

"If you are ready to pay attention, can we move forward now?" Rishi stood a step away from Om, his hands folded behind his back and his gaze fixed on his pupil.

Om got up to find himself lying in the mud near the lake, covered with wildflowers.

"Where is the hut, and the lady?" he asked.

"What lady, and what hut? I taught you to control your senses, not lose yourself in dreams. Now, with your permission, can we march ahead?" Rishi asked in an authoritative tone.

"Did you say the teachings on controlling my senses

7

aren't over yet? Then why are we going forward?" asked Om, beating the dirt off his clothes.

"We will walk for half a day towards a spring. There's a place to rest," said Rishi, completely ignoring Om's question. "Ready yourself; we are leaving soon."

Om prepared a quick meal, and they both, along with Meer, walked ahead. The charming lady from the hut was still on Om's mind.

After half a day's walk among majestic trees and beautiful animals, they finally came to the spring.

"Where would you like me to put up the hut?" asked Om.

"My dear Om, don't you worry. I have everything here."

Om looked around saw nothing and looked at Rishi with round eyes.

"Come with me."

He started walking up the spring, and stopped in front of an old tree that stood gracefully within an arm's length of a silvery waterfall.

"There it is: the path to peace," Rishi said, and pointed to the stairs going from the back of the tree towards the hill behind the waterfall. Leaving Meer there, they climbed the stairs and entered a beautiful cave that was partially lit with sunlight coming from the openings on the side of the mountain.

"This is the place where I learned from my guru and got enlightened."

Rishi and Om spent a few days in the cave. Rishi taught him different ways to control his senses and heighten his meditation. He also taught him how to utilize nature in doing so. The teachings were already having their effects on Om, but he was still ignorant.

Once during that time, Om meditated for half a day and didn't even realize it. The place was mesmerizing, and Om could have spent weeks or even months there. He gathered fruit and some rare roots to cook.

Sometimes, he would simply cavort with Meer, enjoy the misty pool at the base of the fall, and admire the beauty of the landscape. He was among the few who realized that everything in the world is meant to protect its other elements, in a balanced and equal rhythm. As nature was built to protect us, we were built to treasure its beauty.

From the hills of Malla, the journey continued towards the higher mountains. The mountain passage was difficult. There was no snow on the way, as it was summer, but it was still cold. They could still see snow on the mountain tops.

After walking for two days, Om asked, "How much longer?"

"It's time for you to learn patience. The journey forward will teach you everything about patience and how to align with the natural world," said the Rishi. "Worry not, as you are a disciple of Rig Muni and son of Vinayak."

After another two days' climb, they reached an old hut. It had a thatched roof and the front door was wide open. Flocks of sheep and cattle grazed and wandered in and around the house.

"Meet my friend and brother, Dinkar Muni," Rishi said to Om, bringing him back to attention. There was a man with long hair that reached his waist, a long beard that fell to his chest, and black eyes like death. "He will teach you how to master the art of fighting."

"Why can't I continue learning from you, Rishi?" asked Om. He was skeptical of the man.

"I am your guru, and I will always want to protect you. Unlike me, Dinkar has no feelings for you and will be a better master," Rishi explained.

After they had their meal, leaving Rishi to meditate, Dinkar Muni led Om to a nearby hill.

"Here is where you train. I will teach you how to shoot in the dark, by using sound to guide you. I will teach you how to master sounds and the air around you. I will teach you how to predict the movement of the sword of an enemy. I will teach you, young man, how to judge the next movement of your enemy simply by looking into his eyes," Dinkar said.

Thus began Om's mastery of all areas of warfare, including strategies, methods, and skills. He could soon hear and respond to the swing of a sword with his eyes closed. After a month of training, he could hear the sound of an arrow right as it was fired, even if it was a few yojanas away.

Rishi's lessons about controlling his senses aided him greatly. He began to understand why Rishi was so adamant that he learn them. Dinkar Muni taught Om so fiercely and combatively that it sometimes hurt him, but as Rishi had said, Dinkar Muni showed no concern for

Om's safety or well-being.

"You are a good disciple, young man. You will learn quickly," said Dinkar to Om.

Another seven days passed, and Om learned to hear all kinds of voices and to differentiate between them.

"Today will be the last day of your training, young man," said Dinkar. "In order to pass my test, you have to beat me."

Om was a bit worried and nervous—it seemed impossible. He accepted a blessing from Rishi, and the test began.

The first test was to shoot at hanging pots without looking at them. He had to listen for the sounds they made as they swung in the wind. They clattered and clanked, giving Om an idea of their location. One by one, he shot them, and they jangled to the ground.

The next task was to fight with a sword, then to defend himself from projectiles thrown at him. The last one involved shooting a moving object from horseback.

At the end of the day, after the test was over, Dinkar Muni announced, "You have failed the test."

Silently, Om walked away, his heart low.

Seeing him pad towards the hut, Dinkar Muni approached him. "You have passed."

Om was surprised. "How? I didn't beat you."

"I only said that so that you would try your best, and you did. You have passed, and now your guru will continue your training."

The next day, Rishi and Om said goodbye to Dinkar Muni and continued their journey forward. Om had started to feel glum during the beginning of this journey, but after his lessons with Dinkar Muni, he was excited to see what lay ahead.

After crossing two hills, the two reached the home of Om's next tutor.

This time, Om was introduced to Raga Muni, another friend of Rishi's, to teach him the art of strategy in warfare.

Raga Muni was a very different sage. He didn't even dress like other sages or rishis, including Rishi Rig Muni. He was a jolly man and was never serious.

Om spent two months learning how modern warfare was fought. He learned about different field arrangements in a war, and how and why each one of them was effective. There were at least a dozen basic tactics, and several others derived from them. Each war tactic was an arrangement for a different type of enemy. And out of a dozen, surprisingly eight were defensive. As per Raga Muni, warfare should only be a last resort, and it should start with a strong defense to deter your enemy.

Unlike Dinkar Muni's hut, Raga Muni's place was always clean and fresh, surrounded by an orchard of fruit trees. Even Meer looked happier here. Om spent his leisure time sitting in these fruit trees and talking to mountain birds.

Om further learned how communication and exploiting the opponent's secrets was an important part of war. He learned that a soldier's morale rests on his leader and that he will always follow a leader who has no fear. Om had to pass a test here, too, but this was a test of skills—he had to prove that everything taught to him was now in his heart.

After they left Raga Muni's place, Rishi said to Om, "You will be meeting Rudra Muni to learn the laws of nature and how to survive in the wilderness."

The teachings of Rudra Muni brought Om even closer to nature than he already was. From plants that would give life or death to roots that would give special powers to humans, Om learned a lot of things. He learned how to utilize herbs to cure and to kill, and how to utilize them for offense and defense. He learned about herbs that could heal deathly wounds. He learned about roots that offered enough energy to run for days without food, which were found only in certain mountains of the Himalayas. He learned how to check which water was drinkable and which was poisonous, and how to determine if the food was poisoned based on its smell. This was only possible after a few months of continuous training inside the forest among the massive trees. He was now so efficient that he could smell a meal and say what ingredients had been used to prepare the food.

It had been more than half a year since Om started on this journey with his guru. Om often thought about his home, the jungles, his parents, the fields, his friends, and not least of all, his brothers. He didn't know when he would see them again. However, he was excited to learn more and more. His appetite for knowledge was boundless. He had no idea how the future would unfurl for him, and where his path would lead him next.

CHAPTER 2
The Mountains of Rishis

After leaving Rudra Muni's home, they traveled towards the snow-clad Himalayas. After a day's travel, they camped at the foothill of a mountain. A rock hanging from the mountainside provided good shelter. Om went to gather wood for a fire; he had left Meer at Rudra Muni's home, as the path further along was no good for horses.

After dinner, Rishi asked Om to sit near him. "Whatever I tell you now, Om, you must remember by heart. The Mountains of Rishis is no place for men; only very learned hermits make it there. You will encounter guards before we enter the mountains. They will test you before they allow you to enter. As your guru, I am not supposed to help you; you have to pass the test on your own. Once you enter, you will see things you have never witnessed before—but don't show your surprise, and only consult me about such things in private. That's all

15

for tonight; take a rest now, as the path ahead is a tough climb," Rishi said, lying down.

"What will I do in the mountains, Rishi?" asked Om.

"Om, you will know once we enter." Rishi smiled. "Have a good sleep and worry not, my son. You are a superb disciple."

After a day-and-a-half-long climb, Om noticed the luminous mist floating below them. A lush green forest peeked through the holes in this dense veil of clouds. He couldn't bear moving on without taking a moment's pause to draw in the beautiful breeze. The serene scent of freshness that entered his nostrils brushed away his fatigue. But a moment was all he could spare. Om concentrated on the journey, as the climb was steep and arduous.

As the night approached, they camped in a cave to rest. The cave's opening looked like a slit in a rock, which extended inside to provide shelter and enough room for them to walk around. The systematic layout of the otherwise craggy walls gave Om an impression that it was manmade and used in journeys up and down the mountains. The sunset from this vantage was mesmerizing. Each moment brought him immense hope and happiness. He didn't know the exact purpose of his undertaking, but the more he learned, the calmer he felt within.

Om made dinner, and they ate and talked for a long time before he fell asleep. At the break of dawn, they left the cave and continued their laborious journey through the mountains.

And so it went…

After another four days of rigorous hiking, they reached the Mountains of Rishis. There was one way to the top of the mountain, and as Rishi had mentioned, it was guarded by two guards.

Wait, what are those? thought Om.

The majestic creatures guarding the gates were human to the waist, with the legs and bodies of horses. They were twice as tall as Om and heavily armored, and each one carried a spear in one hand and a shield in the other.

"You, human man, wait here. Rishi Rig, you are most welcome to the holy land," said one of the guards.

"I will meet you on the other side," Rishi said as he left Om there.

Once Rishi was nowhere to be seen, the guards approached Om and pushed him down the mountain.

As Om fell from the top, he wanted to scream, but no sound escaped his mouth. He could still see the guards watching him fall. They got smaller and smaller and finally disappeared. A throng of questions crowded his mind, but death squeezed them out.

Rolling down the edge and knowing that death was certain, he closed his eyes and prayed to God when the thoughts of his mother crossed his mind. Right before, where Om would have crashed onto the ground, he felt someone or something catch him, and he landed safely on the ground.

It took him some time to ease out of the shock and into the awareness of what had happened to him. He lay there peacefully on the dirt. The damp caress of grass between his fingers and on his bare feet was all he desired. But soon, realization seeped in: He was nowhere near the mountain top or with his mentor, Rishi. The only way ahead was to head home. He used all his knowledge and tried to determine the way home. Nothing helped. The jungle didn't seem to be the one they had crossed to climb the mountain—even the scent of its air was strange. He considered carrying on towards the sunset, hoping to find a town or hospitable family.

Om started his journey back home. He would need both his oldest and newest skills to survive and find his town. He identified the herbs and roots in the forest that he could use to quell his hunger. To counter any creatures lying in wait for him, he made a bow out of a bamboo tree and made some arrows. He sharpened the arrows with sharp stones and deftly fashioned a long wooden spear from a fallen branch, then hastened forward.

After walking for about a yojana, he felt like he was being followed or watched. Before he could assimilate his thoughts, he saw a dark figure jump from the top of a tree and land right in front of him.

The beast was carrying no weapon, but was almost half as tall as an elephant, with shining claws. With the face, mane, and muscles of a lion on the body and limbs of a man, he was a terrifying figure. The beast bared his teeth at Om in challenge.

Om blocked the beast's first blow with the top of his spear. Spinning it, he struck the monster's head with the bottom end of the spear. Before the beast could think, he fired an arrow that hit the creature's foot. It looked at him with burning eyes, ripped the arrow out and broke it into pieces before throwing it down.

Om aimed the next arrow at the beast's head. "I don't want to hurt you; we can talk. I am lost and looking for the path to my hometown of Medhya," said Om. "If you understand what I'm saying, let's not fight."

After Om finished his sentence, he lowered his guard. He knew he might be committing a mistake. The beast was still looking at him.

Suddenly, something struck Om, and he fell unconscious.

On waking, he found himself lying on the ground. Before him was the same beautiful lady he had met in the jungles of Medhya.

"Who are you?" asked Om.

"I'm the one who saved your life and brought you here," the lady replied.

Om saw a sword and a knife hanging by her side. The last time Om was conscious, the beast had been standing in front of him. However, someone had struck him from behind, so he knew that something was not right.

The lady brought Om something to drink. He was sure that the drink tasted ethereal, and he sensed that it might be poisoned.

With a swift movement, he got up and snatched her dagger.

With the dagger pointed at her neck, Om yelled, "Who are you? Don't make me repeat myself. I know you're not here to help me."

Suddenly, he heard an arrow fired at him; he along

with the lady jumped to the side and an arrow flew past them. Om couldn't see anyone at the arrow's origin point. With the lady still under his blade, he held his breath and concentrated on the sounds around them. He pulled his arm back and threw the dagger at his unknown enemy, letting it spiral through the air.

"Aahhhh!" came a cry, and it felt like ten elephants struck the earth.

Om drew the lady's sword and rushed towards the sound. After walking for some distance, he found nothing. There was a huge fallen tree, but he knew that the dagger would not have caused that. He returned back, but the lady had vanished.

"Om! How have you been?"

Om moved his head and was stunned to see Rishi standing next to him.

"When I heard you had left, I decided not to stay in the mountains any longer," said Rishi.

Om sensed that Rishi was lying. Other than his appearance, he seemed peculiar and strange. There was a hint of magic around him.

"Let's go home, kid," Rishi said.

Om kept all his feelings to himself and followed Rishi. It grew darker as they walked, but they continued forward. Om soon realized that they were going down the wrong path. After walking for a while, Om heard the sound of water—as though a deep waterfall was nearby.

"My dear son," said Rishi, waving his hand towards the waterfall, "our path goes downstream from the waterfall. Go near it and find a way for us to climb down."

It was a sharp fall. He could distinguish the waterfall, but not the spring or source. The sound was almost impossible to trace.

Where is the water coming from? thought Om.

Before Om could climb down, a strong gust of wind pushed him towards the sharp edge. He felt his legs give way as his feet slipped, and he fell feet-first into the abyss.

As Om fell, he took out his sword and tried to plunge it into a rock. Shrieking and sparking against the stones, the sword finally stuck in one of the rock openings.

From there, Om made a great effort, but he couldn't get to the top. He tried harder each time, but failed. Cursing and bellowing, he desperately tried to lift himself up. Right then, he heard movement at the top.

"Help!" he screamed as loud as he could, hoping that it was Rishi.

It was Rishi! He carried a long branch with him. "Hold on to this branch, and I will pull you up," Rishi said.

A few moments later, Rishi asked, "Are you holding the branch, Om?"

"Yes…"

"Let go of anything else you're holding."

Om knew that Rishi could not see him. "I'm hanging on to the branch," he lied.

The tree branch crashed down on Om, barely missing him. There was no sign of Rishi. He had appeared out of nowhere, then vanished the same way. Om let out a sigh of relief and tried to climb up again—but in vain.

After a while, Om couldn't hold on anymore. By sensing the noise of the waterfall and sound of the stream below, he gauged the depth of the water. As there was no way he could climb up, he pushed himself away towards the deeper water channel below, a few feet away from the falls.

Once he was ready, with every bit of strength he still had, Om pulled out his sword and heaved himself away from the cliff. He fell straight into the water.

As he fell, Om saw a bright blue light on the waterfall. It blinded him. He could see nothing, feel nothing, as though he was drifting away…

"Wake up, wake up!"

Om opened his eyes to see the giant guards of the mountain gates talking to him. He slowly rose to his feet and looked at them with surprise.

"Oh, human, you have to answer our questions before we can let you inside," said one of the guards.

What are they talking about? Where am I? What was all that? Who were the people I met? Was I dreaming? How did I pass out? What was the blue light? thought Om.

"Each one of us will ask only one question, and you have to answer it to our liking," said the other guard.

"Why are you here, human?" one of the guards asked.

This was the very question Om had held in his mind from the beginning, but Rishi had said he would get his answers only once they were inside.

A strange situation Rishi has put me into, Om thought. He would surely let Rishi know when they met again. For now, Om didn't know the answer, so he concentrated and recollected Rishi's lessons about places that surrounded the kingdom. Rishi had told him that mountain was only for rishis, sages who had attained siddhi.

"I am here to attain siddhi and gain knowledge," replied Om to the first guard.

"What would you do with such knowledge?" asked the other guard.

Om knew that this was a perilous question. Again, referring to the teachings of his guru, he knew that the purpose of knowledge was to better and enlighten people. Right or wrong, he went ahead with this answer.

"Dear human student, although your answers were not perfect, we have discussed the matter, and you can enter the mountain," said the watchman on the right.

Not perfect?! Discussed?!

Om hadn't even seen them talking. "Thank you," he mumbled.

Om entered the gate, which seemed to be made of ice. Inside, he saw Rishi waiting for him.

"You may now rest, Om. All your questions so far will be answered tonight. For now"—Rishi turned to look around—"I want you to behold the secret mountain and admire its beauty."

From the place where Rishi was standing, Om could see a lush valley. The towering trees and a green blanket of foliage sheltered many kinds of birds and animals roaming freely over the land. It was circled by snow-peaked mountains, plunging waterfalls, and raging rivers cutting through the rock and greenery. The roar of these distant waterfalls greeted Om. He took Rishi's permission, and the two of them climbed down towards the valley.

Clusters of shining orange flowers filled the air with their delicate aroma. The sound of birds flying above carried a trilling melody down to him. As he traveled further, he saw monkeys swinging from one tree branch to another. He could see a beautiful passage among the trees, all lined with flowers. He walked towards it, and it led him further inside the valley. Beautiful huts sat in between trees further inside. Next to them, Om saw many people meditating. Every one of them looked like a rishi, their faces glimmering with the radiance of eternal knowledge and awareness beyond the reality we are aware of.

Om stopped to look back for Rishi, and there he was, silently walking behind him.

"My son, the beauty here is the result of the meditation of hundreds of siddhars," said Rishi, inhaling the fresh scent of flowers around them. "Even surrounded by cold mountains, you won't feel cold—the warmth of the prayers, yajnas, and meditations keeps the whole place warm."

"Here, my dear Om, you will see many yogis and siddhars, and you will meet some of them." He paused and smiled. "Let's continue our journey towards my house." Rishi pointed in the direction they were heading.

"You have a house here?" asked Om.

"Yes, my dear. I am also a siddhar. Let's talk more while having dinner," Rishi replied, and started walking towards his home.

After washing his feet and hands, Om lay down to rest. He had so many questions to which he wanted answers.

Rishi had gone to arrange for dinner, and Om patiently waited for him to return.

The next morning, Om woke up very relaxed, as if the fatigue of his journey had washed away. Last night after dinner, he was so tired that he had slept outside the hut, and even forgot to ask his questions.

Om finally got up and went to fetch some water for Rishi. He came back quickly and started preparing food, wanting it to be ready before Rishi woke up. After the food was done, he went to wake Rishi up and found that he wasn't inside the hut. Om sat down in front of it, eagerly waiting for Rishi to return. As the wait grew longer, he got slightly anxious and began to worry. There was no point looking for Rishi, as this place was totally new to him.

The sun was fully up now. Before Om's anxious mind had abandoned him, Rishi arrived. "Will you accompany me, Om?"

Om followed dutifully. Rishi's hut was near the opening of the valley. Now Rishi took him deeper inside the forest, which was known as the "Forest of Saints."

"Whatever wonders you see, my son, I will explain to you at a latter part of the day," Rishi said.

Om, along with Rishi, toured the area and saw things he had never seen before. Hermits meditated in various postures. Some seemed to have been in meditation for years, not even aware of the birds and insects dwelling on them. One of them had been meditating for so long that a tree's branches had grown around him.

Rishi would speak occasionally, but he never talked

about things they saw.

Maybe Rishi is saving all the strange talk for tonight, thought Om.

Before sunset, they came to a peaceful river with low currents. Om saw a hermit in the middle of it. Undisturbed by his surroundings, he was praying with his hands up and out in the air. Both Rishi and Om sat there and took in the beauty around them.

A few moments later, when Om was still in his thoughts, he heard a voice. He stood up and saw the hermit from the river standing next to him.

"Meet Bhadra Muni, a siddhar and a guru. I have invited him to dinner tonight at our place," said Rishi. "He will be your guru during our stay in the Mountains of Rishis." Rishi and the siddhar talked for a while. Om stood nearby, his mind flooded with questions, eagerly waiting for the day to end.

Evening approached. As the sun was about to set, Om saw a flock of graceful white birds flying high in the sky. It seemed as if everyone was returning home. Rishi asked Bhadra Siddhar to accompany him to his house, and all of them started walking home.

Soon, Om saw a big white tiger following them, appearing from nowhere.

"Do not be afraid. He is a friend," the siddhar said, noticing Om's alert demeanor.

They finally returned home after sunset and sat down for a meal. The meal had already been prepared by one of the other disciples of Rishi. Both Rishi and the siddhar continued their talk as if they had met for the first time in a decade.

The food was delicious. After dinner, they sat around the fire. Om was waiting for Rishi and himself to be alone so he could get all his answers. Om was still waiting for the siddhar to leave, but to his surprise, the siddhar decided to stay with them.

Om went to bed with all his curiosity still burning within. He lay down and slowly drifted into a deep sleep.

Around him, he saw people with darkly painted faces—all meditating, chanting, screaming, and dancing around the field. All of a sudden, the chaos stopped. As one, they stared at him. Their red bloodshot eyes warned him, "Go away. This place is not for you. Go away."

Om started walking towards the fading light in the distance, avoiding every one of them.

Leaping from the dark, a white tiger jumped on him.

Om jolted up from his dream, his eyes wide with shock. He raked his hands through his hair and let out a long breath. For the following few moments, he stared blankly at the formidable white tiger lying beside him. Somehow, the beast didn't seem threatening. After a while, Om fell asleep again.

Early in the morning, Bhadra Siddhar woke Om up. "Follow me," he said.

They reached the side of the same river where they had met the day before. After a quick bath, they started with prayers and paid respect to the sun god.

"We will start your training at this moment," said the

siddhar. "First, let me answer all your questions."

Om was surprised; he had never asked Rishi about his doubts. "This is a peculiar land, and I don't fully understand why Rishi has brought me here," he confessed. "And I've seen so many strange people and creatures. Rishi told me to follow him without question, and I have. However, my curiosity still burns."

"So, here is a quick summary of what's beyond your kingdom. Only a few people know about this, and hopefully it will answer one of your questions," the siddhar said. "Towards the north of your kingdom, there are no kingdoms of men. There are kingdoms of Yaksas, Kinnars, Gandharvas, and Kimpurusas. All of them are demi-gods and have their own powers.

"The Yaksas are spirits who can take any form. The Kinnars are half-human and half-horse. The Gandharvas are close to gods and have different powers. The Kimpurusas are half-human and half-lion. None of them are either friends or enemies to mankind. Many of them have heavenly powers, exactly like the gods. All of them respect the rishis of these mountains.

"On the other side of the western mountains are the evil and unscrupulous Raksas. When they offer intense penance, thereby pleasing either Lord Brahma or Lord Shiva, they have the capacity to attain great powers, beyond mortal comprehension. However, these Raksas are enemies to men, gods, and demi-gods alike.

"The lady you met was an angel, and angels work in the court of the gods and serve them. On the gods' wish and command, they will stop the Raksas or anyone in intense meditation. They only stop those people whom the gods feel could threaten the lands under their protection. This answered your next question. Now, your final question, about why she met you, is not something I can read," the siddhar completed.

Om's eyes were still wide with questions, but he waited in respectful silence.

"Now it's time you learn about the siddhar," said Bhadra Siddhar. "Siddhars are rishis who, after many hundred years of meditation, gain powers that can control and alter the elements—like water, air, sky, spirit, and earth. Siddhars can have other powers as well. A siddhar's curse can change any living being's future, with adversities and misfortune befalling them for their heinous deeds. This is one of the reasons the Raksas fear us. A siddhar can take any shape, be omnipresent, and can control another's body and mind. They can see and hear distant things, even as far as the southern oceans. They can also decide when they want to retire from their bodies. These are not all the powers they have, and depending upon their mastery, everyone's powers vary. This is all useful for the balance of not only our world, but all other universes."

Many of these things were new to Om, and he was eagerly listening to the siddhar without interrupting him.

"I will teach you how to learn and control some of these powers, but siddhars gain these powers by meditating for hundreds of years. There are exceptions, but you cannot learn them all," said the siddhar. "I am also going to teach you how to defend yourself from these powers and be unaffected.

"These teachings will protect you from different heavenly powers and also increase your internal power and self-defense." Bhadra Siddhar finished the introduction, and Om's training began.

In the coming days, Om would learn how to detect and defend himself from heavenly weapons. To defend himself, the first lesson Om had to learn was to control his mind to a level he had not learned yet, not even from Rishi. They meditated for hours, sometimes days—not only on the ground, but also in water.

After some days had gone by, Om could feel the energy coursing through his body. Bhadra Siddhar's supreme expertise was in controlling minds. He could hear events from a long distance away, and even see them happening clearly. Bhadra Siddhar would often unleash his powers on him, and Om would counter them with his newly acquired skills. There was no rest, day or night, awake or asleep.

One night, he retired early. He was drained and tired. He made his bed and fell asleep almost instantly. After a good night's sleep, he woke, feeling fresh and eager to resume training. His eyes were still closed and he was lying peacefully. A strange yet familiar feeling of damp grass between his fingers and under his bare feet jolted his heart.

His eyes fluttered open. There he was—lying in the same place where he had fallen after the mountain guards pushed him off the cliff. He clenched his eyes shut, hoping this was a nightmare. He was still there. After going through all that he had, he would have preferred waking up in hell to this. Strange as it was, the series of events that followed were exactly like those before. He now thought he was trapped in a dream. He answered the same questions again at the gate and the guards let him in. Content, he assumed he had finally entered the Mountains of Rishis. As soon as he crossed the gate, he found himself lying on the ground again.

Clueless, his life was stuck in a loop of events he had no idea how to come out of. After the guards had allowed him in for the third time, he decided to take a different route.

Instead of entering the gates, he closed his eyes and took a leap of faith off the cliff. The impact of the fall snapped him out of the dream.

He heaved a long sigh of relief. Both Bhadra Siddhar and Rishi stood in front of him, smiling, while Om gazed at them, feeling pride in his own performance.

Such were the tests of Bhadra Siddhar. They got trickier and tougher as they went on.

Loka, Bhadra Siddhar's pet tiger, would take part in some of their training. Om had grown to respect the mighty beast. Slowly, Loka had also grown fond of Om. Loka listened to his commands and was soon able to read his signs.

After a few months, the training on self-defense was over.

"Now I will teach you how to use unearthly weapons," said the siddhar. He trained Om to wield these weapons with lethal precision. Each weapon blazed with the light of purity and its divine creation.

This training lasted for another month. Om had now learned how to defend himself and use some of the godly weapons.

"Each one is very powerful, and now you know how to protect yourself from the wrath of each one of them," the siddhar explained.

Learning all these techniques had transformed Om into a different human being. Instead of feeling more powerful, he felt subtly calm and more relaxed than ever. After the training, Om thanked Bhadra Siddhar, and finally returned to Rishi's hut.

After dinner, Om was washing Rishi's feet, when suddenly he saw someone like himself doing the same. A lightning strike ran through his body as he saw that the person washing the feet was none other than himself. The Rishi stood next to him.

Of all the things that he had seen and experienced since last year, this was the strangest. He thought this might be another dream, but the Rishi standing next to him told him it was not.

"Om," said Rishi, "I am also a siddhar, and my supreme powers are astral projection and telepathy. This is something that I am going to teach you to perfect. I have already been secretly teaching you without your knowledge. This is something that can be taught only from inside one's mind. Currently, what you are watching is actually happening, but I am controlling it from within your mind."

Pointing at the scene in front of them, he explained, "With this power, the mind leaves your body and can travel anywhere in the universe. During these travels, one can even control situations far from their current position, and one can travel and know things that would take years otherwise. You can use the powers from any corner of Earth and even the divine realms. I can teach you how to travel and watch, but you cannot change anything," said Rishi.

"After my teachings, you will not be able to consult or talk to anyone; merely to watch them. Since this siddhi would be something that I pass on to you from my years of labor, during these travels, you can always reach out to me. When you wake up tomorrow, you will possess these powers. The other downside of this is that you can only use these powers when I'm not using them—although you can still connect with me." Rishi completed his sermon. "Get up, Om. Time to go home."

Om opened his eyes and realized that the previous day had passed. He remembered everything that had happened last night. He got up and was ready to pack up for home.

"Before we head home, some people wanted to meet you," Rishi told Om.

Om saw that all his gurus from the time he'd started his journey were there, including the demi-gods that he'd met in his dreams and the guards at the gates. Om was surprised by the turnout.

"It's time to say goodbye," said Bhadra Siddhar. "We all have something to give to you, Om. You will carry these gifts for your protection and the protection of people that might need you in the near future."

"Om, my dear boy, here is something that would protect you from any attack," said Raga Muni and gave him a shield.

The shield was made out of the tusks of the elephants who'd once guarded the heavens. The shield was ivory white, and was made in such a way that it could slide and cover his left forearm.

Next, Om received a sword that had been carved from five elements. "The sword was crafted at the same place where the godly weapons like Shiva's trident were made. This sword cannot be destroyed by any power in this universe," said Rishi Dinkar.

The demi-god who was half-lion and half-man gave Om something made out of tiger claws. They extended out from the fingers on his right hand. "This is powerful enough to rip apart a mountain," said the demi-god.

Rudra Muni gave him a colorful headband that had a blue stone embedded in it. "Use the stone's powers when you feel the feeblest and the most defenseless."

"From me, my dear son, you have the best gift I can possibly give you," said Bhadra Siddhar. "You can take Loka with you. After all, he now likes and obeys you more than me," he said. "Loka is not from this world, and he will guide and protect you, as he has been doing for me." Bhadra Siddhar smiled at Om, and Loka came and stood by Om's side.

Om was overwhelmed. "Thank you all for your lessons and gifts," he said. "I will use them for the protection and defense of others, not merely my own power."

Everyone bade goodbye to Rishi and Om, and they started their journey back home. Om now had experienced things that people only heard in stories in his kingdom. From within, Om felt like a changed man.

"Thank you for taking me through this training, Rishi," he said, feeling the deepest gratitude towards his divine guru.

CHAPTER 3

Princess Abha and the Beast

After months of strenuous tasks and training, Om was more than happy to return home. Although he had grown stronger and even matured, at the first sight of his mother, Om ran and embraced her like a child. Tears of joy rained down their cheeks as his whole family welcomed him with joy. His father invited the entire town that night for a grand dinner. They all celebrated Om's return, and Om shared his stories and lessons with everyone. He made sure not to talk about anything that the town people wouldn't believe.

Slowly, the days passed and Om returned to his usual life in the town. Sometimes he practiced the knowledge and training he had gained, but most of the time, he did what he had been doing since he was little. He visited the jungle and the hills he had known since his childhood, now with Meer and Loka at his side. His tiger and his horse had bonded during their journey back home.

However, Rishi was not pleased with Om's daily activities. "Om, there will be more to your life than gallivanting about the hills."

"What would you suggest?" Om asked.

"Come to the city, to the palace, and meet the king. Om, are you paying attention?"

Om was stroking Loka's fur, kneading the scruff around his neck, and finally looked up. "But, Rishi, I belong in my town."

After a few more tries, Rishi gave up and realized that he had to trick Om into leaving the town. He was a siddhar who could even see glimpses of the future. He knew that the people of Malla would need Om soon. Rishi had a plan in mind, and he waited for the right time to put it into action.

Days later, Rishi left for the capital city of Ogana for a brief visit. "Om, take care of my home until I return."

"Of course," Om assented.

This was not a routine visit for Rishi—the king had called for him. Rishi was the esteemed guest of the palace and the king. The king would occasionally call for him if he needed Rishi's advice on the kingdom's affairs.

"Rishi, my honored guest," the king greeted him.

As usual, Rishi found kindness and respect from King Neera and his queen.

The king discussed at length some of the things that he had been hearing from locals from the northwestern part of the kingdom. There was some kind of beast destroying crops, killing farm animals, and terrorizing the people.

"Nobody has seen it, and the soldiers I sent there were unable to spot this beast," said the king. "I need your help to put an end to this cunning creature."

Rishi agreed. "I will visit the place myself and close the matter. I will collect some personal belongings from Medhya, and then head straight towards the northwest."

Before he left the palace, Rishi asked, "How is my dear princess?"

The queen politely replied, "She is in the retreat near Medhya, in the Garden of Flowers."

Rishi smiled and gave his blessings to the king and the queen. He then paid a visit to the royal temple and met with priests before starting on his journey home. This time, he had a task for his disciple, and he thought the beast at the northwestern borders would help him persuade Om to leave town.

Rishi arrived in Medhya late at night and was glad to see that, in his absence, Om had taken good care of his home. Om had already received notice of his arrival and had prepared dinner. The next morning, after prayers, Rishi closed his eyes and searched for Om with his telepathic vision.

Om sat blissfully on the branch of a tree overlooking the spring. His two friends, Meer and Loka, rested underneath.

With his mind, Rishi spoke to Om. "Om, get me the purple rose from the Garden of Flowers," came the order.

Om was a good disciple, and he never questioned

Rishi's orders. He rode towards the Garden of Flowers on Meer. "Loka, head back to the hut," he commanded.

Om had enjoyed this place a great deal before the king had made his palace there. He had avoided the garden since then. Once, he'd almost gotten into a tremendous fight with the palace guards. However, Rishi's orders were sacred words to Om.

He rode at great speed, as he wanted to be back before sunset.

The Garden of Flowers was spread across four hills, with the king's palace near the northern end. There was a stream that cut from the kingdom's leftmost river, Mansi, and passed straight through the Garden of Flowers to meet the Medhavi River in the south.

As he neared the garden, he tied his horse at the foothills a half-yojana away, and started walking. The guards were always near the palace, with occasional patrols all around the garden. Om wanted to avoid being seen by them. He headed towards a section that was full of different kinds of roses. He plucked a few of the purple roses, rolled them up in a cloth, and tucked the parcel in his belt.

Om was about to head back quietly, following the same path, when he heard a faint song. Curious, he slowly started walking in that direction, hiding behind the trees. He came to a place from where he could see a group of around half a dozen women singing and playing sitars. In the middle was a beautifully-dressed lady who looked like royalty.

Om had never seen such beauty before, and he knew

that she had to be the princess. The lady he had met in the forest didn't even come close. He sat on top of the tree and watched silently. Her beauty lit the place, as though he'd been transported to the gods' own chambers.

Rishi watched all this, wondering why Om was still hiding and not showing himself. Rishi called Loka. He turned Loka into a large black beast, gave him some instructions, and asked him to head to the Garden of Flowers.

Loka went straight to the garden and saw Princess Abha. When he was near enough, with a deafening roar, he lunged into the clearing. Hearing the tremendous sound, the guards shuddered with fear, while the ladies screamed and clung together.

The thunderous roar hit him like a wave. Om fell to the ground. The guards rushed towards the princess and formed a line in front of her. "Everyone, run back to the palace!" they ordered.

The fiery black beast jumped and blocked the princess from the other side. The guards had no choice but to form a circle with the princess inside. They blocked the way with the grounded shields and pointed their spears outward. A few guards were in the middle of the circle with the princess and her group.

One of the guards took out his horn and trumpeted to alert the other guards. Immediately a battalion from the palace rushed towards the princess, but it would take them quite some time to reach the garden.

The beast roared again and barreled towards the formation. He rammed into the shields, scattering the

41

soldiers. Om ran towards the beast with his tiger claws in his right hand. The beast ran towards him, and Om jumped, swiping at the beast with the tip of the claw. The impact was thunderous. After a moment, the beast was nowhere to be seen.

The princess watched all this through the openings between the shields.

Om looked at the soldiers. "The situation seems to be under control."

"Form a walking line, with the princess in between you," ordered the soldier's captain. They walked towards the palace.

The princess came forward to reward Om, but he was long gone. She had never seen another man as brave or as handsome—especially one who could knock a beast down with only one blow.

As soon as the princess reached the palace, she told her captain, "Send your men to the town and look for the man who saved me. I want to visit him and express my gratitude in person."

"I will send the men tomorrow to the nearby town of Medhya," he agreed.

On Meer, Om rode back to Rishi's hut, distracted by the princess. When he reached Rishi's hut, he handed over the flowers.

He was about to tell his tale when Rishi told him, "Pack up everything. We're heading to another side of the kingdom."

"We are?"

"A demon is threatening the livelihoods of the people there."

"But…" Om was not in the mood to leave. He hoped to return to the Garden of Flowers the following day. But Rishi's orders were sacred, and Om obeyed.

With a deep sigh, Om packed his things that night. After taking blessings from his parents, Om went to bed.

Before sunrise, Om and Rishi began their journey. Loka accompanied them, along with Meer. The journey was long, and they had to pass through the capital city of Ogana.

In a few days, they reached Ogana, but didn't enter the capital. They stayed with a friend of Rishi's and gathered more supplies for the rest of their journey.

The next morning, they continued their journey. During their travels, wherever they stayed, they met and interacted with the locals. Most of them were afraid to see the white tiger walking calmly among them. Some were interested to know how they'd tamed the tiger, but others ran away.

Meanwhile, the princess's men looked everywhere in the town of Medhya but could not find Om. Other than the description, they knew nothing about him. The captain told the princess, "We couldn't find the man, but were told about a man fitting the description."

Princess Abha and her guards went to Om's home. She met Om's father and heard about Om's journey. The others in Om's family were so overwhelmed that at first, they even forgot to ask her to sit.

The princess asked Om's father, "Would you bring your son to the capital to meet me once he's back?" Thanking his family, she didn't stay long, and started her journey back towards the capital.

After half a month of travel, Rishi and Om reached their destination: the northwestern frontier town of Himal. The head of the town, Dana, greeted them. "You are welcome to stay in a hut near the end of the town, at the mountain's foothills. It's a beautiful sight."

It was true. Around the hut and the town were distant snow-covered peaks, elegant plantations all around, brightly colored homes, and lavish farms with a few animals.

Later during the night, Dana came to visit them again for dinner. "The Raksas you came here to tackle has wreaked havoc in the whole town. He attacks us every few weeks, takes a dozen animals with him, and burns anything that stands in his way. He's damaged most of our crops and fruit trees. This has been happening for a year now. The king sent some more soldiers last month, but they were unable to defend us. The only thing that keeps us here is the fact that the Raksas doesn't kill humans, but we know that it will come for us once all our livestock are devoured."

After dinner, Om and Rishi discussed and concluded that the best option was to wait and watch. The Raksas showed up often, and it was decided that it was best to tackle him right outside the town.

Om passed his time in the new town by practicing with

his sword and ivory shield, and he now also involved Loka in his practice. He had become immensely attached to the white beast and communicated with him using signals or eye movement. Sometimes, Om thought Loka knew things before he'd spoken; the tiger seemed to understand his thoughts. Loka, as the siddhar had said, was no ordinary tiger, and eventually, Om would come to know his powers.

Seven days passed. Nothing strange had happened yet. Both Rishi and Om knew that this silence was a calm before the storm. Something dreadful was on its way.

The next day, Om was lost in thought, resting on the branch of a shady tree and enjoying some fruit. All at once, the tree shook like an earthquake had hit. He ignored it the first time, but soon he realized that the ground was actually shaking.

He climbed to the top of the tree, only to see that a big, brown, hairy devil with hair all the way down to his waist was walking towards the village. The Raksas carried a big, ugly sword that was round on top, and it wore a metal glove on half of his left hand. The Raksas was headed straight towards the farm where Om was.

From the top of the tree, Om readied his bow and shot three arrows in quick succession, aiming for his head. The demon raised his sword and deflected all three arrows.

He turned his eyes in Om's direction. Om could feel his big fiery red eyes piercing through his own. The next moment, the Raksas rubbed his sword on the metal guard on his left hand and pointed it towards Om. A lightning bolt hit the tree branch on which Om stood. Om tumbled

45

out, and the fall broke his bow. The tree was uprooted, and in a flash, it was ablaze.

There was no way he could attack the Raksas from a distance now. Om whistled for Meer to come close and rode towards the Raksas. He had his sword in his right hand, along with the tiger claws and the ivory shield in his left hand. Om stood on top of the horse as he moved closer.

The moment the Raksas was close enough, Om jumped at him. At the same instant, the Raksas turned, and Om missed his strike. Loka took the next blow from the Raksas to protect Om. That sent him crashing to the ground, and he tumbled a few times, until finally he collided with a tree. Om looked at him and signaled him to stand back.

While Om was looking at Loka, the Raksas had turned his sword towards him. It crashed down. Om braced his ivory shield in front of him, interrupting the strike of the Raksas' sword. The clash released a wave of energy that threw both of them backwards.

The Raksas, already back on his feet, quickly fired another lightning bolt at Om. Om wasn't ready for that. But before he could do anything, the gem on Om's head glowed brightly. It formed an orb-like shield around him. The gem's defense absorbed the lightning.

The Raksas had never seen anything like this before. He uprooted a tree and sent it flying in Om's direction. Om tried to use his gem, but it didn't work this time. Having no time to escape, Om held his left hand up again and waited for the impact.

As the tree was about to hit, a trident hit the tree and broke it into two, and both pieces fell on either side of Om. The trident had come from Rishi. He told Om telepathically, "The fight is yours to win! You're not concentrating enough. This will be the last time I save you."

Om stood up and looked into the fiery red eyes of the Raksas, while he planned his next move. He knew that he had to get rid of the demon's sword and the metal on his hand. Om and the Raksas ran towards each other, with swords held high.

Om asked Loka to get on top of a hill on his right and wait for his signal. Om and the Raksas further raised their swords for attack. Loka jumped on the Raksas and tore its back with his claws. The Raksas hadn't anticipated this move, and the attack from Loka made him move to the side, his right hand still held up.

Om took this opportunity and hit the Raksas under his arm. The pain from both attacks was excruciating, and the Raksas could no longer hold his sword. Leaving the sword behind, the Raksas ran towards the jungle until it was beyond their sight.

Om whistled to Meer, and along with Loka, they rode in the direction the Raksas had fled. They searched for it the entire day. They could see spots of blood here and there, but they weren't consistent enough to track. It was already dusk, and they couldn't locate the demon.

They came close to a mountain with a cave and took shelter there. Om managed to eat some fruit and made a fire. All three quickly fell asleep as they huddled around the fire.

Everyone woke up with a jump. A sudden thud echoed and resounded through the cave. The fire was out, and it was dark inside the cavern. It took some time for Om to realize their way out was blocked by a big rock. Om rubbed his gem, and it radiated enough light to see. Along with Meer and Loka, he tried to push the rock aside, but they could not. Out of frustration, Om even tried to push the rock using his mighty tiger claws.

Disgruntled, Om started walking towards the back of the cave to see if there was a different way out. After quite a long walk, they couldn't find anything.

He sat down, calmed his mind, and thought of using astral projection. Om closed his eyes, and soon, his consciousness was out of the cave. It was time to find a way out.

In front of the cave, he saw that the Raksas was guarding the door and sitting in front of the rock. His eyes were closed, and he was bleeding badly. At the other side of the cave, Om saw a stream coming out of the hill.

This could be the way out, thought Om, and he opened his eyes.

Now he had to find the source of this spring inside the cave. A quick walk brought them to the other end of the cave, and he saw a stream inside, but it was far below. The only way was to jump, and the drop was very high.

To gauge the river's depth, Om dropped a rock into the pit. The sound of its splash reassured him. Along with his dear friends, he jumped, dove in, and came out of the rock mountain at a small waterfall.

After a few moments to catch their breath, they hurried towards the Raksas. He lay on the rocks, splayed out and bleeding to death. Though relieved to be safe, Om felt bad for the Raksas. He prayed to the gods to send his soul to the right place.

They all started their journey back to the Himal town. On their way back, Om stopped for some water at the river. He'd had two sips when he heard someone approach him from behind. With one hand touching his sword, he slowly turned back.

There stood a man who had to be a prince. "Thank you, sir."

"May I ask why you are grateful?" asked Om, with one hand still on his sword.

"I was the Raksas that you killed." The prince bowed in gratitude.

Om stood there and stared at him in disbelief, not sure what to say. He was about to ask why, but before he could, the prince answered, "I was cursed by a rishi. I misbehaved with the rishi, and this was a fair retribution for my sins. I then had no choice but to move to the kingdom of the Raksas. There, I was quickly outcast, as I did not fight and kill anyone. I started living in the mountains, and I would visit the village to prey on cattle. Thank you for ending my curse at last.

"The rishi that cursed me also told me that the curse would be lifted if I was killed by the heavenly weapon of a true warrior. Please do not tell others of my suffering."

"That is incredible." Om placed a hand on his shoulder. "I promise, I won't share this tale with anyone.

But I wish you well in your next life."

The prince disappeared in a beam of light that went straight up in the sky.

Exhausted, Om finally reached the northwestern town. There, he was met with a warm welcome and celebrations. He looked at Rishi and thanked him.

At night, after returning from the celebrations, he asked Rishi, "Are we returning home tomorrow at last?"

Seated on the floor, Rishi joined his hands in prayer. Closing his eyes, Rishi said, "Actually, we're going to the capital tomorrow. The palace priest invited me to a great Sun Festival. It'll be magnificent! And you're coming with me—I'm not taking no for an answer!"

This time, Om was happy to obey—this could be his chance to meet the princess again.

CHAPTER 4
Princely Love

The capital was elaborately decorated for the upcoming Sun Festival. Outside the city walls, tents and temporary structures had been created to accommodate visitors from different towns. There would be various yajnas held throughout the first seven days, during which priests would chant hymns to appease the gods. People would participate in cultural demonstrations on the streets. A line of food stalls and gift shops were set up throughout the streets, stacked side-by-side, all the way from the capital's main doors to the stadium. Traders from all parts of the kingdom and even neighboring kingdoms took part in this joyous occasion.

This was also the month for organized games in the stadium. There would be sword fights, hand–to-hand combat, archery, small-scale artillery, horse races, and even elephant fights. On the second to last day, there would be chariot races, which were the locals' favorite event. Finally, the princess would distribute prizes to winners on the closing day of the games.

Om and Rishi stayed with Rishi's friend, a priest in the main temple.

The next morning, Om dressed himself in his finest clothes and brought his weaponry with him. "I'm going to meet one of my older brothers. Gautam is a member of the king's palace guard," he announced to his hosts. He hurried out the door, looking forward to meeting his brother.

On the way to the palace, he stopped at a bowyer's shop and asked for his bow to be fixed. The owner looked the bow over, then looked at Om thoughtfully. "Since the wood is still intact, it won't take long to fix the bow. Where should it be sent?"

Om gave him the address to deliver the bow and a gold coin for his service, then he headed straight to the palace.

At the palace gates, he gave his details and explained to them the purpose of his visit. He had to wait at the threshold for a while until his brother arrived and took Om inside. Meanwhile, all of Om's weapons were collected. He was a bit worried, but he had no choice.

When he arrived, Gautam saw the look on his brother's face and turned to the guard stacking Om's weaponry up with that of the other guests'.

"Keep Om's weapons with my own personal belongings," Gautam instructed. The guards didn't collect Om's headband, mistaking it for a mere ornament.

Om's brother showed him around the palace, but he

avoided an area that led across a small stream.

Om dragged Gautam ahead to get a closer look. "What's across that creek?"

"It leads to the personal chambers of the royal family. Very few people are allowed inside. Only those who tend to the needs of the royalty, or those who are close to the king, are allowed. As palace guards, we get to guard the entrance on rotating shifts. Come, let me show you where the king holds court," said Gautam, pulling Om away from the creek.

The court was beautiful, masterfully decorated with fine gems and intricately crafted golden statues. The throne made of gold was placed high with descending steps of gold, and a massive ruby set on the top. Above the throne stood a golden statue of the king's father.

And yet, all the beauty around could not stop Om from thinking of the princess.

He told his brother, "This has been marvelous, but the tour is enough for today. I should leave now."

"I'll accompany you to the gate."

"Don't worry; I know the way out."

Before parting, Gautam said, "Come to the chariot race. I'm taking part in it for the first time, and I've been practicing for the last few months."

"I wouldn't miss it for anything. I'll be sure to sit in the front," Om assured him. After accepting his brother's blessings, Om walked towards the palace gates.

After crossing the main hall, however, he entered the open garden area and turned to confirm that his brother had left. He didn't see his brother, but he did see a few guards and courtiers sitting in the garden.

Om knew that he could only enter the princess's chambers in disguise. He knew that it could land him in prison, but it was a risk he was willing to take. As his brother had said, the only people allowed inside the chambers were either nobility, courtiers, servants, or maids. The courtiers wore rings that served as their identification for both the king's court and personal uses. Moreover, the guards knew all the courtiers, and a disguise as one of them wouldn't help Om. The slightest suspicious sign, and Om could be imprisoned for life.

The options left were to either be a servant or a maid. Om chose to disguise himself as a servant. He needed a way to the king's kitchen, which was the best way to get in.

In the garden, Om waited for an opportunity to grab a uniform from someone. The garden had lot of trees and tall bushes—the right area for him to hide and attack. He wandered for a while and saw a soldier standing near a tree.

He slowly reached for the soldier from behind and knocked him out so that he would not die, but also so he would not wake immediately. Quickly, he took the soldier's armor, helmet, shield, spear, and shoes. He then hid the soldier's body in the bushes and tied his legs and hands. Om walked slowly towards the kitchen, confidently greeting whomever he met on way.

At last, he found the kitchen. Soldiers were not allowed inside, but he saw the army of servants and smiled to himself. Om knew that with this many servants, it would be nearly impossible for the chamber guards to recognize each one of them.

He found two servants eating food on the other side of the kitchen. He approached them slowly and asked, "Might I have a glass of water?"

After one of them left, he knocked the other servant out and concealed his unconscious body in a nearby trunk full of utensils. In the meantime, the servant's friend returned with a glass of water. Om drank the water and asked him to leave. The servant was about to ask about his friend, but he didn't want to annoy a soldier. Once the second servant left, Om dressed himself in the unconscious servant's uniform.

He blended in with the servants inside the king's kitchen, looking for an opportunity to join the party that brought the food for the king.

Om saw a quiet servant and said, "I'm new. Can you tell me who cooks for whom and who serves for whom? I don't want to make any mistakes."

The servant told him all about the servants' orders and who would cook for whom and who would serve whom. "There are only a few who are privileged to cook or even carry food or water to the king. These servants wear a red band on their right hand as an identifier. The rest are for the nobility, courtiers, soldiers, and guests."

Om keenly started observing the servants with red bands. Clearly, there was a head cook, and all the other servants were acting as his assistants. After a while, he knew that a meal had been prepared and that they were about to leave for the chambers. He followed the large group.

The last servant was carrying a copper tray with silver glasses full of water. Om threw a pebble in his way. The servant stumbled on it and fell flat on his face.

The head cook cast him an angry glance. "Refill the glasses and join me at the chambers."

While the servant rushed to bring the water, Om grazed against him and stole his red band. He picked up a tray and put some glasses on top of it. With empty glasses on the tray, he started walking towards the chambers.

Looking at the band on his arms, the guards didn't ask him anything. They quickly checked him for weapons and then let him in.

Once inside, it wasn't very hard to locate the princess's chambers. Leaving the tray outside, he slipped inside the princess's chambers through a side door.

"What are you doing here? Only the princess's maids and helpers are allowed in," someone shouted loudly at Om.

He turned around to see a noble lady in beautifully draped silk clothes, wearing rubies and emeralds. Om fell silent. He was stuck and didn't know what to say.

But the lady's expression changed from anger to puzzlement. "I know you from somewhere. Are you the one from the Garden of Flowers?" she asked. "I saw how you saved us all there. I was there with the princess. They went looking for you at your family's home, but you were long gone. Come with me." She held his hand and pulled him further inside.

Om didn't remember her; he hadn't noticed anyone other than the princess. She took the stairs and led him upwards to an open area on the other side of the palace, overlooking the great Nanda mountain. The courtyard was stunningly beautiful, and before he could appreciate it, he noticed the princess sitting with her maids on a seat made out of white stone.

The princess wore a beautiful red dress, with her mantle touching the grasses on the ground. She had a delicate headband made out of white and blue stones, with a white feather attached to it.

"Look who I found," said the lady to the princess.

The princess looked at Om, and neither of them could manage a word.

"Would you follow me elsewhere?" said the lady to the maids. With peals of laughter, their jewelry tinkling, and their silk clothes swaying, the young women left.

"Who was she?" asked Om, breaking the silence.

"She is one of my cousins," said the princess. "We grew up together. Who are you? Where were you? What took you so long to come meet me?" she demanded, all in one breath. "After you saved us from the beast that day, we looked everywhere for you," the princess continued. "I met your parents and requested for them to send you to the palace as soon as you returned home."

"Well…" Om walked a step closer, feeling overwhelmed by her presence, "there was something my guru wanted me to take care of in the northwestern mountains, and that took me more than a month. I've also been thinking of you since the day I saw you in the garden.

But after I tackled the beast, I wasn't willing to get into another tussle with the guards, and I avoided meeting you in person that day."

"So you weren't there by accident, but you were already watching me?" the princess asked. "I wonder if the beast was also yours," she said, and then laughed out loud.

Om stood still and watched her as she laughed. He was sure even the gods must be jealous of him.

They talked for the rest of the day, until the sun was about to set. Her name was Abha, and he thought it was the most beautiful name he'd ever heard.

The sun was shining on the waterfall, next to the chambers towards the west. The dimming sunlight cast a red shadow over the palace. The princess looked even more captivating with the evening rays adding to her glow.

They stood at the edge of an extension that emerged from the princess's chambers and ended in the mountain at the back.

The princess showed Om the king and queen's chambers to her left. "Both of them are in the temple with the royal priest," she said.

They watched the sunset together, after which Om asked, "May I take my leave of you?"

"When will I see you again, and how can I reach you?" She walked with him towards the door to her chamber.

"My lady, I am here till the Sun Festival is over, and I will be watching my brother in the chariot race on the last day," replied Om. "My brother Gautam is one of your guards, and for the time being, you may pass your messages through him." Om also told her where he was staying in the town.

He bowed, then left. Om sneaked back to the gates, collected his belongings, and headed straight home.

The following day, Om received the princess's maid in disguise at the doors and collected a letter from her. She had asked him to meet at her sister's house. The spring that formed from the waterfall behind the princess's chambers separated the noble quarters from the rest of the city. Her sister's house was also across the stream, with the houses of other nobles—east of the palace and north of the stadium, where all the games would be held.

Om met Abha yet again, and they continued to talk until dusk. They ate together and told each other stories, and Om told her of his experiences in the mountains.

Abha finally asked, "And who are you, my mysterious savior, who goes by the name 'Om'?"

"I am a student of Guru Rig Muni, or Rishi, as some people call him. I belong to the warrior caste. My father, Vinayak, is a distinguished warrior and a master swordsman. I, myself, am the youngest in a family of seven, with four elder brothers." He went on, eager to impress her. "The day I was born, the sky lit with thunder and lightning. My mother always believed it was a sign from the gods that I was blessed."

"And your brothers? Did they think you were a blessing?" Her laughter tinkled like chimes in the wind.

Om laughed, too. "Fighting with them taught me new

skills. But Medhya is named after my great-grandmother, who once saved the town from a horrific flood. To this day, my father still oversees administration for the town."

The princess nodded. "You are fortunate to live in a place surrounded by wilderness. Unlike Ogana, which is so busy, Medhya is peaceful. I love Medhya's thick forests, teeming with life. It's so beautiful that my father, the king, had a lavish palace built right outside the town near the waterfall. He loves to visit there in summer." Abha trailed her fingers in the water.

Om fumbled, feeling he was losing her attention. "Rishi has taught me many things. I can handle a sword, shoot arrows many ways, ride a horse… but my guru is even more powerful. He can speak to animals, and even the fiercest of creatures bow their heads before him. He's been teaching me about history, different wars, and the tactics used in those wars. One of my favorite stories is about a horseman who once led a small army of peasant soldiers and prevailed against a great empire."

The princess was rapt and took in his remarks with shining eyes.

Over the next few days, Om met Abha at her sister's home many times. One day, Om even took her in disguise to introduce her to Meer and Loka. The princess was ecstatic to meet them.

Loka even bowed his head and let the princess play with his soft ears.

"May I ride with you after the games are over, and when the madness in the streets has settled?" the princess asked.

Om nervously tore his eyes away from her. "I don't know how long I will be in the capital." He aimlessly glanced about the unfamiliar street, focusing on nothing in particular. "But please visit the Garden of Flowers—we can meet there every day, if you like."

She smiled at him. "It is an option, but it will be difficult to leave the palace soon."

That day, they wandered in the capital. As the princess was dressed as a commoner, no one took notice of her.

"These days have been wonderful for me, Om. I don't know how long my duties towards Malla will permit me to enjoy them." She looked away as a strange heaviness gripped her heart, and she left for the day.

Om felt the same way. He felt joyous with her, and for the rest of the day, he would be restless, waiting eagerly to see her again. *What if I never see her again once I leave Ogana? What if we are separated forever?* A storm of thoughts clouded his mind.

The same thoughts were running through the princess's mind as well.

The day after, Abha sent her sister to ask Om to come to the palace. First, the princess's sister took him to her house and dressed him like a noble. They entered the palace in a luxurious carriage. As Om was with the princess's sister, none of the palace guards checked or asked anything. Even the guards at the chambers didn't say anything; instead, they bowed their head in regard.

"You look great," the princess said, greeting Om. The two sisters nodded at each other in agreement.

They ate lunch together, and Abha told Om, "I want

to take you to a wonderful place."

After lunch, they sat and talked outside in the courtyard. This was the same place he'd met the princess when he initially came to the palace. The courtyard was on the third level, and it extended from the princess's chambers into the bedrock of a mountain. A tree grew almost as tall as the chambers, and stood four levels above ground. The courtyard was built around this tree. One of the branches of the tree extended backwards, touched the mountain, and grew towards the sky. The princess took him behind the tree and below this very branch.

"I have already seen everything from here," said Om.

"Not this part," the princess replied. "You will be astonished."

She passed her hand around the rock, stopped at a curve, and moved her hand beneath it. She took out a silver key and inserted it beneath that curve. There was a little rumble, and a door opened in the mountain.

"A door! How unexpected!" Om exclaimed.

"Keep quiet and follow me," said Abha, smiling. She took out a stick with an emerald on top; as she moved her hand, the stick glowed. They entered the cave, and the door slid shut behind them. They continued walking inside for a long time. The inner cave walls were all carved with pictures of animals, plants, and gods; some were even colored.

In the emerald's light, it looked like they were walking under a sky full of stars of different shapes. The only difference was that they could touch those. On the other side of the cave was another heavy door which opened with the same key.

They came out on top of Nanda Mountain, in front of which the palace was built. The waterfall was but a few steps away from the door. The view from there seemed even better than the one Om had experienced in the Mountains of Rishis. The entire capital city was visible. On the other side, he could see a thin road leading towards the great mountains of the Himalayas.

"Do you know where this leads to?" asked Om. Abha shook her head in denial, and he told her more about his adventures in the distant mountains.

They sat there until nightfall, enjoying the weather. It was colder here. The princess told him stories about the king and the queen. Like Om, she was a child of prophecy. They had believed her birth was special, as it had brought peace to the whole kingdom. At nightfall, they walked back to the palace through the same cave.

The more time Om spent with the princess, the more a fear of not being able to do so in future circled his mind.

That night, she asked him, "Would you stay?"

Om knew that Rishi would be waiting for dinner. "I'm afraid I must humbly decline your request. But I promise I'll return tomorrow."

"You must," Abha assured him. "I will be waiting."

The morning after that, Om woke up to a stranger at the door. Every day unfolded a new mystery for him, it seemed. He walked to the door and saw a lady with her face wrapped in a veil, her head covered. She was carrying a bow on her back and a sword by her side. He thought she might be one of the princess's personal guards. He had never met one before, but the princess did mention that these guards accompanied her if she went out of Ogana. In the capital, it was always safe, and the palace guards were in charge of her protection.

"Who are you?" he questioned.

"I need to borrow your horse," the lady stated politely. Without waiting for Om to reply, in one swift motion she drew her blade and severed Meer's rope. She jumped on the horse's back and rode off.

Startled, Om whistled to Loka and ran outside. He found a horse tied next to the door, jumped on it, and rode after the lady. The mysterious lady was a capable rider; she quickly passed through the crowded festival lanes and easily swung below the vendors' shops.

"Watch it, watch it," Om shouted at the crowd in the street, riding faster to catch up to the lady. After some time, he saw that the lady rode out of the main city door towards the jungle. He started riding faster. "Loka, keep up with me!" he urged.

Soon, the lady vanished into the jungle, and Loka, too, was nowhere to be seen.

Om entered the jungle, but couldn't tell which way to go. He went past a lane, occasionally whistling for Loka. He came to the river Medhavi and got down from the horse. Suddenly, he felt something hit his leg, and he fell. He could feel a sword pointed at his back.

He turned his head a little and saw Meer and Loka standing nearby. He understood then at that very moment that it was the princess—otherwise, his friends wouldn't have been so quiet. Om let her play out her ruse without revealing his understanding. "I want you to hand over all your valuables, then run for your life, the same way you came in," she said, making Om smile.

"Certainly, but for that, you need to let me up," he said.

"Don't act clever," said the lady, allowing him to get up.

Om couldn't stop smiling. Knowing that her disguise was no more, Abha lifted her veil and smiled back at him.

"What's next?" asked Om.

"I want to travel with you and spend a few days in the warmth of nature."

Om inquired, carefully hiding his smile, "Won't people worry about you back at the palace?"

"Well, if I can disguise myself as someone else, don't you think someone else can be disguised as me?" Abha answered. She added, "Every one of the royals has their doubles, including the king and the queen. This protects them—and also allows them to 'attend' functions they don't want to go to. Besides, the king and queen are so busy with the festival that they won't notice my absence until the last day, when I need to distribute the prizes. Come with me—I have a secret retreat in the forests."

Both of them rode towards it. After some time, they came to a hidden dock, where the princess took out a boat from a hideout. They dragged it into the water.

The secret place turned out to be an island in the middle of the Medhavi River. They arrived in a rather hilly area which was denser than the forest. Both the horses and Loka had swum to the island, and now they were walking by their side. They climbed to the top of the hill, from which they could see the capital, the mountains, and how the river split before the hill and merged after it. There was a well-built hut on top of a tree. They climbed up, and the view from there was even more breathtaking.

"We have five days before the final day of the games," Abha said, settling on a branch. "The day before and the last day of the games are always interesting. The day before is when the final games of each category are held and the fighters are the finest."

They decided not to miss the final two days and to spend the next three days in the wilderness. Both of them spent their time merrily gathering food and fruits together. Om would occasionally catch fish, and both would swim for a long time. They also spent time practicing archery. Om discovered that he was no match for the princess when it came to shooting arrows; she was faster and more accurate than him.

The day before they had to leave, they went further inside the jungle, exploring areas the princess had never been to. The jungle was full of surprises, and so were the different kinds of trees and animals. Later the next morning, feeling refreshed and excited, they rode towards Ogana.

CHAPTER 5
Save The Game

When Om returned after three days' absence, Rishi didn't ask a single question. He, too, had been busy; he had taken part in prayers and yajnas in the main temple, along with the other priests. But he was aware of all that had happened, and he was happy for Om.

Two days were left until the final event of the festival (the chariot race), and Om was excited to see his brother in the arena. But first, the stadium would host the finals in all the other categories. The finest combatants and contestants were selected from different rounds of games and competitions.

Just as Om's thoughts turned to his brother, someone knocked at the door. Looking, Om saw Gautam waving at him. "Let's go. It's sunrise, and the games have already started," he said. They quickly ate and then rode their horses towards the stadium. They tied the horses in a shaded area outside it.

"Can anyone enter the games, Brother?" asked Om.

Gautam ushered his brother towards the arena. "The king's guards have special arrangements. Other people in the kingdom have to buy their places inside; the sale happens months before the game. Since the games go on for half a month, everyone gets a chance to see them, but not all get to see the chariot races."

Om entered the stadium for the first time and was awestruck by the structural masterpiece. He had never seen anything like it. The stadium could comfortably seat thirty thousand people. The noise from the people inside was already shaking the ground.

The grounds could be transformed in different ways for different events. For a sword fight or hand-to-hand combat, there would be a stage in the middle of the stadium. For an archery competition, the ground could be transformed to include many stationary as well as moving targets. There were also competitions to fight and tame fierce animals, such as wild horses, elephants, lions, and tigers.

The closing day was reserved for horse, elephant, and chariot races.

The finals started with archery. Five of the finest archers had already advanced from the prior competitions. They stood side by side in their marked area, almost fifteen feet apart. The goal of the first round was to hit the painted portion of a stationary target. Each target was placed one after another; some were below eye level, some above, and some straight ahead. For each target, there was a mark from where the archer could shoot. He was not allowed to cross that line at any point. The winner would be the one who shot the closest to the painted portions.

The first targets were paintings of a man, and the area between the eyes was painted red. The other target portrayed a man holding a shield, and the painted area was the man's left eye. The third one was a raised target from the ground; it was of a squirrel, and the painted portion was the nut that it was holding.

As the games began, four of the five archers hit the first target area. The next target was hit correctly by the same four archers. The third one was hit by two among the four archers. The one who hadn't hit any of the targets was eliminated.

In the ensuing round, the target was a painting of a moving lady carrying a pot of water on her head. The colored area was the pot. The next was not only moving, but it was also rotating. The target was again of a squirrel, whose eyes were painted red.

The first target, all four archers were able to hit. But the second target, only two of them could, and these were the same two who'd hit all targets in round one. The third and the final round was a moving target of a hermit holding an apple, and the apple was colored red. The target was moving from left to right, and there were obstacles placed in front of it. There was a myriad of heavy iron rings hanging on ropes a few feet ahead of the target. The condition was to hit the target through the circle. The crowd screamed at the tops of their voices when the final target was announced. This time, only two archers participated, and only one was skilled enough to hit the target precisely.

"This is truly amazing!" Om had to shout so his brother could hear him over the crowd. He stood from his seat to take a better look at the archer. All of this made Om remember his days of training with Rishi.

"So we have a winner now?" asked Om.

"He's the winner, but he isn't yet qualified to take the Honor of the Kings ornament. The ornament is a valuable piece of stone bestowed upon he who passes the Honor of the Kings round. This round is kept until the end of all the games, and it resembles combat in real battles."

Archery was followed by sword fighting, for which twelve were selected. The first engagement would be in a group, and the twelve swordsmen were randomly divided into two.

Om enquired, "Is this a group event, or will there be individual winners, too?"

Gautam inched forward in his seat. "The game requires teams, and the group event resembles more of a battlefield situation."

On one side, Om saw a man commanding and talking to the other five. Soon the group stood in formation—two in front, three in the middle, and one at the back. The group on the left stood side by side, in a row. Whoever dropped his sword was supposed to leave the round. The swords were real, but blunt; it could give someone a bad wound but would not kill.

The groups began to move forward with shields raised and swords clutched tight. The group that was lined up held the line for a while, and then started moving aggressively. They saw only two in front on the other side, and thought they could easily tackle them first.

As the group on the left approached closer, the group on the right swung into action. Two of the warriors from the second line came to the front and combined their shields with the two already there. Together they held and pushed the opponents. The warrior left in the second line knelt down and arched his back forward. The last one stepped on him and lunged at the opponents. He landed on them with his shield facing forward.

At the same time, the four in the front row pushed the other group back. The warrior who had jumped at the group on the left couldn't stand the final blow. Out of the six of his opponents, five had dropped their swords. The man who jumped had also dropped his sword, but the five left in his group were enough to win the round.

The subsequent round was among the six men who won the first round. This time, it was a one-on-one sword fight. The three winners from this round would then fight each other, and whoever was left at the end would be the winner.

The first fight was rather quick; three emerged as winners. Now the three winners had to fight on the stage. Anyone who lost his sword or fell from the stage would be eliminated.

The man who'd commanded the group on the right to victory in the first round was standing on one side. The other two warriors seemed to have joined hands in defeating him. Swords and shields clashed, and the enthusiasm of the crowd reached a new high. The two warriors who had joined forces forced the third to the edge of the stage.

Om named the third person the "Commander," and he told his brother he would win. The Commander's opponents' intention was to push him off stage. From near the edge, the Commander hit the wooden stage with his shield. The impact popped up a wooden piece on which one of his opponents was standing, throwing him off balance and off the stage. The other opponent on his left, caught by surprise, turned in the direction he had fallen; and the next moment, he was lying flat on the stage. In a swift move, the Commander lifted the opponent by his waist and threw him to the ground, as if he was a bundle of hay.

Some in the crowd stood up from their seats to admire the last round, while others clapped and screamed at the top of their voices. The noise only settled after another contest was announced.

The next competition featured hand-to-hand combat, or "mal yudha." Eight people, all of extraordinary size, were selected, and they had to fight in groups of two. The rules were simple. The fighters were only allowed to use their hands and bodies. To win, the person had to force his opponent to the ground. Once on the ground, the rule was to hold the opponent down until he gave up. The first four games happened at the same time. Then, when only four warriors were left, the game happened one at a time.

"Did you select your winner this time?" Gautam asked cheerfully.

Om knit his brows as if pretending to weigh options, and then he shook his head. "It is hard to decide. The group matches finished rather quickly."

This time, Om had no winner in mind. The other two matches began on stage, one after other. The first match was a long one, as the opponents seemed to have similar strength; five times, one of them came down and again stood up. At last, one of them was able to win the match. After this, the next match began between the other two fighters. One of the fighters had long hair bound up in messy knots. He came straight to his opponent, lifted him up, and slammed him down, breaking the stage and some bones of his opponent's body.

The guards rushed in, and the long-haired fighter was disqualified on grounds of not following the rules. The winner from the first one-on-one match was declared as the final winner.

"So, now he has to fight again to gain the Honor of the Kings ornament?" Om asked his brother.

Gautam shook his head. "The king's ornament is given only for archery, horse riding, chariot races, and sword fights, as these are primarily used in battle. Chariot races and horse-riding winners don't have to perform a final test to gain the Honor of the Kings. Whoever is the winner gets the gem."

Next was the javelin-throwing competition. The first round was a contest for the longest distance thrown, as marked by lines on the ground. Five opponents, each standing in line, waited for the call to throw. As they got the signal, they ran and threw the javelins. Almost all of them made it to the first marked line, and one crossed all the marked lines.

"Hmm, this man looks like he drank from the godly river." Gautam stood in excitement to watch the javelin impale the ground.

The second round was similar to the first, but this time, the opponents had to continuously hit multiple targets. The higher the number of targets garnered by a contestant, the better was his position to win. Again, the man whose javelin crossed all markings last time knocked all the targets to the ground. He was announced the winner, and since no one else was close to his score, the third round was canceled.

The final round for the day was beast-taming, wherein a beast caught from the jungle had to be tamed in the open arena. The presence of a huge crowd could trigger any beast's temper, and for that reason, this competition was considered the most heroic. A beast would enter the field from one side, and the man from another side. The man would be provided only with a spear, a shield, and a rope. If the tamer gave up, he was allowed to run towards the gate, and the match would be dismissed. There were also archers with burning arrows on the roof of the stadium to make sure the beast didn't kill the man in worst-case scenarios.

The crowd waited breathlessly for the first round. A lion as tall as a human entered the field from one side. It roared, and the might of its roar struck the audience dumb for a moment. After a moment, they returned to life and started yelling and screaming back.

The first man entered the building and ran straight towards the beast. The beast saw him and unleashed a deep, prolonged roar that promised agony and death. The intensity shook the stadium and drowned out the wild clamor of the audience. Terrified, the man dropped his shield and spear and ran towards the gate.

The lion charged at the second man as soon as he entered the arena, tossing him in the air. Bruised, he landed about twenty feet away. The guards rushed in and saved him. The third man fared no better. He tried to resist for some time, and once, he even struck the beast's back with his spear. Soon, guards rushed in to take him away as well.

"This is not a game. Real soldiers participate for the merriment of the people," Gautam whispered in Om's ear. Gautam returned to watching, resting his jaw on his knuckles.

"So, that means more are going to fail." Om laughed. His brother looked at him with annoyance.

Six men were already down, and the beast was angrier than ever. At last, a wiry man entered the scene and he grounded a shield to his right. He started swinging his rope in one hand and tightly held the spear in the other. With the lion advancing straight towards him, the man quickly fashioned a trap with one end of the rope. While laying the trap behind him, he tossed the other end near the shield. He now held the spear in both hands, and was waiting for the lion.

As the lion jumped, the soldier slipped towards the shield and grabbed the other end of the rope. As one of the lion's hind legs fell into the trap, the soldier quickly pulled the rope, managing to entangle the beast's paw. He planted his feet and tugged the rope with all his might, tying it several times around the shield. The lion roared and kept pawing at the trap, but soon went quiet. The crowd cheered in thunderous applause, and after the final announcement, they departed to make their way home.

Before saying goodbye to his brother, Om asked, "How was the lion tamed so quickly by this soldier, when others failed?"

Gautam smiled and said, "This was merely a game for people's merriment. The lion is a pet, and he was kept hungry so that he seemed fierce. The last one was its trainer, and the lion knew it would get food if it listened to him."

Om laughed out loud. He now knew that the beast-taming was a mere game indeed—a show. Whatever he had heard at the stadium was a lie—simply fabricated to entertain the viewers. He said goodbye to his brother and headed home.

It was almost sunset, and Om could see the moon in the sky. He hadn't been able to meet the princess today, but he knew she would be there for the final games. After dinner, Om went to bed with thoughts of Princess Abha still in his mind.

In the morning, he woke up early and sprang out of bed. Gautam had told him they would ride together to the stadium. After scurrying to get dressed, Om hurriedly gulped his breakfast, and as soon as his brother showed up, both rode towards the stadium. That day, at Om's earnest request, his brother had gotten him a place near the nobility. Gautam showed him the elevated dais with fancy roofing and glossy black carpet where the royals would sit. It was quite near his seat; from there, he could see his love through the bustling crowd. Om waited eagerly for her to show up.

The first game of the final day started. Six lightly armored horsemen entered the arena and greeted the cheering crowd. The first round required them to ride in a straight line, between two wooden poles placed on opposite ends of the field. From the starting line, they would ride between the two poles, pick up the iron rings placed in their track with a spear, and drop them on the poles. They were permitted four attempts to make it from the start to the finish line. The rider putting the most rings down would qualify for the next round. Three of the riders lifted all the iron rings in four attempts and slid them successfully onto the poles. The second round was announced, but Om was still anxiously waiting for the princess to arrive.

Swords were used in the second round, and there were ten wooden poles erected—five on either side of a straight line for each participant. Wooden statues resembling heads were placed firmly on top of each wooden pole. The riders had to topple the statue with one blow without hitting the pole. It would require great strength to topple these statues.

The round ended with one man toppling all the statues; the other two tipped nine. During the announcement for the following round, the royalty joined the stadium, and the announcements were paused. The whole stadium rose to honor their king. The royals sat down, and the games were resumed.

Om was looking at the princess, but she was unaware of his presence. The final round for the game again had ten wooden statues, with each one painted at a different level. The riders had to hit the painted area while riding towards them with a bow and arrow. The round began, and as it progressed, so did everyone's excitement.

At last, one of the two men that had toppled nine out of ten from the previous round was able to hit all the marks. None came close to him, and he was declared the winner.

Once the winner was announced, Om started shouting, in hopes of drawing the princess's attention. The princess and Om saw each other and smiled.

"That young man is really enjoying the game," the king said to the queen.

"I have to get ready as the chariot race will be after the elephant's game," Gautam said as he struggled to make way through the crowd, and he left for the preparation. The elephant show was only for merriment's sake, and not a real competition. The first step was to uproot massive wooden tree trunks inserted deep into the ground. The second round required them to topple huge wooden walls with half of their bases below the ground.

While the people were preparing the obstacles, Om

often looked at the princess to see if she was looking, and Princess Abha often did the same.

After some time, the two obstacles were erected. The final one had not been announced yet, but there were targets placed on each side of the wall. Five magnificent elephants adorned with precious stones and the finest embroidered coverings entered one after the other, bearing their mahouts on their broad backs.

As the first round began, the mahouts guided their elephants to the tree trunks. Soon, all of the elephants were able to uproot them. The crowd cheered the mahouts.

For the next round, the elephants ran and butted the wooden structure with their heads. After four or five hits, all the structures slowly came down. The final one was the fiercest. The archers on the stadium's roof fired a volley of arrows on the ground in front of the elephants. The mahouts had to guide the elephants around the arrows without harming the elephants or letting them step on any. The archers on top were supposed to hit the target on the sides with arrows to bring them down. All the elephants were able to cross all the hindrances on the ground, and the archers shot down all the targets. The mahouts had a real connection with these giants, and all were able to skillfully control them.

The chariot race was announced, and a group of men started planting a circle of tall and hefty wooden poles, forming a circuit in the center of the field. The chariots had to complete twenty rounds of this circuit, and the first person to finish would be the winner. Om eagerly waited, expecting to see his brother win the race.

A total of ten chariots entered—each one driven by two horses. Five chariots were placed in the first row, and five right behind them. His brother's chariot was the last to enter, and it stood at the right in the second line. Om looked at him and waved, and at that moment, a horn trumpeted and the race began.

Six laps had passed, and Om's brother was the one leading in front. The crowd shouted in encouragement and excitement, calling to their favorite racers. This was the noisiest game Om had been to yet. The sound from the wheels, the noise from the crowd, and the occasional chariots clanging against each other filled the atmosphere.

On the thirteenth lap, Om saw his brother struggling to handle his horses. Om came to the very end of the stadium's upper-level fence and looked closely at his brother's chariot. One of his chariot's wheels was not rotating properly, and it was about to come off at any moment. He shouted at his brother, but his voice was drowned out by the crowd.

Om rushed down to the guards at the lower level. "His wheel is going to come off!" he tried to shout, but the guards paid him no mind, caught up in the action, barely hearing him in the crowd's roar.

He decided to take matters in his own hands and jumped down to the lower level.

Two soldiers saw this, rushed towards him, and grabbed him by the arms. "Halt!"

"No—please, I was trying to help my brother in the chariot race! His wheel is about to fall off!" Om tried to persuade them, but four more soldiers came towards him. Realizing that he was losing time, Om shoved both the soldiers holding him away. The four other soldiers rushed behind him, and Om slammed all of them to the ground.

The king rose from his seat and saw Om tussle with the six soldiers, then jump down to the grounds.

"Who is this person? Has he gone mad?" the king shouted.

The soldiers behind the entry gates saw the king's reaction and rushed towards Om. All the attention on the chariot race shifted to their tussle. As a troop marched towards the scene, Om bolted for his brother's chariot.

He saw the wheel of his brother's chariot come loose, bringing his brother down. Gautam's chariot collided with two chariots on his left and sent them swinging. The chariot immediately behind collided directly with Gautam's. Launched from the chariot as the force struck, Gautam went flying through the air. He landed hard on the ground, thunking into the dirt.

Om rushed to save his brother. Gautam was bleeding badly and was unconscious. Om picked him up and started running towards the gate. He saw the guards at the gate blocking the exit and another group still chasing him. Om carefully laid his brother down and charged towards the guards at the gate. Incensed, he hammered the ground with his tiger claws. The first line of guards collapsed around him, every soldier thrown to the ground. He hammered the ground for the second time, now with his ivory shield. The ground shuddered from the concussion of the blast, which felled the remaining lines of guards.

The crowd was aghast—an utmost silence prevailed among them.

Another battalion rushed towards the gate where Om was standing. Before Om could do anything, he heard his brother cry out, and Om ran towards him. His brother passed out again, and Om cried out for help. The two battalions managed to capture Om, and they carried Gautam away for treatment. The games were completed, and everyone left without seeing the final ceremony. The princess watched as the soldiers dragged Om away with them.

CHAPTER 6
Meet The Kingship

Om was thrown and locked in the darkest corner, in one of the jail towers. The stench of raw sewage pierced through his nostrils and made him retch. It was a mostly dark room with only a small opening above for sunlight. He was served food once since he came, and it wasn't too bad. A mud jar for water was kept inside, and it was filled once in the morning. The light did give Om a little hope that his brother would be all right and that he, too would be released soon. *Perhaps it would be best to wait and not cause trouble for now,* he thought. He already had spent one night there, and he was worried about his brother.

Another day passed. Om began to feel that unless he did something, he might never be released. All of his weapons, even his headband, had been taken from him. His only remaining power was that of astral projection. Even with this power, he could not communicate with anyone except his guru. It was time to seek his help. Om closed his eyes and went into deep meditation with hopes to reach Rishi.

On the other side of the jail, Abha made sure that Om's brother was properly taken care of. It would take him a few months to fully recover from his grievous wounds. Since the day Om was caught, Abha had thought only of how to release him.

She sought out her guards for counsel. "Going to the king is your only option," they all agreed. She already knew that—but it would mean telling her father everything. She also thought that under these circumstances, it might not be the right time. Om had injured a lot of soldiers that day. A lot of people had seen a commoner defeat well-trained soldiers with only one blow of his fist.

She finally decided to meet Om in his cell. Dressed like one of her bodyguards, she entered the jail. When she reached Om's cell, she saw him meditating. She looked around, pained to see him in this situation. Without speaking to Om, she rushed back to her chambers and burst into tears.

At last, Om was able to contact Rishi. His guru's reply was clear.

"Stay quiet and be patient. I am with a friend in the nearby town, outside the capital. It will take exactly three days for my return."

Om came out of meditation and prepared himself for

three more dark days.

He thought of his love and wondered if there was any way he could see her. He knew that she would be in a desperate situation, too. He crossed his legs and leaned his back against the wall with the tiny opening. He wondered if his parents even knew about the condition two of their children were in.

The night was very long, and it didn't seem to end. Om tried to sleep, but he couldn't. He had gotten up to drink some water when he heard a voice in his head. It was Rishi.

"Everything will be all right, and you should rest. Do not worry. I will be at the capital sooner than expected."

Om laid down, less worried, closed his eyes, and went to sleep.

There were a lot of people with their faces painted in blue and white, all carrying battle axes. They looked ferocious and strong, and even in broad daylight, the briefest look at one of them would have frightened even the bravest man. They were holding more than a dozen of the king's soldiers as captives. One by one they dragged the soldiers behind a chariot and struck them with a cane until the pain caused them to collapse.

The soldiers were eventually taken to a place where there were more of these strange blue and white warriors. At the heart of that place was a temple, from which appeared a chubby man. He was clad in a white loose piece of clothing wrapped around the lower half of the body, and his hair was tied in a bun held by a string of beads.

"These men are evil and must be punished. Take them to the river and execute them," the man ordered.

The prisoners were dragged to the river, lined up, and were ready to be axed. One among the painted faces, who looked like a leader, took an axe, and chopped the nearest soldier's head off. All other soldiers screamed in horror as the headless torso collapsed.

Om woke up from the horrible dream to find that half the day had gone by; he could tell by the fading light in his room. He saw a wooden plate of food, but he didn't have the energy to even get up and eat. He simply wanted to be out of this hell. Being in jail for a crime was one thing, but to be in jail because he'd tried to save his brother was something Om couldn't adjust to.

At that moment, Om heard heavy footsteps approaching. He knew from the sounds that there were at least a dozen soldiers. With his legs chained and his hands tied, he was taken outside the tower. Once outside, a battalion guided him to the palace. He thanked his guru and felt a lot better to see the sunshine.

In the palace courtroom, King Neera was seated on his throne, with the queen and the princess on either side. With a glance at the courtroom, Om knew that there were only noblemen and people close to the king. Inside the palace, Om was guarded by hundreds of palace guards. Om didn't see Rishi, so he was a little worried whether it was the princess who'd gotten him out or if, in fact, this marked the beginning of his prosecution.

He bowed before the king.

"Get up and come to the front, Om," the king called.

Om walked to the front. He looked to Abha for some reassurance, but she looked worried.

"My daughter talks highly of you. She told me that you were the one who saved her life," the king said. "She also told me that you didn't even give her an opportunity to thank you. Where did you get those powers?" he demanded. "I have never seen a human with such powers before."

"I have a good teacher, who has taught me well," Om replied modestly.

"Om, I know whose son you are and who taught you," the king said. "Rishi has had many disciples, including one of the courtiers, but he never trained anyone to be a soldier. All of his disciples are thinkers or writers or very learned people. There is something that you are not telling me. One of my guards brought me your weapons, and they do not seem ordinary, or of this world."

"My king, I have told you the truth," Om said. "Rishi is my only true guru, and I have no special powers other than that of a good soldier. The weapons were also given to me by my guru."

"I am not satisfied by these replies," grumbled the king. "Your prosecution begins tomorrow. Soldiers, take him away."

"Father, no!" Abha began, but she was silenced by one look from the king.

"My dear king," Rishi interrupted as he walked into the courtroom, "I would not do anything of that sort if I was in your position. This man is my disciple, and I am his guru. I have taught him to be brave and respectful. If it was not for that, he would have been long gone.

"However, you are correct—Om is no ordinary man. I have been training him to be the finest warrior the kingdom has ever seen. Furthermore, he has used his training only for good—the only reason he entered the arena and fought with the soldiers was to save his brother.

"Om would be glad to accept any punishment you give him if he had committed a crime," Rishi said. "Even though his brother was soaked in his own blood, he did not injure your soldiers severely. I think that this kingdom's army can learn a lot from him."

"Rishi, you are a learned man, and I haven't ever disregarded any of your suggestions," said the king. "I have seen the way Om fought in the stadium, and there is obviously a way to utilize his skills. Isvasa, what do you think?"

The king looked at Isvasa, the head of the army. "Perhaps you should keep Om near you and utilize his skills as necessary."

"My king, your wish is my command. I think this would be beneficial for the soldiers," Isvasa replied. Isvasa was himself a great warrior and could easily sense another's great valor.

Now, Isvasa would decide how Om's skills could be put to use. Om, thereby, had to follow Isvasa's orders, and his authority would be second only to the king himself. Om could not say no to the order of the king. And after all the things that Rishi had told them, there was no way he was getting out of this. Om bowed to the king again and got out of the courtroom with Isvasa and Rishi.

Outside, Isvasa told Om, "In two days, I will ride with you to a soldiers' camp a few days' ride from the capital. Be ready."

Rishi and Om left Isvasa and walked towards Rishi's friend's cottage, where they had lodged. "Thank you for coming sooner than expected," said Om gratefully.

"Om, my boy, now you may have understood that everything happens for a reason," said Rishi. "Take a bath, have something to eat, and then we will go visit your brother. Your family is also here, and it would be good to see all of them before you start on yet another adventure." Rishi made it sound as if Om was not just going to a soldiers' camp, but rather setting off on a long journey.

When they arrived home, he tightly embraced both Meer and Loka. It was almost evening by the time he ate. The food was simple yet comforting, the warm meal his first in days.

Soon afterward he left to see his brother. Glad to see others in his family and his brother, he felt his fatigue lift up off his shoulders. Gautam was in much better shape now. He had not seen Om's act of heroism, but had definitely heard stories.

"Thank you for saving me—I'm sorry it landed you in jail. But good deeds are never forgotten, my brother," Gautam told Om, and he lowered his head in respect.

Om greatly enjoyed the time with his family and bid goodbye to them with a promise to meet them again before his journey to the camp. That night, Om slept like a baby—the struggles in that dark dungeon a distant memory.

A while after daybreak, Om went straight to the princess's sister's house and waited there for her. The princess ran towards him and embraced him in a tight hug.

Om looked at her and smiled. "Thank you for the risks you took to get me out of captivity. I missed you so very much—I thought of you every waking moment and dreamed about you every night."

"I couldn't sleep until I saw you. I went to meet you in prison, but you were meditating. I couldn't bear your conditions, so I left," said Abha. "I'm worried that you'll be gone for a long time, but at least Isvasa is a very able general and warrior," she said all in one breath.

Om smiled at her. "I assure you, I am able to take care of myself. The only thing that I will miss is you, my princess," he said.

That day, they ate lunch together and spent time talking about the games. "The accident left a deep scar on the minds of the organizers," said the princess. "For the next festival, there will be stricter inspections of the chariots and all other games to make them risk-free, and the visitors will have to surrender their weapons."

Before long, they bid farewell to each other. "I will miss you more than anyone and anything else," said Om. The princess smiled at him, didn't utter a word, and left for the palace. Om went to meet his brother, took his blessing, and prayed for his good health.

At dinner, after a long silence, Om asked Rishi, "Your preparations and teachings have been extensive. Is there anything you aren't telling me?"

"Om, soon there will be a time when this kingdom will need you the most. At that point, you will need to embrace all the teachings that you've received from your gurus," replied Rishi.

The next morning, one of Isvasa's guards came looking for Om. Without any greeting, the guard hastened to deliver his message: "The battalion is waiting outside the palace, and the orders to march have been given."

Om replied, "You may proceed, and I will join the battalion shortly." The guard left without another word. Om gathered his belongings, got dressed, and rode on Meer towards the gate to join the battalion. Loka followed him behind.

At this early hour, the streets were free of people, and Om reached the capital's gates sooner than he had expected. The gates were already open, and he could see the battalion outside the gate, assembled for the march.

"Om!"

Om looked back, got down from his horse, and smiled at the lady behind.

Removing her veil, the princess said, "I don't want you to go, but it's best for both of us if you do. I'll wait for you. It's hard to imagine life without you now. The last few days with you have been the best days of my life," she said.

"I feel the same way." Taking her in his arms, he held her close, and she stood with him for a moment or two before quickly climbing onto her horse and riding away.

This time, Om couldn't follow her. His path lay ahead, with the battalion waiting outside the gates to march towards the general's camp.

Om saluted the general and took his place beside him. They started their journey with the sound of the horn and the beat of drums following them. The soldiers sang their battalion anthem, and forward they rode.

"Destined to win!
Worship lord and king,
Protect all natives,
Free land of all evils,
Worship lord and king,
Destined to win!"

After two days' march, they entered the camp. It was constructed around the Lake of Sarasi. Looking at the vast lake, Om realized that this was not a camp, but a military city.

At the entrance, there was a magnificent statue of Lord Indra. In his left hand, he held his fabled thunderbolt, the Vajra, and in the right, a sword. The white stone monument filled the soldiers with renewed vigor. It was colossal—so vast that even on horseback, Om could only reach its toes.

The entire battalion, commanded by Isvasa, lived and trained here. To the left of the lake, there were wooden houses for soldiers and captains, with the general's quarters at the end. On the right were all the training fields and campgrounds. There was a huge arena where soldiers trained throughout the day and even night. The lake also served as training grounds for river warfare. All sections were connected by boats across the lake.

It was on one of these boats that Om reached the general's house. There, he was introduced to Isvasa's finest captain, Parvaza. Parvaza was a tremendously large man with two axes and a shield on his back. He offered to show Om his accommodations and the city. After showing Om around, Parvaza showed him his quarters and took his leave.

Om tied Meer outside, and he went inside to rest. Meer seemed to still be confused after riding on a boat for the first time. Loka also seemed tired from this long trip, and he rested in one corner as soon as they entered the house. Om noticed there was already hot water in the tub behind the house. He cleaned himself, put on fresh clothes, and had food brought to him by one of the soldiers.

Isvasa called for Om in the evening. "I have to visit a nearby town, and I will be back in two days. Parvaza will be in charge until I get back."

Later that night, Om found himself unable to sleep. He got up and went outside to feel the fresh air, and he saw some light on the other side of the lake—possibly from a fire. He went inside to look for Loka and could not find him. Meer was gone as well.

Where would they be in the middle of the night? he thought, sitting on the stairs of his house. He decided to wait a bit more. A slight but sudden headache washed over him, and the next moment, he lost consciousness.

The sky had started to turn bright by the time Om woke up. His eyes snapped open, still heavy and hurting, but his mind worked full-speed. He was tied to a dead tree, surrounded by soldiers in the middle of a field.

A young soldier came forward, resting his hand on a coiled whip tucked into his belt. "You were the one who hit our brothers in the stadium and dishonored them in front of all people of Malla. Today, you will suffer, and we will show you our strength," he said without bothering to hide the disdain on his face or in his voice.

Om tried to free himself. He'd expected a wooden pole in the ground, one he could lift or wriggle out of the dirt—but alas, he was not tied to a wooden trunk stuck into the ground, but to a giant tree. No matter how strong Om was, he wasn't getting out of this one without his weapons.

He wondered if Parvaza knew about this; it was highly unlikely for a captain to be on the training grounds. Om was powerless and at the mercy of angry soldiers.

He closed his eyes and thought that if Loka had been around him last night, this would never have occurred. He wished someone could help him.

Loka had been captured as well, and he was held in a darkened iron cage. He sensed that Om was in grave danger. In the blink of an eye, Loka transformed into a big black beast. He ripped apart the sturdy cage and roared in rage—the sound echoing enough to shake the sky. The sound sent shivers through the people of Sarasi. Loka ran towards Om, sensing exactly where he'd been tied up.

Om was astonished to see the black beast running towards him. He realized that it was the very same beast he'd seen back in the Garden of Flowers, where he'd first met the princess. Reaching his master, Loka raised his razor-sharp claws, then cut Om loose and set him free.

Around them, the soldiers formed a protective line on one side, raising their shields and spears. On the other side, archers stretched their bows to open fire.

"I am not an enemy. Please lay down your weapons," shouted Om.

No one listened. The soldier who'd initially been talking with Om shouted, "Archers, open fire!"

Seeing this, Loka roared and thumped both of his front legs on the ground, sending a wave of dust towards the archers. Blinded, the archers were not able to see. Some were still able to fire, but missed by a far distance.

Om snatched a sword from the soldier near him and held the man at the point of his own sword.

At that very moment, Parvaza entered the scene. He ran towards Om. "Om! Don't move, and don't harm him! The rest of you—Om was appointed to serve with us by the king himself. Any harm to him will be a felony in the eyes of the king," Parvaza screamed at the soldiers.

The soldiers obeyed their captain's orders and even apologized to Om.

"I am a soldier, exactly like you. What I did back in the

stadium was to save my brother," Om told the men as they started to leave. "There is something I must do before I leave for my quarters," he mumbled to Parvaza.

Om caught up with the soldier who'd ordered the archers to open fire and said, "Meet me in the evening, before sunset."

Parvaza interceded. "Om, I beg you, please don't discuss the incident with Isvasa. The soldiers were emotional and fought only for their dignity and the brotherhood. This was probably a sort of revenge for their brothers."

"I won't say a word to the general," Om promised, and went straight towards his quarters.

At sunset, the soldier came to meet Om. "I'm Maghavan. I'm terribly sorry about this morning."

Om, however, had another concern. "It's as good as forgotten. But what was mixed in my food yesterday, and who did it?" he asked. Sensing Maghavan's unease, Om elaborated, "I can usually sense or smell something awry in my food, but last night, I could smell nothing."

"Revat, my lord. He is the battalion's Vaidya. He made the herb paste that was mixed in your food," replied Maghavan. "I am the one who mixed it."

"Then call Revat immediately."

"I will." Maghavan called for Revat, and meanwhile, talked to Om about the battalion and the place.

Revat came and bowed in front of Om. "I didn't know that the herb was going to be used on a human," Revat said. "I was told that a beast had gone wild."

"Glad I'm alive then," laughed Om.

"I am terribly sorry."

"There's no need. I am remarkably impressed with your skills, however. Why was I not able to smell this herb paste in the food?" asked Om.

"It took me a lot of time, but I made the herbal mixture odorless," replied Revat. "You see, animals have a better sense of smell and won't eat anything suspicious."

"What other things can you do, my friend, and where did you learn these skills?" asked Om.

"Since I was a child," Revat told him, "I've lived with my father, who was also a Vaidya, in the corners of a jungle. My father taught me about different wild herbs. From childhood, I was curious about herbs, and would try to make different kinds of combinations out of them. With these combinations, I would then perform experiments and try the herbs on house rodents. Now I have an assortment of potions, salves, and elixirs that can be used for a variety of purposes."

"He has one herb that can even make a dead person speak for a moment," Maghavan interrupted. Revat went on, and Om listened keenly, curious about his skills.

"This has been fascinating. I would like to continue these conversations tomorrow. For now, I'd like to go rest."

Isvasa was back the very next day, and in the afternoon, invited all his captains, as well as Om. During lunch, Isvasa sat next to Om. "I'd like you to choose and train a hundred men. Our battalion, Om, is the best in the kingdom but not the best in the Himalayan region,"

Isvasa said. "I want all hundred men to be as fierce as yourself.

"These hundred men would then be placed in forts and the capital city. They would also manage training at all these places. Teach them some of your skills, Om, and then I'll give you the very gift you desire," Isvasa told Om.

He was puzzled by that remark. "I don't know what you are talking about, but I will agree to train the soldiers."

The next morning, a rigorous competition was organized. Om had to choose the hundred best out of thousands of soldiers. The competition went on for seven days, and the hundred were selected from different groups, like the archers, sword infantry, axe infantry, spear infantry, chariot handlers, and cavalry. Everyone had to go through a few rounds in each of their fields.

Apart from competing, the selected soldiers from the competitions had to answer a few of Om's questions. A person who answered Om's questions correctly was selected for the hundred. Om was looking for warriors who were there to serve and who would disregard any odds for the sake of their kingdom. He looked for those with a commitment to and love of the kingdom before anything else.

Om had learned a lot from all his gurus, but he knew that he wasn't a teacher himself and never acted like one. Instead, he acted like a trainer, and he made the hundred sweat with labor.

The archers were taught to fire shots as they had never imagined. The swordsmen learned to fight not only one opponent, but numerous at a time. The spearmen learned not only to throw, but how to fight better and to form an impenetrable line. They formed the line with shields and used the spears to their advantage. The axe warriors learned how to throw and retrieve axes faster. Cavalry and chariots learned to attack in different kinds of formations.

The training continued for two months. At the same time, Om worked with the army's blacksmiths to forge sophisticated weapons. He also sought Revat's help to design special arrows for archers.

In the evenings, Om spent time with Maghavan and Revat. One evening, during a conversation, Om asked Maghavan, "Why aren't there any elephants in the Sarsi battalion?"

Maghavan replied, "Sarsi's battalion is a swift response battalion. As elephants would slow the battalion down, they have never been inducted into it."

Om pursued, "Why, then, was the tusk of an elephant chosen as the battalion's symbol?"

Maghavan answered, "Isvasa worships only Lord Indra, and Lord Indra rides an elephant. That's the reason he chose the tusk as a symbol for the Sarsi battalion."

After a month, the training was complete. Om offered extraordinary gifts to each one of the chosen hundred. Axe warriors were given special thin metal ropes; one end of the rope could be attached to the axe and the other to their hand. This increased the range of the axe warriors and gave them the ability to retrieve the axes faster. Cavalry warriors were given special horse shields to protect against archers during heavy combat. Spear warriors were given unique spears, which could be detached and used as two smaller spears. Chariot riders were given horseshoes that would help them navigate arduous terrain. Archers were provided with different armor-piercing arrows—even some that would burst into flames on impact.

Om finally requested the presence of Isvasa. "At last, I have prepared you the hundred soldiers you asked for in the beginning." The men were then sent on missions that Isvasa already had in mind. The following day, Isvasa convened a meeting of all his captains.

"Om will be a captain in the royal army, not a part of my battalion. He will work closely in the palace as the king's adviser on warfare—the position that has been vacant since I was given the highest military position," Isvasa announced to the gathering.

Om was surprised to hear that.

"Om will be second only to me, and in my absence, he will act as the king's primary adviser on war," Isvasa said, and he came forward to congratulate Om.

"Thank you!" Om said to Isvasa.

"This was the gift. But now, Om, before you accept your new duties, I have a last one for you," said Isvasa. "We attend an annual friendly meeting with the King of Kanika. This time, I will be the one attending it on behalf of the king, and I would greatly appreciate it if you were to accompany me. As for the rest of you, we will start for Kanika in a day. This will be useful to teach Om to deal with foreign affairs and relations."

Before he left, Isvasa cautioned Om, "However, you

can't take Loka with you to Kanika."

Reluctantly, Om agreed. "I'm looking forward to this journey greatly." Hearing that, Isvasa nodded and left the room. After that, every one of the captains greeted Om, and they began to prepare for their travels.

CHAPTER 7
Friendly Visit & Capture

Two days later, Om, along with Isvasa, Parvaza, and two hundred soldiers, marched towards Kanika. Loka was left at the camp, in the care of Revat. The journey was pleasant, with nice, cold weather throughout.

On their way, they crossed rivers and climbed a few hills. It took almost twenty days for Isvasa and everyone else to reach Kanika's capital.

Kanika was a glorious kingdom, its boundaries shared with Malla in the north, the Kutilam kingdom in the west, the kingdom of Anga in the east, the kingdom of Asankh to its southwest, and the vast sea to its southeast. Kanika had a strong navy, and traded to the farthest corners of the world. To reach one of their farthermost trading posts, Kanika's sailors would spend as much as six months at sea.

The Kingdom of Malla used Kanika's trade stations to

trade with the outer and farther world, and the Queen of Malla was Kanika's king's sister. This further strengthened the friendship and relationship between the kingdoms. In exchange for access to trade, Malla guarded the northern borders of Kanika. Each side assisted the other in time of war and disaster.

Kanika's name derived from Kanika Lake, which was so vast that no one could see one side from the other shore. It took two days to sail across it. The water in the lake was salty, and therefore it was not suitable for drinking.

The palace city, Hrada, had been built on the western banks of the lake. A good distance from the shore was an island. At the center of this island, in the shape of a crown and rimmed by delicate courtyards contrasting the bright blue lake, stood the royal palace. The only way to reach the palace was on the king's own boats; the boats sailed through the palace's outer walls to anchor a few yojanas inside.

The palace was a marvel, built from rock quarried from the giant hills of the Southern Himalayas.

Isvasa, along with Om and ten other soldiers, called for a palace boat. The remaining soldiers stayed back at the city of Hrada. After Isvasa's boat anchored in the palace, they were shown their respective quarters. They were informed that the king would meet them in the courtroom after the sunset and dine with them.

After refreshments, Om strolled out of his quarters idly whistling. Unhurriedly, he roved about the palace, appreciating the art, the architecture, and the splendid views from the many windows and balconies overlooking the kingdom. As he wandered, he reached the grand balcony at the top of the palace. Intricately designed with flowers and statues of birds carved in precious stones, the polished white floor reflected the glow from these statues.

Om eased down on a seat near the railing and enjoyed the beauty of the city from the palace's highest plaza. The sun was about to set, and the evening sunlight outlined the palace with mystical hues. After the sun fell, Om finally climbed down and walked towards their quarters to meet Isvasa.

"Parvaza and I were waiting for you, Om," Isvasa said.

The three of them walked together towards the court house. Unlike Ogana, the courtroom at the palace was a round, open-air space. In the middle, one could see the bright skies above. One corner had the king's throne, surrounded by the nobility and his elegantly seated courtiers. The king's son and daughter sat right beside him. Isvasa was given a place close to the king, and Om sat next to him.

The evening started with folk dances performed by a group of women dressed in long white garments elaborately draped over the body and finished with exquisite jewelry from head to toe. Their movements were so enchanting and synchronized that they looked like a single artist, moving as one. After these dancers came the musicians, who performed with different sets of instruments. Then came singers, who filled the palace with their melody; the audience couldn't hear anything apart from their eternal song. Each one of them was unique and ethereal in their own way.

As the music drifted through the room, Om noticed Isvasa and the Princess of Kanika looking at each other several times. After the court celebrations, every one of the guests and royals proceeded towards the dining hall for dinner. The hall, large enough to accommodate a village, was decorated with beautiful paintings of the kingdom. Multiple fireplaces were lit up to ward off the evening chill.

Isvasa saw Om admiring the pictures. "All the pictures you see were painted by the Princess of Kanika," he said.

Om smiled and said, "Yes. You do know a lot about the palace… and the princess."

Isvasa laughed at Om and went ahead to talk to the others.

The food was amazing, and far better than in the stories that Om had heard on the way to Kanika. They only used fish fresh out of the sea, and now Om knew why people visited Kanika for its food alone. After dinner, the party divided up into different groups gathered around the fireplaces. The king, along with Isvasa and the queen, were sitting on one side. Parvaza and Om were talking to one of the courtiers.

After a while, Isvasa came forward and took Om to meet the king and queen. Om greeted them gracefully and thanked them for a wonderful evening. He also met the Prince and Princess of Kanika. The wonders and pleasures of the night didn't seem to end. After a long conversation at a fireplace, Om and his friends walked towards their quarters.

In the morning, Om requested Isvasa's permission to visit the palace city, Hrada.

"Today, you will talk about the kingdom's affairs. I would like to skip these discussions and visit the city instead," Om told Isvasa. "I won't be able to follow much anyway."

Isvasa agreed to it, and Parvaza volunteered to accompany Om. They hired a boat and headed to the city, which looked more like a trading post—although a very big trading post indeed. People from far-off kingdoms came here to trade for different varieties of goods—from leather to wool, precious stones to gold and silver, farming tools to weapons. Each street was famous for one of the trading items. The shops filled with the hustle and bustle of people selling and buying.

Om and Parvaza went to see some of the weapon shops, and they were impressed with the assortment. The quality of weapons was the same as that of their kingdom—indeed, some weapons were imported from Malla. There was a street famous for food, where they sold spices of various kinds from all around the Himalayan kingdoms.

Om and Parvaza spent half a day exploring. At noon, they felt like resting and chose one of the taverns. The tavern served great food and wine. Both of them were thirsty and started drinking. One followed the other, and soon, they were quite drunk.

A man named Amber approached them and started a conversation. He had a clever look and a swift, dexterous way of moving, as well as brown eyes and dark hair, not unlike Om and Parvaza.

After a while, he asked, "Can I interest you in a bull fight match?"

Parvaza looked at Om and noticed that he was all ready to go. "Let's go. It would be fun," Om told Parvaza.

"The place is a few yojanas' ride from Hrada, and the fight won't begin until sunset," Amber explained.

Both of them followed Amber towards the rocky town of Kripan. Everyone in town seemed as if they were waiting for the fight to begin.

Amber took them straight to the arena. It was surrounded by massive rocks on all sides. The rocks formed a boundary, and the seats were carved in them. There was an open area at the bottom reserved as a fighting ground. The rocks were connected via wooden bridges at different levels, which also served as a viewing area.

The group got a place near the edge of a bridge. All of them waited for the fight to begin and continued their drinking. Amber described the place and explained its history. "After the fight, perhaps I could take you to play kaitava, a gambling game?" he offered enticingly.

Soon after sunset, the match finally started. There were two openings in the ground. A bull entered from each opening, and the two charged straight towards each other. The sound of the collision, blood and brains rushing, and the wine and screaming formed an atmosphere of ecstasy. The voice of the crowd shook the huge mountain rocks each time the bulls with huge horns collided into each other. The game concluded after four fights, and then the three went to a tavern to eat something before heading to try their fortune at kaitava.

The gambling games took place inside a private house with a pleasant open garden in the middle. There were a number of carpets, and each carpet had a table, around which people were sitting. The game played was similar to the dice game Om and Parvaza had played in their kingdom. Amber introduced them to the owner—a man with a big beard and black-painted eyes.

As they sat to play, Amber left them, saying, "I'll be right back with some water." The game began with four other players.

Soon, both Om and Parvaza started losing. They did everything they could, but nothing seemed to work. "I was certainly a good player back in Malla," Parvaza told Om.

Time passed, and Om started growing suspicious. Then he caught one of the other players cheating. The garden almost instantly became a heated battleground. Soon enough, both sides pulled swords. The nearby people came and surrounded both Om and Parvaza.

At the same time, Parvaza said, "Om, the band is missing from your forehead!"

That drove Om to madness. "Did someone among this group take my band?" he demanded.

The argument went on, but so far, no one had actually raised their swords on each other. A consensus was reached that the parties would return all the winnings, and that people could leave with their original money. Om agreed, and they took back their share.

After the restitution, while walking towards their horses, Om opened the bag of coins. "These are cheap metal, not our gold!" Both of them turned back and saw that everyone in that garden was standing in line with their swords held high.

"Time to teach them a lesson, my friend," Parvaza told Om, and drew both his axes out.

At that moment, Om witnessed how unrivaled and perfectly coordinated Parvaza was with his axes. It would have taken Om a few moves to destroy the group of people; instead, he chose to fight like an ordinary soldier and dashed ahead with his sword and shield. Parvaza was surprised, but watching Om fight like a commoner inspired him.

The fight continued, and neither side seemed to gain on the other. One of the opponents ran and rang a bell on top of the house, signaling for all the thugs to join. A swarm of displeased men surrounded them within moments.

"We won't win if we fight like this!" Parvaza told Om.

"Run, Parvaza!" Om whistled for the horse. He forgot that he had not gotten a response about his headband.

Both continued to fight and jumped out of the premises, over the fence, and started running in circles inside the town. The thugs signaled without delay, and more joined them. On horseback, they chased Om and Parvaza through the streets of the town.

One of the thugs fired arrows at Parvaza. An arrow struck his back, and one of the axes fell to the ground. Another arrow grazed his shoulder, and his clothes were soon soaked with blood.

Seeing this, Om took a piece of burning wood from the tavern next to him and threw it at the thug. The burning wood missed the thug, but landed in one of the houses.

The thugs chased Om and Parvaza down an alley, surrounding them on all sides, except for the house at their backs. Om signaled their horses to run in front, and both of them jumped inside the house through the windows. They ran towards the back and climbed up the walls to the roof. Precariously racing, Om and Parvaza jumped from one housetop to the other.

"This is terrible!" shouted Parvaza.

Om grinned back and said nothing, enjoying every moment.

They crossed a number of houses, jumping from one to the other. Below, the horses were still following their signals. After a while, at the end of a row of houses, they jumped onto the horses to ride towards the city's entrance. They were still at a great distance from the gates.

As they approached a bridge between two houses, on the opposite sides of their path, Om saw men with flaming arrows aimed at their heads. He signaled for Parvaza to get behind him, and he lifted up his left arm, the one bearing his shield. Before Om could assist, an axe flew at the bridge and severed one side of it. The thugs lost their balance, staggering on the wobbling bridge.

"I know a few tricks as well." Parvaza smiled at Om and collected his axe.

Moments later, they heard the sound of a battle horn.

Both of them knew something bad was going to happen. Sword held high and shield in one hand, Om started riding slowly towards the end of the street. Parvaza had already lost one axe and held the other one firmly in his right hand. He prayed to the gods to get them out of this mayhem.

In the next street, almost forty men stood with blazing arrows, and the same number of cavalrymen stood behind them. On one side were the houses and on the other side was a hill. The only way out of the town was now blocked by these men; to fight or surrender were their only choices.

"It is time to show your true self, Om," said Parvaza. He looked at Om meaningfully.

Om dashed towards his rivals with the shield in front, riding at tremendous speed. He stood up on the horse and landed right before reaching the archers, striking the ground fiercely with his tiger claws. The impact of the tiger claws striking the ground blew the archers away, scattering their arrows in every direction. The squealing, terrified cavalry horses scattered, some throwing or entangling their riders. The flaming arrows rained down around them, landing on nearby houses and setting them on fire.

Om and Parvaza climbed the hill and looked at the town behind. Both of them rode towards the palace. Om still did not have his headband. When they reached the palace, it was already morning, and they were ordered to clean up and meet Isvasa.

Isvasa came to see them. After hearing the story, he

couldn't stop laughing, though he was sympathetic for the loss of Om's headband.

He said, "I left you for one day, and you both brought the whole town down! However, I was busy with useful matters. I had an elaborate discussion with the King of Kanika on strengthening the northern border. We also talked about trade and discussed including a trade route that would directly take our goods to sea.

"The king said that the new trade route was very close to the Anga Kingdom. Anga is hostile to both Malla and Kanika. The king also told me that they have been unsuccessful in preventing skirmishes and lootings near the border facing the Anga Kingdom," Isvasa told Om. "This is something you may discuss with the king and his advisors once you are in Malla."

Om listened to Isvasa carefully.

Isvasa continued, "Om, the king also told me that there were rumors of Anga joining hands with the evil Paksi Kingdom. I assured the king that Malla would do anything to protect Kanika from any foreign attack."

Afterwards, the three of them talked about the Paksi Kingdom.

"Let's go and meet the king. We have to start our journey back home tomorrow," said Isvasa to both Om and Parvaza.

Om had one more stop to make. "Instead, I'd like your consent to visit the city of Hrada. I want to buy some silk from the town for my pr... parents." He couldn't tell them about himself and the princess! Hiding his relief, he continued, "I'll be joining the king's court soon, and I don't want to disrespect my family by not sharing my good fortune with them. Which are the best silk merchants?"

Isvasa agreed and laughed, then he gave him recommendations. Om went straight to look for them.

While he was purchasing silk, he felt a dagger pointed to his back. "Don't you move," came a voice from behind. The next moment, the person pointing the dagger was on the ground, and the dagger was in Om's hand.

"You, where were you? I know that what happened yesterday was your fault!" shouted Om.

The man lying on the ground was Amber. "Hear me out. I returned to tell you the full story."

After buying some of the silk clothes, Om walked with Amber to the nearby tavern, still suspicious. "I'm willing to hear you out, but this had better be good."

"Here is your headband," Amber said, handing it over. "May I have your forgiveness?"

Om crossed his arms.

"In truth, I am a master thief, and I can steal anything from anywhere. All the things I've done since yesterday were because I wanted to have your headband. I nicked it when you were drunk at the bull fight, and you were busy shouting. I slipped it in my pocket and kept it until I introduced you to the gamblers. Whatever ruckus transpired there was not my fault," said Amber.

"Why should I forgive you, and why are you returning this to me?" asked Om.

"My lord, forgiveness is up to you, but if I wanted, I could have kept the headband with me," said Amber.

"While I am a thief, I never steal from the poor. However, my friend Samva, an astrologer and a learned man, asked me to return this. My friend also believes this gem is not of this land, and that it is sacred," said Amber. "He urged me to return this to you soon—otherwise, something horrible might happen to myself or this kingdom."

"I have to say that I'm impressed with both your talent to steal and your courage to return my headband," replied Om. "However, I would like to meet with your learned friend."

"Samva doesn't meet anyone, my lord," said Amber. "He lives with me in a distant cave, outside the town, and studies astrology."

"Convey the message to him that I would like to meet," said Om. "Tell Samva that it will be good for him as well as you, and that this is the only way you will get my forgiveness," Om told Amber and left.

The rest of the night was ordinary; most of the time was spent in preparation for the following day's return. Everyone in Isvasa's camp was busy gathering things for the journey. Om spent some time on the grand balcony, and then enjoyed a great dinner with Isvasa and Parvaza.

The next morning, everyone woke up before dawn. Isvasa and others in the palace reached the shores of Hrada and joined the remaining soldiers. Everything was set for the long journey, and all of the two hundred soldiers started the journey back to Malla.

They marched for half a day and stopped in a grassy sunlit clearing for food and rest; Om sat under a tree to have the meal he had wrapped for the journey. He had developed a sense of caution, and liked to prepare his own food. Before he could start, he saw someone on horseback riding towards them. The archers drew their arrows, and one of the soldiers called out a warning.

The man came closer, and Om recognized him as Amber. "I assumed I was about to die from the moment I saw fifty arrows pointing to my head! Samva would like to meet you, my lord, but he said that he would only meet you," Amber told Om.

"Excellent. Come! Dine with me." Om offered food to Amber, and both sat down to eat. "I will ride with you to meet Samva, and then later join the troop on their journey back home."

"I am yours to command," assented Amber, winking.

After finishing his food, Om updated Isvasa, and he rode with Amber towards the cave to meet Samva.

Om was impressed immediately. Samva indeed was a great astrologer, and to an extent, he could even predict the future. He was also capable of talking with animals and could use their abilities. Samva and Om continued their conversation on various matters, and Om told him about the teachings he received from the gurus, but he never mentioned the Mountains of Rishis.

Samva showed him some of his skills and introduced him to his pet hawk, Marak. "I can not only control and command the hawk, but I can even feel what it senses," Samva told Om.

"Ah! I myself have a white tiger for a companion," said Om, leaving out Loka's powers.

"Excellent. By the way, are you in need of a place to

rest for the night?"

"Certainly. I believe I'm only half a day behind my troops, and it won't take me more than a day to regroup with them."

Their talk continued to various philosophical topics. Meanwhile, Amber prepared dinner for them.

"Amber is a great cook, and he takes good care of me," Samva said. "Amber came to me to learn my tricks, but his skills were too advanced for him to learn anything new from me."

"How did you meet?"

"Amber was captured by a group of a dozen soldiers not too far from here. He was being carried to prison, and I happened to be there. I was returning home after running a few errands of my own. He begged me to help him get released and said, in return, that he would do anything. I bought Amber's freedom with a sizeable bribe."

Amber laughed, embarrassed.

"The irony was that Amber was not caught stealing. Instead, he was fighting with a person who had stolen from a poor man. I saw a good person in him, and I thought he would be of great help," said Samva.

"He still continues to steal from people," Om interrupted Samva, and pointed towards his headband.

"Amber is a kind man and never steals from the destitute," said Samva. "He grew up with an empty stomach and would steal only to fill his belly. Slowly, that turned him into a master thief."

"I only steal things from people who do not deserve

them," Amber said, jumping into the conversation.

"Anything powerful in the hands of a wicked person is extremely perilous," Samva said to Om. "Amber also helped me prevent people from practicing wicked arts and black magic."

They spoke at length, quickly developing a friendship. Finally, dinner was ready, and all three sat to eat. The food was wonderful. After dinner, they sat inside the cave around the fire and drank wine.

"Why don't you both join me in the journey to Malla?" Om asked both of them. "You could live at my home and practice your arts there."

"I must never leave this cave," said Samva firmly. "This is the very place that gives me the power to fight injustice."

"That is well, but you must promise to visit me once during winter," Om said in return. He told the man where and how to find him if he ever needed his help.

It was late at night. Samva continued his talk about stars, and he told Om how he could utilize their alignment to predict the future. Om was already impressed with Samva and thought that he would be of great value at the capital city.

Amber also talked about a few of his experiences, where he'd stolen things that others said were nearly impossible to steal. One of Amber's stories took place in the Paksi Kingdom, where he stole from a noble who went out of his way to hurt poor people; he even used them in place of bulls in his fields.

"On the way out, I burned down the entire fort; I still

cannot describe the feelings of the people when I told them they were free," Amber said.

"I also stole magic charms from a witch. She was using them to harm the nearby people and animals. She would kidnap young girls, trying to make them like her; and in the process, she killed a few. It was one of the toughest jobs that I had to execute," Amber proudly said. "Her dark house was guarded by giant owls, bats, and foxes. She had layers of defenses that would easily have killed an ordinary man.

"I sneaked in as her servant to help her keep the place clean. I worked there for a month before I could finally lay my hands on these charms. After the people knew she had no more power, she was burned to death."

The conversation continued until midnight, when at last, they all fell asleep.

Om woke up early in the morning, before the others, and gathered his belongings. As he was about to climb on his horse, Amber woke up. "I would have loved to accompany you to the capital."

Om smiled. "I will seek your and Samva's help whenever needed in the future."

Meanwhile, Samva woke up. "We must surely ride with Om until he rejoins his troops!" The new friends swiftly agreed and set off.

The three rode together for a full day, but they couldn't find the troops. Om was worried; this was the only route they should have taken. There was no way the troops were riding faster than them, and they were supposed to be merely half a day ahead.

"Let's relax under a tree for a while. I'll have a look around," Samva advised. He whistled for his hawk, Marak, and ordered her to look in the direction of Malla. The hawk returned soon after with no signs of anyone.

"We should go back to the place where I parted from them and look for a trace from there," Om mused.

They rode towards the location. It was already evening when they arrived.

The hawk screeched. "She's seen something," Samva said.

The three ran in that direction. The hawk pointed, and they saw a soldier lying down with an arrow in his back.

Om went closer and found Parvaza. He was prone, bedded in a puddle of blood.

CHAPTER 8
All of Your Strengths

Samva sent the hawk to bring his bag from the cave while Om tried to revive Parvaza. Om carefully removed his armor, then snapped the shaft without disturbing the arrowhead.

Parvaza was still breathing, but he was unconscious. He had lost a lot of blood. Samva applied healing herbs on the wounds, and after a while, Parvaza opened his eyes.

He recognized Om with his half-opened eyes and asked, "Where are the others?"

"I didn't see anyone else," said Om slowly.

"There was something in the food that we ate, and everyone started falling sleep. I and a few of my men didn't eat anything because we were the ones serving... Oh! I remember," said Parvaza. "We were surrounded, and only a few of my men could fight. The others were lying on the ground, deep asleep."

121

"What happened next?" demanded Om, deeply concerned.

"The fight was short, and my men were killed. I continued to fight with almost a dozen men who had surrounded us from all directions. I could see the assailants loading the soldiers on bull carts. Then something hit me from behind, and I passed out. I seem to be the only one left behind. The attackers took everyone else, living or dead."

"Samva, take Parvaza with you and then bring him to Malla once he regains strength," Om said. "I will head in the direction that Parvaza mentioned and find his men."

"Om, let Amber accompany you. He knows the lay of the land," Samva instructed, looking around at the trees. He made some strange clicking noises, followed by what sounded like a howl, and he continued to do so, until soon, a pack of seven wolves appeared.

"These are my friends, and they will help you find your men," Samva told them. Samva instructed the wolves to follow Om's orders. "As you can't interact much with the wolves, you must remember to raise one hand towards someone to attack and show your fist for them to stand still. The wolves will also attack anyone who attacks you. My prayers are with you. Marak will keep a vigil from above, and I will know about your well-being," Samva told Om.

Taking Parvaza with him, Samva left Om with Amber and his wolves and rode towards his cave.

The wolves had already caught the scent and sped off to follow it. Om and Amber rode behind them. They rode all night, as they didn't want to rest, and sought to cover the maximum distance between them and the captors.

Even as the sun rose, there was no sign of his men, but Om somehow knew that they were getting closer. It seemed that the captors hadn't rested at night either.

The chase brought them near a stream of water, where they stopped, drank, and filled their water bags.

"Beyond these waters is the Kingdom of Anga," Amber told Om.

Om remembered his discussion with Isvasa about the daily skirmishes in Kanika's border areas near Anga. "I'm convinced that the raiders were definitely Anga soldiers in disguise," he said.

After a brief rest, they crossed the stream and continued to follow the running wolves. The journey seemed endless, and they were getting tired.

A few yojanas inside the Anga Kingdom, they saw smoke to the west. Towards its source, the smoke grew thicker and a fetor of death hung over the land. Coughing, the two brought their horses to a halt, as they had entered what seemed like a cremation ground. Smoke rose from pyres in front of them and at a distance. Unable to find another living being, they returned to their path. Around a dozen yojanas further inside the kingdom, they found a hut, and they saw the wolves running towards it. Om stopped to see if there was anyone inside—perhaps someone who could tell them of any troops' movements nearby.

Meer was behaving strangely, dragging himself backwards. He even tried dragging Om back. Om ignored

Meer's strange behavior and knocked on the door. An elderly man came out.

"Hello, sir. Have you seen any troops?"

The old man replied, "I have seen no such thing, but you may rest inside if you want."

"We *are* tired. Perhaps we should rest and wait a while," Amber suggested.

They entered the hut, and the old man gave them some fruit to eat. Amber grabbed Om's hand right as he was about to take a bite. He seized the man by his tattered garb and held his sword at the old man's throat.

"Tell me if you saw the troops. Were there captured soldiers on bull carts?" said Amber. "Om, search the man's trunks."

Om opened a storage box in the corner and found a bag of coins. He opened it and found Anga gold.

"Yes, fine, I saw them. They went there." The old man pointed out the direction in which they had gone.

"We will spare your life," said Om. "Amber, let's go." Om didn't even ask Amber how he sensed that the old man was lying.

They started in that direction, as they were very close. A brisk ride brought them to the edge of a cliff, and from the top, they saw the captors. There were dozens of them—a few on horses in the front, a few on foot beside the bull carts, and the rest following behind. The troops had moved forward from where they stood on the cliff, and the last row was now in front of them.

"Amber, about a hundred feet to your right is the ideal location where you can hide and shoot arrows from," said

Om. Om gave Amber his bow and arrows.

"Why are they painted in different colors?"

"The red ones are bee stings; the orange ones are fire bursts; green will render the enemy unconscious; and black ones are bodkin arrows to pierce the enemy armor. Now, here's my plan…" Om gestured towards the army. "Don't fire the orange arrows in the middle, where the bull carts are; it would harm our own men. Fire the orange ones in front, the green ones in the middle, and the red ones in the end. Target the cavalry in front first, then the middle section, and finally, the back. I will charge after you have fired on the last section," said Om. "Don't let anyone escape, as they might bring in more soldiers."

Amber took his position, ready to fire at Om's signal.

Om came close to the final line and hid behind a small tree. He gave Amber the go-ahead. To Om's surprise, Amber's aim was impeccable. He fired in quick succession and targeted each of the three sections.

Below, Om charged in and wounded as many captors as he could before the enemy came out of shock. The front line of cavalry recovered sooner than he had anticipated. The leader of the enemy sent five of his men in the eastern direction for help.

This meant that Om had to finish the fight before others joined the captors. Amber was already helping him with black arrows. He signaled Amber to fire all he had towards the five men that had gone for help.

Amber took a deep breath and fired a black arrow, the only color he had left. He struck one of the men, but after missing the rest of them, he gave up.

Meanwhile, Om and the wolves had put down all the men except the cavalry. It was not surprising to see wolves bring down so many heavy men all on their own.

Om used his tiger claws once again and smashed the ground; the shock from it threw all the cavalry off their horses. In no time, every one of the enemy was either dead or tied in ropes.

Amber climbed down the hill and helped Om untie their men.

Om found and untied half-conscious Isvasa first. Om instructed him, "Take the men back to Malla as fast as you can. I'll follow the four soldiers that escaped, surely to return with copious numbers. Wait for us in the eastern fort once you reach Malla."

"Let the hawk guide Isvasa and his men. It can fly back and alert us if they are in any danger," Amber advised.

"Indeed. Isvasa and the soldiers are still weak. Now, let's go," Om agreed.

Along with Amber and the wolves, Om marched in the direction the four soldiers had gone. The wolves had picked up the direction of their quarry, and soon, Om saw four men riding ahead of him.

"How many arrows do you have remaining, Amber?"

"Only two."

He handed them to Om.

Om fired both arrows at once. One arrow hit one of the soldiers, and he fell from the horse. The second one wounded another soldier, but he did not fall. The remaining three of the enemy left kept riding. Retrieving the arrows, both Om and Amber followed as fast as they could.

"In thirty yojanas, we'll reach a fort city of Anga. It's full of assassins and corrupt soldiers," Amber warned Om.

"We have to catch the three in front or fight every soldier in that fort, but we can't let anyone follow Isvasa and the troops until they reach a safe distance."

Om caught his gaze, smiled and shrugged, and neither of them spoke a word for a while.

Their quarry disappeared into a narrow path among overhanging trees and hills. When they reached the path, Om examined the passage and said, "We'll have to take this on foot." Both slid down from the horses and entered the narrow path. The wolves all around them kept a sharp watch for their masters.

In the middle, there was a wide opening surrounded by hills. The eastern side of the opening was the ruins of an old temple. It appeared to be an ancient Shiva temple that might have been abandoned for years. Strangely, moments after they entered the opening, the wolves formed a circle around them. They had lost the scent of the three soldiers, but they were sensing a horde of men scattered around.

"Om! Look at the wolves!"

"I know. I'm ready."

In a moment, they were surrounded by hundreds of men on all sides of the hills. A few even stood on top of the ruined temple, with arrows pointed at their heads. The only way out was the path behind, but they would be dead as soon as they moved an inch.

Even the tiger claws wouldn't stagger an enemy that far away. A straight battle with everyone on the ground would have been altogether a different scenario, and Om would have finished them all.

"If they strike, I want you to lay low on my horse and ride back," Om told Amber. "Take my shield. It will protect you from any incoming fire."

"No. If it can protect you, it can protect both of us."

As they were planning what to do next, a person from the ruined temple came forward. "Who are you, and why did you attack our people?"

"We're travelers from the south, and we're here for trade," said Amber.

The person from the temple replied, "Traders come in carts and not horses; traders don't carry heavy weapons; and traders don't have wolves."

Seeing no way out, Om told Amber, "Move between the horses."

As Meer wore his own armored plates, Om held his shield up to cover Amber's horse. The wolves were in between them, and slowly, they started to move back with the horses, sheltering Om and Amber on either side.

Om saw the man standing on the temple signal something. Hundreds of savage arrows pointed their way. Other than prayers, they only had luck to get them out alive. Both of them also prayed for the safety of their soldiers riding back to Malla.

The enemy leader ordered, "Fire!" As one, the archers released the volley, and arrows flew towards Om and Amber, blotting out the sun in a hellish downpour.

128

In that moment of defeat, a bright light descended from the sky and struck the land in front of them. The arrows fell harmlessly, like tiny drops of rain. Om saw a lady dressed in lustrous white, emanating an ethereal glow all around her. She wore a silver headband with a bright red gem embedded in it and a peacock feather in her hair.

She carried a silver trident. Om had not seen a trident like that before. It was like a spear in the middle, and it had an axe-like structure on either side. The lady lifted her trident and stuck it again on the ground, sending a thunder across that shook not only men on the hills, but also uprooted a few trees. The enemies were either dead or fleeing for their lives.

Om tried to look at her face, but he couldn't manage, due to the bright light that surrounded her.

"Take this as the last time, Om, that someone from the heavens will save you," the lady said. "We will watch over you, but no one from the celestial realm can always come down and save you. You are destined to do more, but you should treat this as a lesson and make all your decisions wisely. We have been watching you since the day your training started, and we have been helping you without being seen. I will pass some of my powers to your sword, and you can use it in the same way I used my trident." She walked towards Om and touched Om's sword with her trident.

"Use this new power wisely, and only if you have no other choice. But I have one last gift for you." She held out a bow and a handful of arrows. "A gift from the gods. The arrows are divine and can be recalled once fired. As for the bow, you will learn its powers eventually."

The lady disappeared the same way she had appeared. Om didn't even realize that Amber had been unconscious all along. When he finally noticed, Om didn't want to further frighten him by telling him precisely what had happened. He hid the bow on the left side of his horse and woke Amber.

"What happened?" Amber demanded, blinking furiously.

"The jolt from my tiger claws frightened everyone, and they fled. We're safe now."

However, the wolves had seen everything and were still wary of the bright light. They were acting strange, lagging behind, as if dazed.

On their way back, Om finally asked Amber, "How did you know that the old man back in the hut was lying?"

"Before we entered, the old man might have been playing with the coins, as he may not have seen so much his entire life. When we knocked, he put everything down in a hurry, and one of the coins fell underneath the trunk. I can recognize a coin from a distance, and I knew it was not earned honestly. An old man who earns a coin will always keep it by his side, tied to his clothes," Amber said.

"Then I must thank you for your wits, my friend."

They rode towards the eastern fort of Malla.

After a rest that night, they arrived at the fort the next morning. Om relieved the wolves and hawk of their duty. "Now you may return to Samva."

"Wait!" Amber tied a message to the hawk's feet to be delivered to Samva.

After a day of rest and wonderful food, Isvasa and his men were back in shape. "How on earth did you rescue us?" Isvasa asked at length. "And where is Parvaza?"

"He is safe and will return in a few months," Om answered, watching the hawk fly off.

"Very good. The soldiers will march towards Camp Sarasi tomorrow, and both of us will ride to the palace."

He dismissed Om, who turned back to his friend.

"Amber, stay with us. Come to Ogana with me."

He clapped a hand on Om's shoulder and smiled. "Absolutely. I'm thrilled to be in your company. It's far more adventurous than my routine life with Samva. I have the highest regard for Samva, but I want to be part of greater adventures."

In the evening, the fort's captain gave Om a tour of the mighty structure. This fort was the second largest in the kingdom and was well engineered and protected. The captain also gave him a tour of the escape routes in case of an unforeseen invasion.

After a hearty dinner, everyone slept, so as to rise early in the morning. Om was eager to meet his love again. He had not seen his family or guru in a while, either. He had asked one of the soldiers to bring Loka directly to the capital city, Ogana.

Isvasa and Om, along with Amber and a few others, rode towards Ogana. As they'd already had a tiresome journey over the past month, they took chariots from the fort city. Isvasa rode in one with his soldiers, and Om, with Amber, in the other. They would stop at intervals to

131

take rest and eat.

After riding for eight days, they were in the capital. Om was shown to his new quarters, which were some of the finest in the west wing of the main palace. "Stay with me as an associate," Om suggested.

"Of course," Amber agreed.

"But first, I have a private matter to attend to," Om said, with complete seriousness.

"Enjoy time with your princess!" Amber called back, letting his friend go.

Before meeting King Neera and Isvasa that evening, Om went to see the princess. "Where is she?" he asked one of her handmaidens.

"She has gone out, but no one knows where."

Om knew where she was, but today, he would not be able to make it to her and back in time to meet the king. By now, Isvasa had already groomed Om for his role as advisor to the king. Om had spent a great deal of time with Isvasa while training the special force and had learned all about politics in the king's court.

Isvasa and Om were greeted by the king in his private chambers. Isvasa updated him on his Kanika visit and their northern border skirmishes, and he also described their capture by Anga soldiers in disguise, and Om's bravery.

"Thank you for your heroism once again, Om. I can now formally present to you the ring marking your role as my new advisor."

Om accepted in silence, with a deep bow.

"Your Highness, we also need to strengthen the

eastern fort with more soldiers and start regularly patrolling the borders with Anga. Anga soldiers come and burn the villages, loot the harvest, and steal the cattle," said Isvasa.

"Anga soldiers don't dare plunder on Malla territory. They only attack villages past our borders, on land belonging to Kanika Kingdom."

"Kanika is a friend, and we must defend them from these skirmishes," said Isvasa firmly.

The king agreed. "Station more troops in the eastern fort. I have heard about the Paksi Kingdom growing stronger. Paksi is the biggest kingdom under the Himalayas, and their alliance with Raksas makes them more threatening. They have captured all of the west and south, and soon they will eye the eastern kingdoms," said the king.

Isvasa said that the king of Kanika had expressed the same thoughts.

"I have a messenger who will arrive in two days. I would want both of you to be present once he is here," the king said.

Isvasa and Om left the king's chambers after the discussion. Om went to find out about his brother and family, and enquired in the temple about Rishi's whereabouts. To his surprise, his family had taken his brother Gautam back to Medhya, and he wasn't a palace guard anymore. Rishi was also back at his hut in Medhya.

The next morning, before sunrise, Om rode towards the jungle, hoping to meet the princess. Abha was indeed on the same island inside the jungle where they had spent time during the festivals. She looked up with a true smile as he found her. She greeted Om graciously, and extended her hand as he strolled towards her. Om could sense by her actions how elated she was to see him.

"I've brought you a present from my travels." Om gave her the embroidered scarlet silk vesture he had brought from Kanika, and she handed him a bracelet she had made for him.

"You have a new bow! How did you come by it?"

Om told her the story, and she was both amazed and thrilled. "But I don't know how to recall the arrows yet," he admitted.

"We can stay one more day in the jungle and practice tomorrow."

They spent the rest of the day talking about what they'd done after they left each other. Om narrated to her the complete story from the camp to Kanika and back home. He also acknowledged that the beast back in the Garden of Flowers was Loka, though he didn't know about it then.

"We were destined to meet," the princess said. "If it wasn't you, then who gave instructions to Loka at the Garden of Flowers?"

"Rishi is the only person who could have done that," Om replied, laughing. "He saw our future together; all he did was help us meet each other."

Abha told him all about the month she had spent living in one of the villages, in disguise among the farmers. Om knew these small things brought her great happiness.

The night passed by, and neither one left the other for

a moment.

The next day, the princess and Om tried the new bow. She tried, but she was unable to recall the arrows.

"This might only work for you," she said, and handed over the bow to Om.

Om tried a few more times, with no success. They tried showing their hand towards the arrows, putting hands up in the air, and even whispering to the arrows, but nothing seemed to work. After some time, Abha lifted the bow and shot an arrow straight towards a target. Before reaching out for the next arrow, she stretched the string of the bow, and the arrow fired earlier came back to her hand.

They tried again and again, and the tiresome venture soon became merry. That night, both of them returned to their kingdom. Om showed her his new quarters and introduced her to Amber. Om then accompanied the princess to her chambers. On the way back, he found Isvasa and was invited to meet the king next morning.

CHAPTER 9
The Ganas

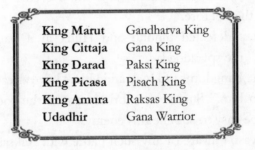

King Marut	Gandharva King
King Cittaja	Gana King
King Darad	Paksi King
King Picasa	Pisach King
King Amura	Raksas King
Udadhir	Gana Warrior

Early that morning, both Isvasa and Om were summoned to the king's court. Two finely dressed noblemen stood in front of the king.

"Here are my warriors," King Neera greeted them. "And this is my head minister, Susans."

Om had heard about him from a lot of people, including Isvasa. Susans was said to be the wisest person under the Himalayan peaks. Om looked at the other person. He was familiar.

"Your spies, Isvasa, bring rather evil news this

morning, and that's the reason I summoned you at once," the king said. "The Paksi ruler is going to attack us, and he will be accompanied by all the Raksas."

"How is this possible? If they attack, we will defeat them again!" Isvasa said with a jolt of anger. "We were victorious over Raksas and Pisachs once, and our men are capable of repeating history."

"Times have changed," Susans explained, as he paused and took a seat behind him. "Darad, the Paksi king, has grown more powerful. The Paksi king commands the greatest force that these lands have ever seen. He has powerful allies, the Raksas and the Pisachs, who are fiercer than before."

"They defeated Sindhu and Huna in a battle last winter," the spy added.

"The Kingdoms of Doab and Uttara have already bent knee to him." Susans now briskly paced the room. "It won't be easy to subdue this enemy."

"I wasn't aware of any such battle with Raksas," Om said in a questioning tone.

"The kingdom's allies from the mountains will come to our aid when called upon," Isvasa said.

King Neera arose from his throne and walked down the steps as calm and composed as ever. Everyone else rose with the king. "The mountain treaty was broken after my father's death. No one will come to our aid. Discuss and come up with a solution," said the king. "Let us then meet again in the evening."

The spy was relieved, and three of the king's most trusted men continued their conversation.

Om interrupted the talk and asked them to explain a few things. "Who was the spy, and why did he look familiar? When did we fight with Raksas? Who are these mountain friends of ours?" Om showered them with his questions.

Isvasa answered, "Spies are soldiers of the king who perform duties beyond our borders. It was my idea for a way to learn the secrets of enemy kingdoms. These spies make themselves local residents, and a few have even joined high ranks in enemies' courts. They are highly trained to be in disguise and gather important information. There is also a channel to pass on the messages swiftly," said Isvasa. "All the soldiers you trained back at the camp are spies now."

"They are? Why?"

"The spies are good at information gathering and relaying, but they weren't as physically strong as their core unit. I required you to train some of the spies, and now they can fight their way out of difficult situations," Isvasa told Om.

"But how? Each one of the chosen soldiers had to pass the test," Om questioned. "How come only your spies got selected?"

"The other soldiers were asked not to perform well in order to let the spies pass," Isvasa replied.

Om didn't look happy.

Isvasa consoled him. "At that point, it was the king's secret, not to be shared with a commoner. But you are now a part of the king's court, and now you know," said Isvasa.

"All right. So when did we fight the Raksas, and who are our mountain friends?" asked Om.

"This is something you have to hear from Susans, who was among the people who witnessed it," Isvasa said, and looked at Susans.

Susans was already sitting in his chair, hands folded and in deep thought.

"He wants to know the story, my lord," said Isvasa.

Susans looked at Om and gestured for him to sit in the chair by his side. "This happened almost a hundred years ago. No commoner alive today knows about it. All that the people know are the tales and stories that the king's court has passed on for years. In the king's own library are books that tell tales as they happened. I was the advisor to the head minister for the king's father, who was then the King of Malla, after whom this very kingdom was named. Well, this was something everyone knows," said Susans.

"The King of Malla was a great warrior and a devout follower of Indra, the thunder god. As you know, Indra is the head of the gods. He was always pleased with the king's worship and offerings. Happiness reigned in the kingdom, and every child lived life without fear. Despite being a mettlesome warrior, the king never believed in war, and the army was only used as a defense. He never threatened any other kingdom. We were living happily, and offering our prayers and worship to the gods. Yet in a not-so-distant world, people were also praying—not for good, but to bring evil upon everyone.

"There were two unholy kingdoms, which were not of

men, but of demons. On one side, there were Raksas, and on the other side, Pisachs. The Raksas were demons that could take any form and size. They were friends with the ruler of Paksi and Pisachs. These odious beasts were powerful. Their power grew with meditation, and they pleased the lord of the lords, Brahma, enough to attain unearthly powers. Raksas King Amura had pleased Brahma more than once, and had been blessed with mystical powers. He could push mountains with his feet and turn anyone blind with his powers to control the air. He could even command fire and dust together—and unearth the dead from the underworlds.

"Pisachs were also demons, but they were said to be already dead. After years of devotion and prayer by King Picasa, they were created by Brahma as a favor. These unholy creatures, dark as night, drank the blood of the innocent and had vivid red veins and eyes. They were lighter than air, and could even fly. They talked the language of the dead, known as Paisaci. They lived in darkness, and their powers knew no bounds at night. It was hard for humans to defeat them, but at night, they were undefeatable even by the gods themselves. They mostly dwelled underground and would occasionally rise up. They were horrific to look at and had long, sharp tails."

Om and Isvasa silently looked at Susans as he continued the story. "On the other hand, guided by his greed and lust for power, Darad, the King of Paksi and slayer of kings, worshipped Lord Shiva. He was granted the power to live indefinitely without aging. Darad had made a pact with the Raksas and Pisachs against their common enemies: men and demi-gods. Their pact was so strong that none of the kingdoms on land could defeat them. Some rose against them and vanished into dust, with no remains or history of them to be told. They would burn down everything and kill everyone. Every kingdom in the Himalayan region was captured, except the kingdoms of Northern Himalaya.

"At that time, Malla was a big empire, with Madhya as part of it. In the Himalayas, our kingdom and the demi-gods' kingdoms remained out of reach for these demons. But then marching orders towards Malla were given. The enemy rode for a day, then called a counsel between their leaders. They decided to attack the mountains before the rains began. The Raksas King Amura told the Paksi King Darad that Malla could be defeated easily, but that once it rained, capturing the mountains would be impossible.

"There were only two ways to the mountains and the kingdom of demi-gods—one was through Malla and the other was upstream on the Devprayag River. The path upstream to Devprayag River was through a series of caves, and it was difficult. No one had tried it before, but it was wise to attack the mountains before rain. Once the rains started, the snow would follow, and the enemy would have to wait for another year. The path through Malla was home to four demi-gods' kingdoms, but the path via the river was home to only one—a fifth demi-god kingdom, the Ganas, which were some of the strongest of the demi-gods.

"In the past, King Amura had suffered several defeats

by the Ganas. Amura was not willing to wait at all, and wanted to put an end to the Ganas to send a strong message to the world. The message would be that the undefeated Ganas had been conquered, and no one among the rest of the demi-gods would be spared. All preparations were made, and they rode towards the caves upstream of the river Devprayag.

"Ganas were known as architects of the gods. They were masterful warriors and marvelous builders. They were direct descendants of Indra and Varuna, the god of water. It was said that they could build an entire city in merely a few days. It was also rumored that the city of Ogana was built by Ganas. The Gana land was said to be even more beautiful than the land of the gods. They built godly structures and had used all their skills to carve out a great kingdom in the Western Himalayan Mountains.

"Their kingdom was built of gold and precious stones. The first light of the sun would make it glow like an ember on a throne of snow. The buildings were majestic, and there were statues in every corner of the kingdom. Some statues rose like mountains above the ground, but the royal palace was the tallest of all. They used floating, horseless chariots to travel, driven by the force of a Gana baton.

"The Ganas regarded themselves as different from the other four demi-gods and had chosen this secluded land to live in peace and prosperity. Their land was so secluded that only gods and demi-gods could travel to their kingdom. The path through the caves of Devprayag was dangerous, and no non-god had ever crossed it.

"The unholy army marched towards the Gana Kingdom, led by the three powerful evil rulers. The Pisachs were in the front lines, as they could fly, and they were a few yojanas ahead to watch any movement. Soon, everyone arrived at the mouth of the Devprayag Cave. Rope bridges were built by Pisachs in no time, and the ascent towards the great kingdom began.

"The Ganas were alerted by their watchmen, and they prepared themselves for the arriving army. They knew that their enemy was many times stronger. Some of the Ganas would be fighting for the first time. However, the Ganas had sent for help from the Gandharvas and patiently waited for them to arrive. At this time, almost half of the evil army had reached the mountain cave, and the other half was still climbing.

"The Ganas, however, had strategies to thwart the enemy. As they climbed, the evil army heard the rushing water, but they thought it was the river clashing with stones in the cave. Slowly, the sound grew louder, but the evil army was too consumed in their efforts to notice.

"Before long, they saw waves huge enough to swallow the cave rushing towards them. The force was devastating, and the deluge unrelentingly hurled the evil army to the base of the fall. The rope bridge was broken, and a great number of the evil army's soldiers were dead even before the fight started. The Raksas King Amura saw the growing dissent among his soldiers and decided to climb up himself. The Pisachs laid out another bridge, and the great evil warrior climbed. That moment brought enough motivation to the evil armies that they started climbing back. An army is as good as its leader; a powerful leader can strengthen a weak army enough to take on even the titans.

"Once the Raksas King Amura was up along with Pisachs, he carved out a path inside the cave. Each one was tied by a rope and pulled up so that the gushing water wouldn't wash away any more of the soldiers. King Amura used his mythical powers to slow down the flow of the water and, thereby, help his soldiers climb.

"Soon, every last soldier had climbed up and moved further inside the cave. In a few yojanas, they had left the river behind, and now they were on a dark road ahead. After another yojana, they entered a large hollow space inside the cave. It resembled the ruins of an ancient city, and the height and depth of the opening could not be measured. There were a series of stone bridges and rope connectors, and the path ahead wound like a serpent. King Amura inquired with his advisors, who gathered information from the Pisachs, and they were divining the route. They said that the only way forward was through the bridges and the ropes. The army continued the march. The paths narrowed at the bridges, and only one man at a time could pass. Soon, all the army was on some kind of bridge or connector and moving forward. Only some from the evil armies in the front line had crossed the bridges when they heard a rumble. Within moments it had escalated to a thousand thunders through the caves.

"The evil kings witnessed some of the bridges collapse, and saw the soldiers plummeting to the bottom. The Pisach King Picasa ordered his aerial troops to go after the befuddled soldiers and lay out Pisach bridges. These, unlike the rope bridges, were formed by Pisach bodies cinched with each other. The armies were ordered to move slowly and be silent.

"After crossing the bridges, they came to a muddy morass, and it seemed like a river had once flowed through there. The wetlands were full of insects, which drove the evil army insane. After walking a few yojanas inside, they were attacked by black, monstrous flying beasts. They were as tall as five Raksas on top of each other, and they could seize at least four men at once. The wetlands were filled with screams and blood. Soldiers fought with the creatures and insects at once. Amura, the Raksas king, started using his mystical powers to fight these creatures, but their numbers were large.

"Seeing nothing work, Darad, the Paksi king, took out his trident. A gift from Lord Shiva, the trident could be used only once, and it would have devastating effects even on gods. Darad saw no other option, and he used it. The wave of light that came out from the trident burned down all of the black creatures in the blink of an eye. The impact was such that it trembled the entire Kingdom of Ganas. Finally, when they came out of the cave, more than half the evil army had been destroyed. The remaining half was drained, but when they saw the glimpse of the kingdom and its beauty, all rejoiced at the prospect of living in lands of such unparalleled beauty.

"From there the Raksas King Amura divided the armies into three. The Pisachs were front in line, followed by Raksas, and then the men. The Pisach army marched towards the Gana soldiers. The Ganas used all their weapons, but they were unable to hurt a single Pisach. The Pisachs were able to strike fear into even the most powerful Gana soldiers. The Ganas fought with all their might, and soon, they started gaining on Pisachs.

"King Amura saw this and sent a wave of Raksas at them from two directions—east and west. The Gana army was now divided into three, and they were fighting on all the three fronts. Darad held back and signaled his archers to fire flaming arrows. The arrows filled the sky in such a huge number that it left a shadow on the ground.

"Udadhir, leader of the Gana army, was motivating his army in every possible way. Determined to confront the leader of the enemy, he dashed towards King Amura. Udadhir took Amura by surprise and jabbed him with the hilt of his sword. The impact slammed the Raksas king to the ground, and for a moment, everyone stood still. Seeing their leader fight the evil king, the Ganas fought with their supreme strength.

"On the other side, the Gana King Cittaja was preparing to enter the battle. He had been waiting for the arrival of his Gandharva allies. The Gandharvas didn't arrive, but a letter came. His minister told him that Gandharvas were engaged in a battle with the Nagas—one so fierce that they couldn't leave the battleground. The letter also recommended he reach out to other demigods, but King Cittaja was too proud for that.

"Ready for battle, he entered the battleground in his flying chariot, with his shining battalion following him. The arrival of their king boosted the morale of the soldiers, and they were able to gain ground on several fronts. Darad mobilized his Paksi army to help Raksas and Pisachs. The archers stood back, but the swordsmen gathered in a semi-circle and marched towards the northern line. The northern line was crushed, and there were no Gana soldiers left to fight. The few that were left joined the western fight zone with their king, or the eastern with their leader, Udadhir.

"Darad and the Pisach King Picasa challenged the Gana King Cittaja, and a combat between them began. Both sides used mystical weapons and brought down showers of fire and thunder on each other.

"The Raksas King Amura took advantage of the distraction and used his mystical powers to pass a poisoned arrow to one of his soldiers. Udadhir, fixated on the Paksi king, was oblivious to Amura's cleverly devised ruse. On the other side, King Cittaja was inflicting heavy blows to the army of men and Pisachs. He would use the wind to clobber soldiers' formations into pieces, and then the Ganas would strike them. He accomplished all this while still fighting with two evil kings."

Susans rested for a moment, drank some water, and continued his story: "The Raksas king knew that the Gana king was more powerful than both the Paksi king and Pisach king. He had to end his fray with Udadhir. He signaled the soldier with the poison arrow, who covertly trained the arrow at Udadhir. Udadhir charged at Amura, and as he raised himself, the poisonous arrow struck his leg. He fell to the ground.

"King Amura rushed towards the Gana king, firing a

fusillade of poisonous arrows. King Cittaja averted them, hurling fierce winds to scatter and shatter the arrows. All around them, the Gana soldiers fell. The head minister in the palace saw this and knew it was time for the emergency protocol. All the people in the palace, including the queen, were asked to enter the escape route. The minister joined the battle and lied to King Cittaja about an attack on the escape route. Once the king was inside, the minister closed the grand mountain doors and went back to enter the fight.

"King Cittaja had no choice but to retreat. He and his people followed the escape route towards the Gandharvas' land. The fight ended with the victory of the evil rulers, and the beautiful Kingdom of Ganas was divided among Raksas and Pisachs. The Pisachs acquired the eastern realm, while Raksas remained in the west.

"King Amura and King Darad discussed strategies for their next battle, but the Pisachs were busy in their new worldly fervor. They were underworld dwellers, and after seeing the luxuries of the Gana Kingdom, they forgot everything else. The Pisach King Picasa told both the Raksas and the Paksi kings that they were not yet ready for another battle. Amura knew that more than half of his soldiers were dead, and it wasn't the right time for another attack. He returned to the Raksas Kingdom, and Darad, to his human kingdom. The three agreed to meet in six months, near the Kingdom of Uttara. As winter began, they would march through the Uttara Kingdom and towards Malla.

"The news of their victory had already spread across

all the Himalayan Kingdoms. Fear gripped the rest of the holy world. The four demi-gods were devastated above all others. A few might not have liked the Ganas, but all of them knew the power they possessed. The Gandharvas were still fighting a long battle with Nagas, which didn't seem to end."

"How do you know the story in such great detail?" asked Om.

"He knows because I told him," came a gentle yet strong voice.

Susans gestured magnificently. "Meet Udadhir. He has always been there to help this kingdom and, fortunately, he survived the battle."

CHAPTER 10
A Special Alliance

Everyone greeted Udadhir, and he took the seat next to Om's.

"The rest of the story you can hear from the great Gana himself," said Susans.

Udadhir continued. "Gandharvas were ruled by a powerful demi-god, Marut—the greatest among the demi-gods. King Marut always used his powers for spreading peace and slaying all that is evil."

Om looked at Udadhir, curiosity burning in his eyes. "Tell me more about Gandharvas."

Udadhir smiled at Om. "Gandharvas are demi-gods that act as messengers for gods. They are the bridge between men and the divine. A few were married to apsaras, who tend to the court of the gods. One of the most vital roles of Gandharvas is to prepare Soma for the gods. Soma is a blessed drink which bestows powers to the gods and demi-gods alike. The Gandharvas are also regarded as descendants of the sun god and are called "rays of light" by other demi-gods. Their appearance is second to none, and they are as beautiful and irresistible as the gods themselves.

"Their clan is divided into warriors, poets, musicians, and authors. The warriors guard the kingdom and are protectors of Soma. The warriors also possess mystical powers and are crafters of weapons beyond compare. Their weapons are uniquely built to destroy evil forces like the Raksas and Pisachs. The poets, musicians, and authors also belong to the court of gods. Many plays and epics performed in the lands of men were written and orchestrated by them. The main enemy of the Gandharvas were Nagas, the unholy sons of the underworld, who are half men and half snakes from the waist."

As Om appeared content with this part of the narrative, Udadhir continued the story from where his friend Susans had left it.

"I was knocked down in the battle by the Raksas King Amura. Assuming that I perished, he set off to besiege the Gana king. After the battle, a few of my loyal soldiers revived me. They carried me far away, to the land of men, and finally to the Gandharva lands. When the group reached the Malla Kingdom, I was shivering with fever and pain, covered in bruises and severe battle injuries. The soldiers carrying me arranged for a local Vaidya, who took care of me for a month. After weeks of intensive treatment, I had regained strength, and I went to meet King Malla.

"I was welcomed, and as requested, I was taken directly to meet the king in his private quarters. King Malla was with his friend Madhva, the governor of Madhya province. I explained that an alliance between men and demi-gods would be necessary, as the Gandharvas possessed weapons and powers to defeat the Raksas and Pisachs.

"King Malla understood the severity of the situation, but he wasn't convinced that a treaty could be forged. I pointed out to him that Gandharvas' worst enemy were Nagas, and even with all their powers, they had been unable to defeat them for years. King Malla's assistance in defeating the Nagas would be the beginning of a holy alliance. King Malla argued that his soldiers were not equipped enough to fight such a battle. At that very moment, Madhva told the king that he might have a unique solution to this problem.

"The governor of Madhya said that he knew a group of tribesmen who had mastery in training snakes, and at the sound of their music, even the fiercest snakes could be controlled. Madhva ordered a few of his men to visit the tribesmen's chief with his personal letter. They would join us during our journey. King Malla ordered his army to assemble and for all civilians to take refuge in their nearest forts and castles. After a few days, they marched towards the battleground of Gandharvas, which was to the north, towards the Mountains of Rishis. It would take a few months to reach the battleground.

"When we reached the battlegrounds, we met the Gandharva King Marut, and camped by his side. The following day was spent discussing and outlining battle strategy. King Marut explained that he was tired of this war and that he wanted it to end once and for all. A strategy was discussed and agreed upon; the Gandharvas had to lure the Nagas further in towards their campground. The tribesmen would be placed on the hilltops above the valley. Once the Nagas were near the campground, the forces of men would surround them and fire ignited arrows to block their exit. At the same time, the tribesmen would begin playing their enchanting tunes to confound the enemy.

"It took the Gandharvas a month to trick the Nagas into appearing at the right location. The tribesmen were ready, and Madhva's plan worked. Most of the Nagas were either killed or captured; those who escaped never left the underworld again. This brought an end to the countless years of war with the Nagas. King Malla and his men were invited to the Gandharvas' sanctuary city. The Gandharvas, King Malla, and his battalion all marched towards their kingdom. I accompanied King Malla, along with Madhva.

"We entered the Gandharva Kingdom via a narrow pass opened by King Marut's spear. It was said that this pass could only be used by the king or whoever he designated. After the narrow pass, we came to a ravine. On either side of the ravine stood a gilded statue of the god of fire, in his armor, hefty javelin in one hand, and the other hand risen to impart blessings. The statues rose to the clouds; no man could see their peak.

"From this spot, one had an unrestricted view of the

Gandharva Kingdom. The capital was built on the slopes of a mountain, and it was surrounded by the Himalayas and wondrous waterfalls in every direction. These waterfalls fell into lakes and emerged as other waterfalls—a series of falls and lakes with small palaces dotted between them.

"The king's palace was astonishingly beautiful, built in the center of the highest lake. There were trees as tall as mountains all around—some with yellow foliage, and some with green and red leaves. Passing well-carved walkways lined with lifelike sculptures of Apsaras, celestial nymphs of Gandharvas, we reached the main gates of the palace. The main palace gates had a statue of Lord Indra, with the thunderbolt, Vajra, in one of his hands, and the other raised towards the sky. The kingdom was nothing less than the seat of power of Lord Indra.

"After taking rest for half a day, both the kings met in King Marut's study. The study held all the ancient manuscripts that gods or men had ever written. They discussed at great length the upcoming war with the evil army, following which King Marut offered his help to King Malla. He concluded that to defeat the evil army, they would have to use both their blessed weapons and Soma. Soma would strengthen the Malla soldiers so that they would match the evil army; their weapons gave them the means to finish the task. Soma was meant only for divine beings, but King Marut knew of the evil army's devastation of the Ganas. It was decided that the armies of Gandharva and Malla would join forces at the Malla Kingdom, before the onset of spring. After visiting for a few more days, King Malla and his men left for his kingdom, with myself in tow, to prepare for the battle.

"Everyone who couldn't fight was brought into the capital city, Ogana, and provided with shelter and supplies. The three eastern fort cities were reinforced with numerous soldiers, plentiful rations, and new weapons. The three forts would act as the supply line for the soldiers in battle. The plan was to fight the battle across the river Uttara, and into the Kingdom of Uttara. This would place the battleground within the range of the battleships, fort catapults, and longbow archers.

"To fight along the river, temporary bridges were constructed. The distance between the three forts was hundreds of yojanas, and ships were lined between them to supply food and weapons to the armies. Outposts were built across the river.

"When the work was finished, they settled in to patiently wait for the winter to be over. The soldiers had never faced a demonic army before, and stories of Raksas and Pisachs spread amongst them like wildfire. Not one of them was afraid to fight men, but facing the demons had everyone worried.

"The Gandharva army had arrived before the outset of the war, and they were housed in the northernmost Fort Himal, along with King Malla. I was given the command of the central Fort Uttara, and Madhva was in command of the southernmost Fort Sarit. King Marut, ruler of the Gandharvas, believed that the Raksas and Pisachs would attack Fort Himal first, as it was closest to the path into the lands of demi-gods.

"Soma had already been prepared; it would only take a few drops to strengthen the mortal soldiers. Barrels were sent to each of the fort cities. The commanders were instructed to mix them up with the victory drink. The Gandharvas had brought weapons made out of the five elements, stronger and heavier than ever. They had chariots equipped with prolonged arrows around fifteen feet in length. A separate archer battalion was prepared that would ride chariots to enter the fray. Others still rode on giant mountain lions and carried mighty spears.

"Unaware that they would be encountering an army already well-equipped and trained for months, the evil army marched towards the Malla Kingdom. It was decided among the three evil kings that Raksas and Pisachs would ride and enter the kingdom between the northern and the middle forts. The armies commanded by King Darad would enter in between the middle and southern forts. Both divisions had to finally converge outside the capital city of Ogana. They expected the real battle to be at the capital.

"At Ujcha, a city in the Uttara Kingdom, the evil armies parted in two directions. It was still a ten-day ride to the Uttara River. Pounding on their war drums, they marched ahead. Darad rode an elephant—the beast fitted with gorgeous trappings—and hundreds of thousands of his men on horses and chariots followed behind. Men carried weapons of war, including bows, spears, daggers, and shields. With them, they had an elephant battalion, with multiple archers on top capable of firing volleys of flaming arrows.

"The Raksas, on the other hand, rode gigantic bulls with long, curving horns. The Raksas King Amura rode a chariot pulled by eight gigantic, monstrous bulls. The Pisachs either flew on their own, or rode alongside Raksas. The Raksas carried two-sided pikes, shields with demonic faces carved on them, two-sided swords, daggers, bows, and arrows. A few of the captains on their side also carried special axes attached to ropes to be used at range.

"The Pisachs carried iron chains with cruel daggers on both ends; they also had their sharp tails to attack with.

"The day had arrived; the sound of war-horns filled the air. The victory drink and Gandharva-forged weapons were distributed to the men alongside King Malla. Though surprised, the evil army was prepared for any challenge in front of them. The battle began on two fronts—one in the north with Raksas and Pisachs and the other down south, where Madhva and I fought with King Darad. The battlefields stretched between the forts, and the fort soldiers couldn't intercede, other than by supplying weapons and food. It was also at a great distance from the warships, forcing them to wait unabatingly.

"In the south, the war quickly turned in favor of Malla. The strength of new weapons and a gulp of Soma was enough to crush the evil army of men from Paksi. After half a day, I charged towards King Darad with all of my men. Seeing this, he ordered his elephant battalion to attack us. They managed to gain an edge in the beginning, but they couldn't hold for long. By the end of the day, half of the Paksi men were either dead or injured.

"On the northern side, the war brought havoc on King Malla's men; his soldiers fought mystical beings and weapons they'd never encountered before. Even Gandharva weapons and Soma couldn't avert their plight, but only lessen it. The Raksas launched a gale of shield-piercing arrows which would burst into flames on impact. This was followed by giant orbs of molten lava that incinerated and swallowed whole formations. Their bulls were stronger than even the elephants in the Malla army. The bulls brought down the elephants twice as huge as they were with the merest strikes of their horns.

"Pisachs, on other hand, were teasing their opponents with tricks. They would run towards the formation of men, and as the men readied their weapons, they disappeared and emerged from behind. The spikes on their tails were the worst—strong enough to throw aside five soldiers at once. The Pisachs would suddenly swoop down on the soldiers, carry a few of them several feet high in the air, and drop them from above.

"It was becoming more difficult to tackle both Raksas and Pisachs at the same time. Until the evening, the men had sustained the fight, and thousands of soldiers lay dead or injured. The Gandharvas, on the other hand, had suffered minor injuries, and were not fighting as a team alongside men. The war halted in the evening, and each side carried their dead soldiers home.

"At night, King Malla urged King Marut to change his strategy and fight as a team. He told him that the morale of the soldiers was broken. King Marut agreed and said that he would change his tactics and become the enemy's worst nightmare.

"On the second day, the arrow chariots of Gandharva lined up on an elevated surface. Their goal was to injure the bulls, to give the war elephants a chance to crush the Raksas. The Gandharvas fought the Raksas alongside the elephant battalion of men. The Raksas used all the mystical power they had; this time it was not enough. The Gandharvas rose in the air and sent showers of weapons on them. The Raksas conjured illusions, but the Gandharvas struck them all down. If they projected illusions of themselves, imaginary copies, the Gandharvas would use weapons to fire in all directions so that the Raksas couldn't hide. It seemed the Gandharvas had a remedy for whatever wretchedness the Raksas brought upon them.

"To fight with Pisachs, men and Gandharvas formed into lotus formations. Each lotus was typically forged such that on all sides, the enemy would simply see the shields, while the Gandharvas aimed at the Pisachs from the center. Their enchanted arrows strangled the Pisachs, rendering them unable to use supernatural powers. Some would fall on the ground and succumb to that grip.

"On the southern side, the second day was no different from the first. Three out of four soldiers of the Paksi King Darad were dead, and his entire elephant battalion was wiped out. At night, King Darad marched his men towards the northern battlefields, hoping that his allies might have done wonders. I left Madhva at the southern battleground and marched towards the northern battlefield.

"The two evil kings met in the camp; the Raksas King Amura asked for the whereabouts of the Kumbha army. The Kumbhas are Raksas giants and have the strength of a thousand elephants. They are, however, very slow and ponderous. King Darad answered that the Kumbha army was a few yojanas away and would join them in a day. Amura smiled at the reply, looked at Picasa, and they planned their strategy.

"The next day, both Gandharvas and men were surprised; the enemy had changed sides. Pisachs were fighting Gandharvas and elephant battalions, while Raksas fought the lotus formation. The lotus formation didn't work against Raksas. The Raksas would disperse the formation with their blows and never allowed enough time for the archers inside to secure their aim. On the other side, Pisachs would hit Gandharvas and soar into the air; the Gandharvas were merely able to hold them back. Soon, the balance shifted in favor of the evil army.

"Seeing this, King Malla ordered the two groups to join into one. The soldiers at our side formed lotus formations close to the elephant battalion. The Gandharvas and men once again inflicted heavy damage on the evil army. The balance had shifted again; the Gandharvas and men started pushing ahead.

"But just as victory seemed certain, the entire battleground felt tremors under their feet. Growing every moment, a thick, thumping sound suffused the atmosphere. The Kumbhas were there. Some were carrying heavy iron chains and some huge maces, and a few held whole uprooted trees.

"King Marut signaled the arrow chariots to fire. The arrows struck true, but none of the Kumbhas looked gravely injured. The next moment, King Marut witnessed the obliteration of all his chariots. The armies of Gandharva and men continued to sustain terrible damage until the day end and had to retreat.

"The evil army rejoiced that night at the great blow they had given their enemy, and King Darad joined them. Amura asked Darad to bring in more forces from Paksi, as they would need them on their march towards the kingdoms of demi-gods. He also told him that the battle here would last no more than a day, and that they would march towards their destination soon.

"On our side, we repaired our chariots and prepared peculiar arrows that would burst into flames on impact. Men were praying to their gods to give them strength to fight another day.

"On the fourth day, the Raksas and Pisachs took the back; Kumbhas occupied the front lines. The battle turned into a massacre. The casualties on the Gandharvas' front rose drastically. The fight now was mostly between Kumbhas and the king's elite men, along with the rest of the Gandharvas. It seemed as though the fight would not last another day. At that very moment, I joined them with fresh blood from the south. This was the much-required boost for our army.

"The chariots were now pointed to hit the Kumbhas in the legs. The hit was sufficient to stagger them, and the Gandharvas would utilize this momentary weakness to surge forward and strike them with heavy blows. The war went on, but still was in favor of the evil side.

"Meanwhile, on one side of the battle, King Picasa attacked King Malla with his cryptic powers and wounded him. King Malla was rushed back to the camp.

"The Gandharva King Marut was separated from his army and surrounded by the Kumbhas. The Raksas king directed a fusillade of arrows from all sides. The rest of the Kumbhas prevented the Gandharva army from protecting their king. One of the Kumbhas held Marut down, and the other one raised his leg to finish him."

Om was at the edge of his seat while Udadhir narrated.

"Aware that there was no escape, King Marut raised his sword in the air, closed his eyes, and prayed to his father, the sun god, Surya. In the blink of an eye, an onslaught of heavenly fire descended from the sky, striking the evil army. Seeing the fire, I, son of Varuna, the god of water, used my abilities to prevent the fire from hurting anyone on our side. I created a halo of water that surrounded my army to protect them from the heavenly fire. The fire immolated most of the Kumbhas; seizing the opportunity, the Gandharva army brought down the rest of them.

"With all Kumbhas suddenly dead, the evil army was hopeless and in disarray. A horde of men and Gandharvas charged at them in joined formations and ravaged the diabolical army. Soon after, Amura and Picasa were ambushed. A surge of arrows and javelins flew at them from all sides. The Raksas King Amura took to his illusions, forged a cloud of smoke over the entire battleground, and escaped. The army of men and Gandharva wanted to chase the retreating evil army, but King Marut wouldn't permit it. He said that once King Malla recovered, they would regroup and march towards the west.

"After a day's stay in Malla, King Marut received a message that his son's condition had worsened, and he left without delay. His son had been wounded by an envenomed arrow in the fight with the Nagas. Even all the divine powers possessed by the Gandharvas couldn't save the prince."

"What happened after that?" asked Om.

"King Marut never recovered from the grief of his son's loss and never joined forces with men. Men, without the help from demi-gods, were unable to march towards the west to defeat the evil army. I continued to strengthen the remaining Ganas and persuaded them that, one day, they would win back their kingdom," Udadhir said. "The evil army had scattered for now; the Raksas king and Paksi king went to meditate for a hundred years. The Pisachs went back to worldly pleasures, and an era of peace began in the kingdom of men."

CHAPTER 11
A Great Expedition

We will defeat them again if they come. We have the powers of rishis, and we can ask the Gandharvas to join us," said Om.

"But the Raksas King Amura and the Paksi King Darad have become more powerful—more than anyone living on this land. They have crushed all empires west and south of the Himalayan Kingdoms. Both of the evil kings have secretly worshipped for years, pleased Lord Brahma, and now have powers that no one knows about. It is said that both of them have immortal blessings of some kind," Udadhir exhaled. "No one knows how they can be defeated. We would not only need the Gandharvas, but all of the demi-god kingdoms to fight alongside us."

A heavy silence descended.

"Why don't we approach all the demi-gods and ask them to fight?" Om suggested at last.

165

Udadhir answered, "I have tried to persuade them for a hundred years, and it is unlikely that they would listen to anyone else. All the demi-gods can only be called upon by King Marut himself, as they are obliged to answer his summons."

Before Om could speak again, Udadhir said, "I know what you are thinking. Why don't we talk to the Gandharva king? Gandharva is a fort, and no one is allowed inside, including demi-gods. It has been the same since the day the prince died. Now the king only confers with his reliable group of advisors and only tends to the needs of his kingdom. The only way to get to him would be to defeat the Gandharva gatekeepers. It would be a war against them, and we would need to reach the king before the alarm was raised," Udadhir explained, nodding his head thoughtfully.

"And there is no guarantee of reaching the gates of Gandharva," Udadhir continued. "The kingdom lies on the divine road which begins behind the Malla palace and goes through each of the demi-gods' kingdoms. Even if someone reaches the first kingdom in the path, the Kingdom of Yaksas, it is highly unlikely for anyone to make it through. They would not even allow me, as they believe I might incite a rebellion among the demi-gods. If one crosses Yaksas, they still would have to make it through the Kingdoms of Kinnar and Kimpurusa. That would mean on one side, you would have a near-deadly and impossible way through, and the other side, it would be a fight to the death with the evil army. With the power of the rishis and my fellow Ganas, we could only hold the evil army for a while."

As they continued to deliberate, King Neera entered the palace hall. "What consensus has been reached?"

"Greetings, Your Highness."

As everyone welcomed him, they looked at each other, trying to apprise the king of the situation they were in. He was briefed on the rising powers of the evil army. An army of men, Ganas, and rishis could only extend the battle. In the end, they would lose. They also kept forward the alternative of persuading the Gandharva king to join their forces, but that was a suicidal errand.

King Neera listened to everyone. At last, he said, "I will convene a gathering again tomorrow, and will invite Rishi Rig Muni, too."

In the morning, everyone gathered in the court hall. Rishi Rig Muni joined the group and the discussion on how to challenge the evil army began.

"I have seen many forms of the future, and in each one, the attack is inevitable. Currently, we can only prolong the war, but we will not be able to change the outcome," said Rishi.

"It is time all the kingdoms in the Himalayan lands join forces," King Neera said earnestly. "I would appreciate your suggestions, Rishi, on our next move."

"I agree with Udadhir that the only choice we have is to call upon King Marut and ask him to command all the forces of men and demi-gods combined. We have to take the divine road to Gandharva without fighting any of the demi-gods and sneak past the gates of Gandharvas," said

Rishi. "Om would be the best person to travel this path, and to travel, he would need a group of specially skilled people."

Udadhir immediately stepped forward, volunteering to accompany Om, but he was stopped in his tracks by Rishi. "I suggest you stay back and strengthen Malla's defenses. This group of people has to be small enough to sneak through the demi-god's kingdoms and strong enough to tackle any obstacle.

"I would also have one of my other disciples, a demi-god, join this expedition. He is familiar not only with the divine path, but he also knows many secret passages. Om, according to my best predictions, you have a month to form this group and then continue to this path. Once you have made up your mind, come see me," Rishi said to Om. "The attack will commence right after the winter. It might take half a year for you to return; it's hard to know for certain, as none of the living have ever conquered this path."

After that, Rishi left the palace.

Om was supposed to meet this disciple of Rishi's in a few days. After the king's court was dismissed, he went to the princess's chambers. They talked at length about the discussions that Om had that day, but Abha seemed to know about the past. "I'm worried about Rishi's visions where the attack is imminent," she said.

There was a silence.

"There might be no return from the venture that I have chosen," said Om heavily.

"We should spend a few days together," Abha

suggested, forcing a smile she didn't feel.

Three days later, Om answered a knock on his door and saw a hermit. The man looked bedraggled, with long, disheveled hair tied at his back, a long beard, and a dual-sided voulge as a weapon.

"Greetings. I am Jabala, and Rishi Rig Muni asked me to meet a man named Om."

"I am Om. It's a pleasure to meet you. Come in and rest for a while." Om was a little alarmed by his appearance. "What type of demi-god are you?"

Jabala replied, "I'm not any type of demi-god, but the son of a god in Indra's court. My mother belonged to the land of the men."

Om told him about their expedition. But Jabala already knew everything.

"You have a great burden placed on you, to fulfill this critical errand," he acknowledged.

Om offered him food and water and told him that they would continue their conversation the next day.

The next morning, Jabala woke Om up while it was still dark. "It is time we discussed the situation at hand and our approach."

They walked together outside, engaged in a lengthy conversation.

Jabala said, "The divine path is no game for men. It is full of illusions and deviations; all signs will try to deviate you from the path. There are traps meant to capture or kill. And even if we cross all the hurdles and traps, the

169

gatekeepers guarding the entry to the demi-god kingdoms will fire arrows first and ask questions later."

Jabala continued, "My task is to make sure that the group doesn't die and is able to cross the demi-gods' lands without being caught. It is best if the number of people is not more than a dozen and if all are close accomplices of yours."

"Who will we need?" asked Om.

"An astronomer to guide the path. An Ayurveda practitioner and chemist to protect us from any sort of malady. A cook for the journey, a few brave warriors, and an astute group of communication experts."

"I already have a few people in mind." With that, Om went to find Abha for her counsel.

"I can think of a few ingenious people who would be ideal as communication experts," she affirmed.

Om had sent urgent-marked letters to people he already knew would join him. The team was asked to assemble in two weeks; then they would have another week to plan their journey. The warriors Om selected were winners from the festival games: the archer named Sarvin and the swordsman Arin. The astrologer and cook were his new friends Amber and Samva from Kanika. Revat was his Ayurveda expert, and he also called in Maghavan from the Sarasi camp as an advisor.

The princess gave two of her best bodyguards as communication experts, who used birds for sending messages. "The bodyguards are shadow killers, specialists who ascertain significant damage without detection," Abha told Om.

The wait for the next two weeks began, and Om kept on planning the journey over and over with Jabala. By the end of two weeks, the entire team had arrived, and everyone was briefed about the seriousness of the situation and the risks of the journey. The plan was to start the journey in five days, and everyone was assigned special tasks.

Om spent a few days with the princess, and on the final day, he went to see Rishi.

"Om, I have a gift for you." Rishi handed him a precious red stone belonging to King Malla. "This brilliant carbuncle was a gift from the Gandharva King Marut to King Malla, and it will be of great help."

At last, the time had come; the group had collected all necessary equipment for the quest. Taking the blessings of everyone, they picked up their belongings, and the group of ten extraordinary, talented people headed off for the journey.

The princess went all the way up to the cave behind her chambers. "I wish you all success."

"I bid you farewell, princess," said Om, and he left before she could say anything else. He was apprehensive of the journey to come, but he could not afford any hesitation. Hence, they started the divine expedition towards the demi-gods.

The road was beautiful, with high, snow-covered mountains in the north and sky-high trees everywhere. The path brought them to places full of different kinds of animals that didn't seem alarmed by the presence of humans.

They started their journey by the side of the stream that fell from the mountains to become the Medhavi River in Malla, and continued upstream. It was already summer, and the river water was gushing past them. There was some snow still on the trees, and as the sun shone, it melted and formed small rivulets that snaked into the river. Throughout the whole day, they could hear water trickle and fall.

The group kept to the side of the river to avoid the deep shade of the canopy. Revat was captivated by the place—everywhere he found trees and plants he had only studied, but never seen. He stopped here and there to collect roots and leaves.

Jabala, on another hand, led the group confidently.

"How long again?" asked Om.

"Thirteen to fifteen days to reach the Yaksa Kingdom, through the Jungles of Himalaya."

Jabala had yet to elucidate his plan to enter the kingdom. Om waited for the right time before he pressed him to explain. Jabala worked with Samva at night to study the stars and to determine their path for the next day.

Amber and Maghavan always walked by Om's side, and they would talk about great things back in their kingdoms.

The shadow killers were the ones Om knew nothing about, and they followed silently, close but behind.

Arin and Sarvin cautiously followed the group and kept a keen eye on the surroundings for any threat.

The first two nights went quite well, as the walk was

next to the river. From the third day on, they had to move west, away from the river.

In the camp, on the third night, Jabala and Samva prepared their plans for the next day. The warrior Sarvin, along with one of the shadow killers, had brought in game from their hunt to cook for the night. Amber cleaned the kill and started preparing a meal for everyone. Revat prepared Ayurvedic medicines from the leaves he had collected. He handed each one a strange pungent root to chew that prevented mountain sickness and kept their insides warm.

While at rest, the warriors evaluated their weapons. They were carrying some unique arrows, which Revat had made especially for the journey. Each of the arrowheads was painted a different color, and they were still memorizing what each color meant. Om also had his divine bow with him, which he had not yet used in a fight, in addition to his already existing divine weaponry.

While the food was being prepared, Jabala went into meditation, and Om went to talk with the shadow killers. It was always a good idea to know the strengths and weaknesses of the soldiers one accompanies into battle.

"So, what are your names?"

"Idha."

"I'm Rabia. We're part of a special guard battalion for the princess. We belong to Kanika, and the same battalion protects the princesses in both the kingdoms."

Idha continued, "The battalion is formed only of women, and in addition to protecting the princess, we're used as silent weapons."

173

With a grin, Rabia added, "During war, we smother the most eminent enemy leader in order to triumph with the least possible bloodshed."

"We are masters of the art of disguise, and we can sneak into highly guarded forts without being noticed—as well as blend in with local folks to avoid suspicion."

Om was impressed and intrigued.

The food was served, and tales were shared—both of past glories earned by their forefathers and the battles that they had seen with their own eyes. Samva shared his experience about astronomy and narratives of Amber that Om had already heard.

In the silence of the next night, Idha, one of the shadow hunters, heard something strange. She noticed a silent movement in the grasses nearby. "Be on guard, everyone."

They all pointed their weapons in that direction. The movement ceased, and the group slowly began to circle the area.

Sarvin moved back with an arrow notched on his bow. He hit a rock and tumbled. Finding his balance again, Sarvin accidentally released the arrow.

Immediately, a great beast jumped out and landed near the camp fire. Om ran toward the beast. "Everyone, lower your weapons!"

It was Loka, Om's tiger, who had followed Om all that way. Everyone calmed down and finished their dinner. Loka had followed the divine path all the way, and finally he had reunited with his master and best friend. That night, everyone slept and prayed to the gods to guide them through this precarious journey.

It had already been ten days, and they had not encountered anything beyond strange wild animals in the jungles. As they continued, it became difficult to ascertain the right path at night and to follow the same in the daylight. It was agreed that the group should instead rest during the day and walk at night.

On the thirteenth day, as Jabala had said, traveling during the day was tricky, and they waited for the sun to set. Idha and Arin were on watch, while the others rested.

"A hawk has been following us for a long time," noted Arin to her.

Idha saw a hawk circling above them. She threw her boomerang in its direction, and the hawk came down, screeching. The sound made others wake up, and Samva ran in the direction of the hawk. It was Marak, and now she was badly injured. He cast a fierce look at Idha.

"I'm terribly sorry," she apologized. "I didn't know she was yours."

"It will be okay," Revat told him. "With my medicine, the hawk should be able to fly in a day or two."

The group went back to rest and waited for the sun to set. At night, they began their journey without any other surprises.

In the middle of the night, Rabia, one of the shadow killers, heard a strained voice, like someone was hurt. She alerted the others and ran in the direction, only to find Samva trapped waist-deep in a bog.

Jabala was near him, but his voulge was not long enough to reach. Sarvin fired his rope arrow, and Samva used it to climb out safely.

While the rest of them tended to Samva, Rabia got their attention. Nervously, she said, "We're surrounded by bogs all around us, with no way out."

Everyone sat down to discuss their next plan of action.

Om asked, "Jabala, how long will it take to reach the Yaksas Kingdom?"

"Not more than two days or nights from here."

They had to devise a plan to cross this bog. Maghavan went to talk to Sarvin. "Can you make more rope arrows?"

"Maybe. Why?"

"I have an idea. To cross the bog, we could use ropes stretched from one tree to another. The rope arrows would be fired, and once everyone had crossed one tree length, they could pull out and fire the arrows at the next tree."

Seeing no other option, Om asked Sarvin, "Make at least four of those rope arrows."

Sarvin already had one, so he quickly started preparing three more and was done in no time. The group was divided into five people each, and they took to parallel trees. One group was led by Om, and the other by Sarvin.

"Now Loka, stay behind," instructed Om—even though everyone agreed that it would be easy for Loka to cross the bog with his swift paws. "Once we are comfortably on the ground on the other side, you can join us."

The arrows were fired, and each one of them crossed the distance between two trees.

"It is going to be a very slow process," Amber noted to Om.

After each one of them crossed, Om and Sarvin fired their arrows to free the rope from the previous tree, and then they untied and collected the rope that had been cut by the sharp arrows. The arrows were fired at the next tree and the next, and after seven trees, Revat said, "The ground seems fine."

Samva threw his dagger on the ground to see if it would sink, but it didn't. The group started dismounting cautiously.

Sarvin was the first to reach the ground, but the moment he landed, a burst of arrows came shooting towards him. He fled for the shelter of a tree trunk, while everyone else was still in the trees above.

They could see the arrows struck below, but the trees were so dense that they could not see whether Sarvin had escaped. Sarvin's voice couldn't reach them; no one was willing to climb down. Nobody knew what else was waiting for them beneath.

Samva stood silently, thinking, then he said to his hawk, "Marak, survey the area to see if there are people firing at us."

The hawk had still not fully recovered, but was able to fly. There was no one firing at them, and the hawk didn't see anything ahead.

Samva said, "Om, it seems something triggered those arrows. It could be a sudden movement on the ground, or it may be a certain weight. The weight had to be significant, since when I threw my dagger, the arrows

177

were not fired."

To prove that Samva was right, Om said to everyone, "Drop whatever weight you are carrying on the ground at the same time, all at once."

As soon as the objects landed, the arrows were fired again. The arrows were made of solid metal, and they fired at a great speed. Escaping them would be nearly impossible.

Om descended a few branches, and he heaved a sigh of relief when he saw that Sarvin had escaped. He signaled Sarvin to climb up. Sarvin waved his hand to tell him that he couldn't, one of the arrows had pierced his shield and injured him.

"Everyone," Om alerted them, "Sarvin is on the ground and cannot climb. The only way is for one of us to go ahead and cut off the source of these arrows."

Crossing trees by ropes was very time-consuming. Before proceeding, Om asked Jabala, "Is there any other way or direction we could take?"

He shook his head in refusal.

Om fired the rope arrow to the next tree. After crossing two more trees, the branches were now close enough to cross from one to the other easily. Om continued without the ropes, and soon he saw a series of wooden logs stacked neatly next to each other. He moved to a lower branch and carefully leaned on it to look around closely. He was sure that this was the source of the arrows.

With swift steps, he climbed down on the other side of the logs, highly cautious with his movements. From behind, it looked like a ditch running throughout the length of the only passage.

Om slowly entered it from behind to see a series of metal bows, each one with its own metal string. The metal strings were stretched to a hook, and the hook had a string threaded below and then forward. These wires ran along the front, and anything heavy would trigger the arrows. Om saw the self-loading mechanism, from the quiver below, driven by the same string that was firing the arrows, and he was spellbound for a moment by the beauty and complexity of the trap.

He severed all the metal strings and whistled for his friends to climb down and walk ahead. He also whistled to Loka, and Loka ran towards Om swiftly, crossing the bog without any problem. After a long time, all of them were finally on the ground, safe and sound.

Revat quickly tended to Sarvin's wound. "Make sure you don't shoot arrows until your wounds have healed." Revat had to sew his wounds closed, and any strenuous activity could rupture the stitches.

After going through a seemingly endless struggle, they all decided to rest for a while and continue further at night.

CHAPTER 12
The Mines of Yaksas

That night, after dinner, Om and his group continued their journey. The night passed without any disturbances, and they were able to walk through the whole night.

In the morning, they pitched their camp on a hill, hidden amongst a belt of trees. Witnessing the sublime beauty of the Himalayas, the view itself was enough to take all their fatigue away. They were now near the snow-covered lands and approaching a steep mountain. The early morning sunlight turned the snow into glazed gold. They sat down to rest on the hill after a quiet meal, and they impatiently waited for nightfall.

"We're near the Yaksas land," said Jabala, "and in next two to three days, we will be at the doors to the demi-god kingdoms. There is only one way across, and that is through the doors. Behind the doors, there is a passage which will take us to the Yaksas Kingdom."

Jabala prepared the group for the path ahead. "The passage is a gold and gems mine, and it is heavily guarded by Yaksas. We have to sneak past it without being noticed.

"The passage itself will take two days, and after that, the kingdom is three days' walk away. Remember, the Yaksas can take any form—from giant mountains to trees, from statues to animals—anything living and lifelike. Not all Yaksas can take any form, but they are all powerful. It will take all of us to maybe defeat a single one of them."

The group was already tired, and listening to these details further exhausted them. They traveled at night, in the snow, which made their quest exceedingly difficult. Other than the hawk and Loka, everyone struggled.

It was now the sixteenth night. Jabala announced, "We should be near the gate by the morning."

This excited and invigorated them. If there was even a hint of fear or nervousness, no one showed it. They reached the foothills of the great mountain, but they could not find the entrance. Jabala asked everyone to rest and started working with Samva to come up with an idea to locate the entrance.

The first ray of sun fell on the group, and everyone slowly woke up. At last, Jabala had figured out the entrance. Walking along one side of the mountain, they found a discreet cave that was deliberately obscured by a cluster of thick foliage. Next to the cave were two iron statues, twice the height of the nearby trees. Both armored statues were seated on a carved throne, with one hand on their thighs and the other holding the shaft of a mace resting on the ground. But Jabala and Samva were still unable to figure out the exact means to gain entrance further.

Arin went near the statue and tried to go behind it. There was a sudden tremor, and both the statues stood up, shook the dust off their bodies, and let out a deafening roar. One was taller than the other; the taller one lifted his weapon to them. The smaller statue opened its large mouth, and Om could see fire blazing out of it.

The taller one charged towards the group and hammered its feet on the ground; the shock waves kicked dirt and dust through the air, hurling the group off their feet. Before anyone could get up, the fire giant belched out bursts of fire at them.

Luckily, everyone escaped the first attack, and they prepared to fight back.

"Samva and Revat! Get behind and seek shelter!" Om commanded. "Loka, stay back. This isn't your fight."

The group could now see the passage hidden behind the statues. Arin was standing next to it, but he wasn't yet able to open it. No one else was even thinking about the entrance—only how to escape these giant statues. Om's divine weapons, swords, and arrows weren't causing any damage. They all tried their best to distract and attack.

Revat quickly came up with an idea. "I have something that will help us." Revat passed Om one of his arcane concoctions. "Fire it at the giants' eyes. It's a special venom."

Om aimed it as told. The giants seemed annoyed, and

they couldn't see well for a few moments. The taller statue was still swinging his sword around. The other giant kept breathing fire in all directions. Revat's solution hadn't worked perfectly. However, Om knew that, if properly utilized, it could help them escape.

The fight went on for half a day, with no one standing down. Most of the area between them was either chopped or burned to shreds.

Jabala used his divine powers and the voulge, but nothing worked. "These are gatekeepers and Yaksas; there is no defeating them! We have to keep them busy fighting, while I go and see if the door can be opened. The gatekeepers are not allowed in!" Om engaged the giants and strafed them with venom-laden arrows.

As Jabala was about to reach the gate, the fire giant grabbed for him. Seeing this, Om fired one of his divine arrows straight into the giant's mouth, forcing it to swallow its own fire. The giant released Jabala and let out a screech of pain, with both hands wrapped around its neck. It choked for a while, dropping to its knees, but it recovered within moments, and was angrier than before. Om tried the same tactic again, but it only bought him a few moments.

Jabala signaled to Om that the gate wasn't opening. Om quickly walked to Revat. "Do you have something that will quench the fire?"

It seemed as if some heavenly light struck Revat. He took out another bottle. "Om, dip your arrows in it and fire at them. The arrow should hit exactly when a fireball is coming out of the giant's mouth," said Revat.

Om doused his arrow, waited for the right moment, and fired. This time, there was an ear-piercing explosion inside the giant's mouth, and it collapsed to the ground. The other giant ran towards it, screaming.

Seizing the moment, everyone ran towards the door. The door was still not moving, despite countless efforts. While Om was busy with the door, Arin shook him and pointed in a direction.

The fire giant was still on the ground, but the other giant had charged towards them, with its weapon in one hand and a tree branch in the other. Om pulled out his sword and stuck it in the ground ahead. The abrupt shock struck the giant off its feet. This again didn't cause any damage to the beast, and it rose up yet again.

Meanwhile, as Om was about to pull his sword, the red gem fell from his pouch. Revat handed it over to him. Om took it out from the cloth and raised it to ensure it wasn't damaged, and suddenly, the doors squeaked. The gem was the key to the entrance!

Seeing the door open, the giant quickened its pace towards them.

Barely had everyone made it inside when the doors closed behind them, shutting out the giant. Dropping whatever they were carrying, they sat down to gasp for air. The group was worried that encountering any more creatures like the gatekeepers would be the end of them.

"Jabala," Om asked, "do you know the path inside the mine and out again?"

"I know nothing. I have studied the path, but I have never crossed the gates," he said, still panting.

The ceiling of the cave was unusually high, and there were torches on each side, which lit up the place. From a distance, they saw a stream of light and cautiously walked towards it. What they saw at the source was beyond anything they had ever encountered so far.

A city of gold lay underneath them. A plenitude of overhanging houses had passages and bridges connecting them. Each one shone brighter than the other.

"What is that?" Om asked Jabala.

"The city is the next home for Yaksas, and to my knowledge, we have to walk through it to get out."

Om was a little worried, as going through the city would mean chances to encounter more Yaksas. All of them were still looking at the city from the top.

Maghavan was in a corner, and when someone tapped his back, he simply brushed the hand aside. But the next moment, Maghavan was thrown into one of the cave walls.

Hearing his scream, everyone turned to see two human-like figures standing next to them. They were almost twice as tall and appeared to be covered with gold. Arin ran and struck one with his sword. The gold figure lifted its hand to protect himself, throwing Arin away; he landed near Maghavan.

These figures were not covered in gold, but were made of solid gold. The group had encountered another pair of Yaksas.

Sarvin fired a burst of arrows, but they all bounced off without even leaving a scratch, like nothing.

One of the Yaksas bellowed deeply, "Surrender or

die!"

Jabala hurled his voulge at him, and it struck the Yaksas hard, making him stumble. The shadow killers distracted them further with their weapons.

"Loka, take one of them down!" Om called. Loka leaped and pinned one of the Yaksas. He followed suit with the second. Both of the Yaksas got up, grabbed Loka by his leg, and threw him to the far side of the cave.

Loka seemed hurt, and that infuriated Om. "Sarvin, make a trap from the metal wires we collected from the arrow trap," Om said quickly, and he dashed towards the Yaksas. Om and Jabala attacked both of them, and the others helped. Whenever the golden Yaksas would attack, the shadow killers would strike with their boomerangs to distract them. Om and Jabala brought them down many times, but there was no defeating them. It was taking everyone's efforts to keep these two Yaksas from hurting them. Om was grateful that there weren't more of them.

And then, as if on cue, Om saw another golden Yaksa climb up. This one had a horn tied to his waist, and he raised it to alert everyone. Once the horn was blown, there was nothing the group could do to avoid being captured.

As soon as the Yaksa raised his horn, an arrow fired by Sarvin broke the horn and tangled around the Yaksa. Sarvin had completed the metal trap. He rushed up and tied the Yaksa with the metal wires. He fired the next shots at the remaining Yaksas on Om's signal. All the three Yaksas were now tied. But the metal wires weren't enough to hold them for long, and there wouldn't be enough time to cross.

Jabala, standing close to a shackled Yaksa, brushed his fingers on his head and walked back.

"Why did you do that?"

"One of my abilities is to read minds," Jabala told Om. "I now know the way out."

"Even if you know the way out, these Yaksas will be out of the shackles before we cross, and they will alert everyone," Om said in a hushed tone.

"We have to either carry them or lock them in a safe place," said Jabala.

They all agreed to carry them down and lock them in the first house they saw. The group slowly climbed down and took one of the bridges into the city. There were series of houses made of gold, connected by bridges, so that each house was connected to two others on either side. One had to cross every house and an untold number of bridges to get to the other end.

The first house they saw was empty, and they decided to hide the three Yaksas there. "There are only a handful of Yaksas in the mine," Jabala told everyone. "All of the others have assembled at the capital for some kind of a celebration."

Om wondered how Jabala knew this, but he thought that if he could read minds, there was little he could not do.

There was a layer of gold dust in the house; in fact, everything in it was made of solid gold. The Yaksas were now well tied to the pillars, so that they wouldn't be able to move. As per the directions from Jabala, everyone rubbed the gold dust on their bodies. After a lot of struggle, all of them finally looked somewhat similar to the gold Yaksas. They even rubbed it on Loka to avoid getting attention from a distance.

The group began their journey slowly, hiding from one house to another. Whenever they saw a Yaksa, they would keep quiet and let them pass. Jabala had told them not to attack unless necessary, and no one in the group was even slightly interested in another encounter.

By the time they had made it out of the cave, they had to tackle two more Yaksas and had tied them up in another empty house. Finally out in the open, they ran towards the path that would lead them to the Kingdom of Kinnars—both excited and relieved to leave the mines behind.

Outside, it was already dark and snowing. The group started walking straight towards their path. They only took short rests as required and kept on walking among the trees and snow-covered bushes. No one made a sound, as they were still in the Kingdom of Yaksas. The path, as Jabala had told them, was a two-day walk; and from there, the Kingdom of Kinnars was another fifteen to sixteen days' walk.

The two days passed without any further encounters with Yaksas. Jabala again reminded everyone, "Yaksas are nature lovers and can take any form. Being cautious is in our best interest."

Near the passage that Jabala had mentioned, the group could see the capital city of the Yaksa Kingdom. The kingdom's palaces and homes were carved beautifully into the mountains, and the rest was made out of stone. On one side, they saw Yaksas bathing in gold, and on the other, it seemed as if they were glorying in pure nature. There were statues everywhere. They didn't want to lose any more time, so they continued on the path towards Kinnars.

Another two days passed, and now the kingdom's tallest structures were also no longer visible. Everyone sighed in relief that the worst was over, but no one knew what waited for them ahead.

The next day, Samva got a signal from his hawk to be cautious—the hawk had seen Yaksas coming towards them.

Samva told the group, "Hundreds of Yaksas could be here in moments."

"Your friend is right. Come with me if you want to live," said a voice from behind them. Everyone turned to see a strange human-like figure, but made out of a *tree*. He was taller than them and had hair made of grass. Threatened by the creature's presence, everyone drew their weapons.

"Stand down," Om told them.

"Why should we listen to him?" asked Amber.

"So far, he's the only one who hasn't attacked first and talked second," Om pointed out.

The figure said, "My name is Valka, and your group has no choice but to come with me if you want to live. I am an outcast, and I live in the jungle instead of the kingdom."

"Why are you an outcast?" both Amber and Jabala asked Valka at the same time.

"If you follow me, I can explain on the way."

"We'll follow," Om told them, "but be vigilant."

After walking for some time, Valka lifted a wooden sheet from the ground and showed them a way beneath. The group entered along with Valka.

"I am a tree Yaksa," he began to explain. "I got into a fight with one of the gold Yaksas because he was destroying trees with gold dust. The council found me guilty of not reporting but indulging in a fight, so I was cast out for several years. Even though my punishment has long since been over, I love being in the jungle and traveling around the whole kingdom."

"But how will we find our way to the Kingdom of Kinnars, and can you lead us there?" Om inquired.

Valka said, "There are a series of underground passages that will lead you to the gates of Kinnars. I will guide you to a passage, but from there, you will have to walk to the Kinnar Valley on your own. No Yaksa is allowed inside without the consent of the king. However, the Yaksas following you wouldn't dare cross to the Kingdom of Kinnars."

Valka added, "Please, rest for the night."

Valka served them some roots and berries that he had determined were safe for humans.

Om's group was already tired, and they could not refuse a night of good food and rest.

The next day, Valka led them inside an underground

passage towards the gates of the Kingdom of Kinnars. Conversing with Jabala and Samva, Valka explained the path that would finally lead them to the Gandharva Kingdom. "There are many different hurdles, and this is a very painful journey that you have taken upon yourselves."

After walking for about a day, they came to the end of the underground passage. "The gates of the Kingdom of Kinnar are half a day's walk ahead. We should rest for the day and start in the morning again."

Knowing that the gates would be guarded by multiple Kinnars and the only way in was through them, Om asked Valka, "Is there any other way inside, without encountering the guards?"

Valka replied hesitantly, "I can help defeat the Kinnars, but if anyone comes to know that a Yaksa helped, there will be a problem between the two kingdoms. Let me think, and I will let you know in the morning, before you start your journey towards the gates," he said.

In the morning, when the group was ready to walk towards the gates, Valka gave Om one of his hairs. "There is a hill right before the gates. On the top of the hill is a river that rushes down towards the valley of Kinnars. The hill is too high and steep for anyone to climb, but one of my tree friends close to the hill will help you get to the top," said Valka. "Once you are at the top of the mountain, you can climb down using ropes. However, by using this path, your chances of encountering Kinnars in the valley might be great."

"We thank you with all our hearts," Om said, and the group continued their journey.

Near the hill, as he had said, was a tree. Om stepped forward and showed Valka's hair to the tree. The tree lowered one of its upper branches for them to climb on. When everyone had mounted, it softly rose high enough to touch the top of the hill. The group climbed from the tree to the top of the mountain, and the tree returned to its normal shape. From the top, they could see the Valley of Kinnars below them. Next, they would have to climb down next to the waterfall into the Valley of Kinnars.

CHAPTER 13
Valley of Kinnars

The Kinnar Valley, surprisingly, was not covered with snow, but was lush and green. For a moment, it seemed like they were in their own kingdom. The Kinnars were half-horse and half-human demi-gods—one of the finest among the demi-gods. Their speed was no match for anyone on land.

From above the waterfall, the Kinnar Valley spread before them. They could see the palace and the city in between, surrounded by the vastness of the open land. They decided to slowly climb down the waterfall using rope arrows. Soon, they were in the Valley of Kinnars.

By sunset, they were tired and longing for rest. To the east of the waterfall, they quickly set up tents and covered them with leaves. Amber prepared dinner, and the others sat down nearby. After his discussions with Valka, Jabala had a finer sense of the area. It was agreed that the group would walk during the day and rest at night. Although it

195

was hard to hide in daylight, their watchmen were more attentive during the night. Their torchlight would also glow brightly and attract unwanted attention.

At the first light of the sun, Sarvin woke up and went to wake everyone else. Loka heard his movements, quickly woke up, and started stretching his legs. Both Sarvin and Loka heard a faint noise coming from a thicket nearby. Sarvin signaled for Loka to walk in that direction, while he leaned to grab his bow.

As Loka moved toward the bush, something kicked him and ran in the other direction. Annoyed, Loka chased the creature, and Sarvin got ready to fire a rope arrow. As soon as Loka cornered the unknown creature, Sarvin fired his rope arrow. The cord wrapped around the creature's legs, and Loka stood guard.

Everyone else had heard the noise and came out of their tents. Om ran towards Sarvin and Loka. The creature they had caught was a Kinnar.

"Wait, this doesn't look like the Kinnar I saw," said Om.

Jabala came running as well. "It's shorter than a normal Kinnar. It's still a boy."

Om discussed what to do with this Kinnar boy. "We can't let him go. Otherwise, he will bring company, and we can't tie him here, as it's too far from the kingdom and he might die of starvation," Om said.

It was agreed that they would tie him up to a tree and leave food enough to last several days. They thought someone might come looking for the Kinnar child and rescue him.

The defenseless young Kinnar struggled to free himself from the clutches of his captors. "If anyone finds out about this, you'll all be dead!"

The group ignored him, and after tying the Kinnar, they continued their journey towards Gandharva.

After crossing the trees, they came out in a vast open field. It was the Kinnar Grasslands. The grasses were a little taller than waist-high and provided decent cover for them to silently keep walking towards their destination. Amber was concerned about the Kinnar boy, but they all understood that any other alternative could have put their mission in peril.

"Don't let the sorrow overwhelm you, as we might have to face even tougher decisions on our journey ahead," Om counseled.

It had already been two days into the journey, and they had almost reached the heart of the Kinnar Kingdom: its city.

"The kingdom is beautiful," said Samva. The others were surprised to see him holding a looking glass. Samva had asked Valka to help him gather the resources, and he had crafted binoculars during the last two days. Everyone took turns looking through the glass. Samva's creation was unbelievable. The distant vista looked so close; it seemed they could touch the walls of the kingdom.

The kingdom was made of wood. The houses were conspicuously tall, large, and surrounded by vines on all sides, which added to their austere beauty. There were admirable wooden carvings all around the houses.

"The Kinnars first carve their trees and then use them

to make homes," Jabala explained. "They are such skilled craftsmen that they can carve both the inside and outside of a log at the same time. The incised logs are used to build a house in such a way that the outside and inside carvings come together to form meaningful drawings."

The palace was higher than the houses, and had massive statues of kings and queens in front of it.

"The Kingdom of Kinnars is currently ruled by their queen, Kinnari," Jabala further added.

After admiring the exquisite architecture, the group resumed its course.

Four more days passed, and now the kingdom wasn't even visible through the viewing glass. They were glad that the journey of the past few days had been drab and dreary after their eventful and parlous venture in the Yaksas Kingdom.

On the seventh day of the journey, the hawk warned them that they were being followed. "But she isn't certain," Samva told everyone.

To be completely certain, Om asked Sarvin and Idha to stay back and join them at nightfall. Leaving Sarvin and Idha behind, the others continued on the journey. The two waited until night, but they did not encounter any strange movements and walked towards the group to join them.

Idha told Om, "I think the hawk was mistaken, and we weren't being followed."

Still suspicious, Om suggested, "We should take watch in turns."

Om and Loka were to take the first watch. After dinner, when everyone went to rest, they stayed for the first watch. Om saw something twinkling in the woods. "Loka, follow me there."

A few steps in, Om saw a falling star in the night sky. He felt that the journey was blessed by the gods. He continued towards the light, and as he came closer, it moved away further. Om was getting more and more suspicious, as he was getting further away from the rest of the group.

Right as Om decided to turn back, he saw the same lady he had seen multiple times during his training. Om suddenly had an urge to know who she was and kept following her. She was dressed in white, the same way he had seen her before. Occasionally, she would look at Om, smile, and keep walking.

Loka wasn't seeing anything and merely followed Om. Soon, Loka felt something and tried to stop Om. But there was no stopping him, as he was already mesmerized by the lady's presence. Loka turned into a big black beast and roared at Om.

Om came out of his delusion and knew that something was wrong. Om jumped on top of Loka and rode towards the camp. From a distance, they saw that the whole group had been captured by Kinnar soldiers.

Om was still trying to devise a plan, when he suddenly saw Loka storm towards the Kinnar soldiers. There were more than a dozen. Loka engaged with three of the soldiers, and Om ran towards the remaining nine.

Seeing Om, the Kinnar captain ordered one of his

guards, "Handle him!"

Om lunged at him with the shield in front and knocked the Kinnar to the ground. The Kinnars were stunned, as they had never witnessed such human strength before.

"Six of you, attack him!" the Kinnar captain commanded. The other three were holding the prisoners. Three Kinnars were fighting Loka, and one was sent to bring in more troops. Om knew he had to finish this quickly, before the army of Kinnars arrived.

Om fought hard, but fighting one Kinnar alone and fighting a group was completely different. His every strike was dealt with a balanced shield movement and swift spear attack. Om would often dive behind them and inflict some damage, but the Kinnars were swift enough to turn around. A dozen more soldiers joined in, and two of them joined hands in the fight with Loka and the others with Om. He was now surrounded by the Kinnars, in the center of the circle they had formed.

Om struck his tiger claws into the ground, striking a puissant blow, but it wasn't enough to throw and uproot the opponent altogether. It merely gave Om a chance to escape the circle. The Kinnars soon joined hands and encircled Om.

The fight went on, and Om saw an entire battalion of Kinnars approaching them. He struck his sword in the ground, looked up, and prayed to the goddess who had provided him with her powers. A heavenly light originated from the sky, entered Om's sword, and struck everyone surrounding him.

All the Kinnars fighting Om fell unconscious. The

captain and a few soldiers fighting with Loka charged at Om. Loka seized this opportunity, and struck down the rest of the Kinnars.

The battalion of Kinnars had already reached them, and took a complete defensive stand. Their captain approached Om.

"I saw a godly weapon being used. These are not possessed by humans. Who are you, and what are you doing in the lands of Kinnars?" asked the captain.

Om answered the captain in detail and finished with, "…and that is why it's so important that we reach the Gandharva land."

The captain understood, but he wasn't convinced. "I, Captain Azvin, must present you to the queen, according to our laws. She is the only one who can decide your fate. I do not want to force you to fight with me. But you must accompany us to the Kinnar capital and face the queen."

Om restated his purpose. "We must not lose any time."

Both Om and the captain were rigid in their stance, and neither gave up. One of the captain's subordinates approached him and whispered something.

"I will have one of my men escort you to the lands of the Kimpurusas," the captain said, "but you must help us with something."

"As long as it doesn't go against our interests or take a lot of time, certainly."

"There is an outpost on our way towards the land of the Kimpurusas. The outpost is occupied by Kinnars who are outcasts. These Kinnars don't follow the laws of the land and are a nuisance in the neighboring kingdoms," said Azvin. "Some even travel down south to human settlements, destroying their farms, burning villages, and killing at will. Their leader long ago signed a pact with our queen, which gives them immunity from us. We all, including the queen, have been worried by their actions, and we regret signing the pact in exchange for a peace treaty. If you can help us free the land from these outcasts, we would be grateful forever, and we will help in any way."

Om knew that the journey ahead was still tough, and they had to cross one more demi-god land, not to mention entering Gandharva lands, which would not be easy. "Captain Azvin, how can you help our group get to the destination safely, and without any harm? I will interfere with the outcasts only if we are convinced of your scheme in aiding us and our cause."

"We know a path and a person who can guide you to the Gandharva lands without crossing through their gatekeepers."

Om knew that the demi-gods kept their promises. "Then I agree."

It was already sunrise, and the group was up and ready to travel. Some of them didn't quite realize what had happened. Om was accompanied by a few dozen of the Kinnars, who were supposed to guide him to the outpost, and then show them the path to the Gandharva Kingdom without going through the gatekeepers.

The ride to the outpost took them two more days. The outpost looked more like a fort, with stone-lined and well-built boundaries surrounding it. Om checked with Kinnars to find out whether they knew a way in, but to his disappointment, they didn't.

Om asked Samva to send the hawk and gather some details about the fort. The fort was massive, and the outcasts numbered in the hundreds.

"It took me almost a whole night to fight a handful of Kinnars, and I don't know what it would take to fight hundreds," Om worried.

"The only way for us to have peace of mind is if these Kinnars leave the place or yield to the Kinnar queen willingly," the captain had told Om.

Om decided that having these outcasts leave the place was a better option than having them yield before the queen.

With the help of Jabala and others, Om started to devise a plan. "Revat, do you have something in your cabbalistic arsenal we can use against the outcasts?"

"I have a medicine strong enough to send a human into a deep sleep, but I don't know if it would work on Kinnars."

"Let me take a small sample." Om flicked it at one of the Kinnar soldiers behind him. Within moments, the Kinnar was unconscious. The other Kinnars saw this, withdrew their spears, and came forward in anger. "I was only checking to see if the medicine would work on a Kinnar," Om explained nonchalantly.

It took a lot of effort from Jabala to calm the Kinnars down. Soon after going to sleep, the Kinnar soldier got up.

Om walked towards one of the Kinnar soldiers. "What are Kinnars afraid of?"

"We are the bravest of the demi-gods, and we fear no one in this land!"

Om knew that they didn't have time for combat, as it would take days. He wasn't even sure they would win. Then, all of a sudden, he had an idea. "Revat, do you have more of the medicine that knocked me and Loka out when we were in Sarsi, at Isvasa's campgrounds?"

"I have a few vials of those, but it only works if mixed in a meal or drink."

"There are hundreds of Kinnars," Jabala said, "and we can't possibly mix this in their food or drink without being caught." Various schemes were laid out on how to swiftly, without warning, subdue the outcasts or persuade them to surrender.

Om again asked the same Kinnar soldier, "What would happen if the outcast captain died?"

"All outcasts would surrender. We are not here to kill them," the Kinnar added.

"Don't worry," said Om. "Unless necessary, no Kinnar will be killed."

Om went back to his group. "We will have to fake the killing of the leader of outcasts and force the Kinnars to surrender."

After a few rounds of discussion, everyone agreed on a proposal. Amber, the expert thief, would go inside the fort palace and mix the medicine in the outcast leader's drink or meal. "Once the leader is unconscious, I will announce his death from the fort palace and seek surrender of the rest."

"Unless they see him dead, no one will believe you," a Kinnar soldier said. The proposal remained the same, with the addition that someone would drag the leader to the outer gallery and show his face soaked with blood.

"The best way to climb is from behind, but we would still need a diversion to distract soldiers in the back," Amber said.

"Maghavan, along with Rabia, will help create a diversion at the front gate," Om said. "Sarvin and Idha will accompany Amber to the fort palace; Sarvin has particular arrows that will knock the guards unconscious for a while, giving them enough time to climb inside. I and others will remain to capture the rest of the soldiers and tie them up."

Maghavan, along with Rabia, cuffed one of the Kinnar soldiers and dragged him in a way that made it seem as if the Kinnar was captured by them. They walked close enough to the fort, so as to let the gatekeepers see them. When the gatekeepers saw them, they sent out two of the Kinnars towards them.

When the two outcasts were close enough, Om knocked them unconscious using Sarvin's arrows and signaled for Maghavan and Rabia to tie them. The Kinnars in the fort could not see what had happened, but they saw their soldiers captured. They sent ten more this time, and some of the soldiers guarding the back gates came out front to find out what had happened.

This was the window for Amber and his party to sidle in. Sarvin shot the remaining guards at the back, tied them, and moved straight towards the fort palace.

At the front gate, the ten Kinnars that were coming towards Maghavan already had their weapons drawn. Maghavan and Rabia split from the others and ran on a different path towards a ruin nearby; the outcast soldiers followed them. In the ruins, Om and others were already waiting, and didn't take long to control the outcasts and tie them up. Revat's potion was working like a charm, but it would only hold them unconscious for a very brief period of time. The group had to secure them all before they could recover. They used ropes provided by the Kinnar soldiers, which appeared to have divine strength.

Amber had entered the chambers of the leader and mixed the medicine in his drink. It was then a wait-and-watch situation.

Soon, someone entered the leader's chambers, and it seemed that it was one of his close aides. Amber saw that instead of the leader, his aid drank first, and dropped unconscious. The leader shouted, and soldiers rushed towards him.

"I suspect he is terribly drunk," the leader asserted. The soldiers carried him outside and closed the door.

Amber breathed a sigh of relief and kept waiting. After a while, the leader poured and drank the same drink.

Meanwhile, Sarvin fired an arrow at the ruins where Om was, and signaled them. Idha closed the inner door of the leader's room and smeared some animal's blood on his face. Idha and Amber then dragged him to the gallery.

"Your leader is dead. We demand your complete surrender!"

At the same time, Om and his company were already near the front gates. Om shot his divine arrows, which shattered the gate into pieces. A few of the outcasts had already seen their soldiers captured. Now their leader was dead, and before them stood a deific man using divine weapons. Each one of the outcasts surrendered and let themselves be bound.

Om went to the leader's chambers and waited for him to wake up. Once the leader was up, Om told him, "I have defeated your soldiers, and no one remains to protect you. Surrender to the Kinnars or die."

"I refuse!" the leader indignantly replied.

"Do you have another alternative?" asked Om patiently.

The leader thought for a moment. Glumly, he said, "Fine. I agree to surrender to the Kinnar queen."

Handing the outcasts to the Kinnar soldiers, Om asked, "May we now return to our quest? We need directions to the path to Gandharva, without going through the gatekeepers."

As promised, one of the Kinnars gave him a map that showed a path through a lake towards the Kingdom of Gandharva without passing through their gates.

"Take also this gold statue of Queen Kinnari, and give it to the boatman. He will help you sail without any questions. The lake is called Lake Manas, or 'Lake of the Mind,' and it ends in a waterfall. We don't know how to get down from the waterfall, but the kingdom is right below it."

"How can we cross the Kimpurusa lands safely?"

"Alas, we know nothing of the Kimpurusa Kingdom," said the Kinnar.

Om and his group started for yet another kingdom— the final one in their journey. They were glad that, at least, they wouldn't have to fight their way to the Gandharvas Kingdom.

CHAPTER 14
The Kimpurusa Caves

After walking for a few more days, they reached the land of the Kimpurusas. As agreed, one of the Kinnar soldiers guided them to the lands of the Kimpurusas, and left them at the foothills of a rugged mountain. There were no guards or gatekeepers.

The kingdom was on a row of mountains, and the terrain was so laborious that they never needed any gatekeepers. Om bid goodbye to the Kinnar soldier and thanked him for his help. The group started the grueling climb of the snow-peaked mountains. The road ahead was dangerous, and they made all attempts to reach the top before nightfall. Their journey was full of narrow paths bordering the mountains and the narrow paths connected one mountain to another.

It had been three days of climbing, and nature was still not on their side. At night, they would find shelter in the mountain openings and light a fire to warm up and cook.

On the fourth day, in the Kimpurusa Kingdom, the journey became almost impossible, with the wind too bitingly cold. The roads were getting onerous, and the group tied each other with ropes and continued slowly.

One evening, they came across a narrow opening. Maghavan walked inside and found a vast cave, with an opening to the sky. Weary of the rigorous climb, they decided to rest in the cave. The cave provided enough shelter and warmth for them to regain strength. The fire was lit, and Amber prepared for a meal.

Inside the shelter was a web of caves. Maghavan went inside to explore them. Soon, Maghavan returned, horrified. "I saw bones all over the place!"

Everyone went to take a look, but the bones were mostly those of dead animals. The possibility of them dying of cold was higher than anyone killing them. They all returned to the shelter and took seats near the fire.

Idha sat on a small rock, gazing at the night sky through the opening above. She felt something moving very quietly. Looking around, she saw that none of them was even standing. She drew her sword to alert the group. Everyone stood up and faced towards the narrow opening from where they had entered.

Soon, they heard Loka growl from behind them, and turned. A leap of monstrous snow leopards was crawling out from every corner of the cave. They eyed the group hungrily, the fire gleaming on their teeth and their claws peeking through their wide paws. Some even seemed bigger than Loka. After hearing Loka's roar, they replied with an ominous thundering chorus of their own.

Soon, the shelter turned into a man-against-beast battleground. The leopards were not only fierce, but also clever—they would attack from one cave and enter another, and return from a third one. There were four lower caves, four middle, and four upper caves. The only way in for the leopards was the lower cave, but they could come out from any of the caves. The group divided into two and each one took to the openings in the lower cave—one facing towards the cave and another one opposite. Om and Sarvin stood in between, with bows held high.

Once their entry to the caves was blocked, the leopards were quickly injured or killed. With no other disturbances for the night, the group rested well. Maghavan and Samva stepped out to take a peek at the weather. It was still snowing. They decided to wait for another day and continue once the weather improved.

Two more days passed, and there was no sign of the weather improving.

"Marak has surveyed the area," Samva told them, gently stroking the hawk's beak, "and the weather is better to the east, three to four mountains away."

Everyone stood up, prepared for a difficult climb ahead, and tied themselves in the same way as before.

After half a day's climb, the weather grew unbearably harsh. The cold winds slashed their faces. They covered themselves from head to toe.

While they were walking on a narrow path on the side of a mountain, the ground shook, and the path beneath their feet washed away, into a void. Maghavan, Rabia and

Arin, walking in the middle, fell from the path into the void, and the rest were on either side. Idha quickly severed the rope so they could use the attached rope and climb to the other side. Idha was among those left behind, along with Om, Jabala, Amber, and Loka. The three that fell slowly climbed on the other side.

In a little while, there was another jolt. The narrow path started to slide. The group, now divided in two, rushed on either side and braced themselves. The gap grew wider, the space between them so wide that the group behind couldn't see the ones in front.

Om, along with others that were left behind, decided to use daggers and climb down. The other group in front decided to walk forward and wait for them at a safe location. Samva led the charge of the front group. "We'll meet by the edge of the path!"

Om was concerned about the group in front. "Both Jabala and I are behind everyone else!"

Preparing to begin his descent, Jabala told Om, "Don't worry! Most of us, excluding Samva, are warriors, and Samva himself is wise enough to guide us through!"

Om and his group started the descent carefully. By nightfall, they had finished the downward climb and prepared to rest for the night. On the other hand, Samva's group reached the edge of the path by the evening.

Exhausted by the weather and their climb, they were all fatigued and off-guard. Without noticing their tracks, they ran headlong into a troop of Kimpurusas training in the jungle. Most in the group had never seen a Kimpurusa before, though they had heard stories from Om and

Jabala. They were at least as tall as two men put together and were half-lion, half-men, with faces like a lion's.

The Kimpurusas attacked them instantly, without giving Samva and the others any time to react. The fight ended almost as soon as it began, and all were captured. The Kimpurusas tied them up and dragged them towards their kingdom. The hawk saw everything, and Samva signaled her not to attack, but to inform Om and Amber.

The way forward for the group behind was to climb across the rock slide and then follow the same path the others had taken. They rested inside a narrow opening and avoided lighting a fire. While they slept, the hawk circled above, searching for them. After multiple attempts, unable to find them, the hawk perched on a tree to wait until sunrise.

Samva, Rabia, Maghavan, Arin, Revat, and Sarvin walked ahead, their hands tied. Chained one behind the other, they reached a gate heavily guarded and brimming with Kimpurusa soldiers. Inside was a fortification built into a cavern, brilliantly lit using a skillful alliance of mirrors and openings in the ceiling. Samva knew that it was a godly creation. The mirrors captured maximum sunlight from the openings, and kept the place as bright as it was outside. The walls inside were embellished with rich illustrations: Kimpurusa battles and war, gods, and scenes of other living creatures. Parallel to the walls ran a series of alluringly carved pillars with exquisite tiger symbols. The cave was deep, with a liberal opening in the middle, and a maze of paths going all around and under each other. Unlike the Yaksas' mines, this cave looked natural.

Unaware there were Kimpurusas all around, Samva and his group had been taken captive by the guards, and were marched ten paths below the one they had entered, to almost the lowest path. The opening in the middle formed a beauteous lake, and the pillars in the midst of the lake rose to the ceiling of the cave. The admiration of the cave ended when they found themselves in a prison abutting the lake.

Samva could see shadows of the stars in the mirrors and in the lake. He prayed and hoped that the hawk had delivered their message.

Om's troupe got up the next morning, and after a quick meal, started to walk towards the path. The hawk, fervently circling the area, saw them right as they had crossed the rock slides and started the climb back up to the path. She quickly conveyed the message to Amber about Samva and others.

By evening, they were near the end of the path, and they cautiously walked towards the cave. From the hills near the cave, they saw the heavily guarded gates. The hawk kept an eye on the surroundings. The group needed a map of the place so that they could devise a plan to enter and rescue their team.

Om looked at Amber. "Can you break in and find a way to our friends?"

"Heavily fortified places can only be broken into by using disguises, but there is no way you can disguise me as a Kimpurusa. We might capture one, but there is no way a Kimpurusa would help us."

The discussion went on, with no discernible solution. Seeking his guru Rishi Rig Muni's guidance, Om said, "I am going to meditate. Please don't disturb me."

Om reached out to the rishi. "Rishi, I desperately need your help."

"Alas, there is no way I could be of any help in the demi-god's lands," Rishi's voice replied.

"Wait. Remember the Kimpurusa we met during my training? Could your friend in the Mountains of Rishis give us a way into the cave?"

After his discourse with the Kimpurusa, Rishi got back to Om. "He does know the way into the cave—but he refused to help." Om was excited, but at that, his excitement switched to rage.

"Be reasonable," cautioned Rishi. "The Kimpurusa took an oath to guard his kingdom. Aiding you would have been treason."

"I understand, but I'm in serious trouble," Om admitted.

"One last thing. Though I can't help, meeting the king seems propitious. It is said that the Kimpurusas king is kind and noble," said Rishi.

Om got out of meditation. "Someone has to go in and talk to the king."

"What if we are captured?" Jabala waved his hands in denial, looking at Om as if unable to fathom anything around him.

Om replied, "Whoever goes to meet the king should take the hawk along, and if the person is imprisoned, the hawk will show us the way in."

"I will try and cajole the guards into letting me in to meet the king," Idha decided. She hid the hawk inside her bag and walked towards the gate. The Kimpurusas did not pay any heed to what she had to say, and she was thrown in the same prison as the others.

In the prison, Idha found her comrades. "Om is planning an escape, but I don't know how yet." She let the hawk loose. Marak flew out from one of the openings in the cave, and expressed to Amber everything she had seen on her way out.

The group outside had now finally gained some understanding about the inside of the cave, but they still didn't know how to enter without alerting the guards. From the gate to all the openings, the cave was heavily guarded, and even a single imprecise, fortuitous step would land them all in prison. Nobody had lost hope, but everyone was a little disconcerted at the news that Idha, too, was now ensnared by the Kimpurusas, and they'd allowed it to happen. It was up to Om, Jabala, Amber and Loka; everyone else was in captivity.

They found shelter among dense trees nearby, and everyone retired for the night. They were still thinking about how to get inside. Soon, everyone fell asleep, except Om.

Restless, he stood and paced back and forth. Suddenly, he saw the lady in white standing in a narrow clearing, as if waiting for him to find her. She smiled at him and walked away.

As usual, Om followed. This time, she wasn't going fast. Om asked her from behind, "Who are you, and why

216

are you following me?"

The lady didn't stop walking as Om barraged her with questions that had troubled him for so long. She turned to look at him at last. "The lake inside the cave has a source in the nearby mountain. Find the source; you will find your way in."

She lifted her hand in the direction of a burly mountain nearby, then disappeared.

The lady had left Om with his questions still unanswered, but she had sparked a new hope in him.

It was still night, and he sprinted back to the camp to rouse the others. Om told them, "I now know a way in, but we would have to leave immediately, without delay."

They had always known that Om had powers beyond those of an ordinary human, and they never doubted or hesitated on his judgment. Jabala was a demi-god and knew that Om had some help from the divine. The group started their climb towards the mountain.

By sunrise, Om and his people arrived at a waterfall on the side of the hill. Now they had to find the passage that fed the lake inside the cave.

The group climbed down to the bottom of the falls and started to look for a passage. A few hundred feet from the falls, there was an area where the water was deep. They found a passage inside in the depths of the pool, but they didn't know the length of the tunnel, and if they could make it without breathing for so long.

Jabala gathered everyone around him and stood in the middle. "I will be the one to dive into the tunnel and find our way into the cave. I have mastered the art of holding

217

my breath for a long time. If it takes me longer, my body will merely go into a deep sleep, but the lack of air won't kill me."

Agreeing with Jabala's suggestion, Om and Amber had to wait for Jabala's return and the way forward. Om tied a rope around Jabala's ankle, and they reevaluated the strategy before he was ready to dive in through the passage. If he went into sleep, Om and Amber would pull him back up.

Jabala came back up sooner than they had anticipated. "The passage leads to another opening inside the hill, and there is another spring there."

Without further delay, all of them, including Loka, dove to the inner opening in the hill.

Inside the hill, the water from the passage formed another spring. After looking around scrupulously, they found another adroitly hidden underwater passage.

Jabala dived into the passage again. He took a lot more time to return. Om and Amber had almost decided to pull him out when he finally came back. Breathing heavily, it took Jabala some time to recover. Once back to normal, he had a triumphant grin on his face.

"The passage did lead to the lake inside the cave, but it is too long for either of you to survive. We have to devise some other plan, as I alone wouldn't be able to free our team trapped in the Kimpurusa prison. Even if I could, there was no way I could return with them using the same path."

Amber stood in a corner, mulling over the situation. After giving it a lot of thought, he cleared his throat to draw their notice. "I have a considerably unconventional idea about how we could survive the daunting swim through the passage." He paused to look around, and continued, "…without having to hold our breath for too long. We could dive in using a big pot that would fit our faces. The pot would carry more air for us to breathe."

Both Jabala and Om looked at him in astonishment while he explained. The plan was set into motion, and Amber made a dozen clay pots for the group—including the others, if they returned the same way. The pots were dried thoroughly, and after almost half a day, the group was ready to get inside the cave.

Om and Jabala walked to the mouth of the passage. "Take as many pots as you can, and tie the rope to the other end inside the cave," Om said.

Om tied his end of the rope at the opening where they were standing. Loka was signaled to guard the area and protect it with his life. The rope would guide Om and Amber through the tunnel.

Soon enough, all three were inside the cave. The lake inside was, in fact, larger than other cave lakes that they had ever seen in their lives. They swam to a nearby pillar without making even the slightest noise and looked for their friends.

Om had located the group. "The way in through the same passage is the only way out for them."

Jabala worried, "What if something happens at the other end, and there is no protection for Loka?"

"No one can defeat Loka," Om assured him. "If the opponent is strong, he will simply survive longer."

219

"But Revat isn't with us, so there is no way we could use his alchemical compounds or arrows."

"Next time," Om mulled, "it would be better if everyone carried some potions with them. The only option now is for Amber to steal the keys and let everyone out."

They hid behind a pillar near the edge of the lake. After a long stint of observation, they saw that all guards who were patrolling entered a corner chamber and stayed there for a long time. It was already night, but the whole area was abundantly lit and heavily guarded. Near the chamber, however, the light was dim compared to the rest.

Om told Amber, "You have to find the keys—so we must get into that chamber. There's a high chance the keys are kept there, or are with someone inside."

Amber swam to that part and patiently waited for a chance to get in. At last, he stood behind a Kimpurusa and walked behind him—his every single movement coinciding with that of the Kimpurusa, like a soundless shadow. The Kimpurusas were so tall and broad that Amber couldn't be seen. This Kimpurusa entered the chamber, and walked towards his left.

Amber saw an old, dusty wooden table, laden with scrolls and glasses on the right, and stealthily sneaked under it. From there, he could see at least a dozen Kimpurusas sitting in the middle of the room on wooden seats, with a similar wooden table in between. Most of them had their backs turned towards Amber. The Kimpurusa whom Amber had followed poured himself a drink from a large pot and joined the ones in the middle as well. There seemed to be no way to find where the keys to the prison were.

After waiting for some time, Amber saw one of the Kimpurusas enter and put one of his keys on a wooden board on the other side of the room. Amber knew that it was the area where all keys were stored. He waited for the right moment to slink towards the board and steal the keys. Soon, all the Kimpurusas were drunk, and a friendly brawl ensued.

Outside, Om and Jabala were getting worried. "I simply knew that Amber wouldn't get a chance to steal the keys—otherwise, he would have been out by now," said Jabala.

"I'll make a distraction," Om whispered. He took an arrow and struck the lamp posts outside the chamber, then recalled his arrow. Three lamp posts fell, and made a deafening noise as they crashed.

All the Kimpurusas rushed outside to see what had happened. In this short window, Amber took all the keys and dumped them in his bag. The Kimpurusas didn't find anything suspicious that would tell them that the lamps were purposely broken, went back inside, and resumed drinking.

Amber waited for a while and then sneaked out, dragging his body like a snake and making as little noise as he could. Amber reached the pillar inside the lake where Om and Jabala were waiting for him.

"Now we have the keys, but have to draw the guards away from the prison," said Amber.

Om used one of his divine arrows and fired straight up through the opening in the cave, angling it to land somewhere near the main entrance. The impact of the arrow touching the ground in front of the entrance struck like thunder, followed by a quake that shook the whole cave. "I didn't even know they could do that," Om admitted.

"Whatever you want them to do, they perform it very well," asserted Jabala.

The Kimpurusas, guarding the cave inside, ran outside towards the entrance. Two of the Kimpurusa guards were left behind. Om shot two arrows at once from behind the guards and wounded their legs. Jabala held them down by pointing his voulge at their faces, and Amber tied them up quickly, using the same ropes they had used on the Kinnars.

Amber went ahead to open the lock, but he had too many keys, and only one lock to open. Amber started trying the keys one by one, but his anxiety caused more delays. Jabala and Om were guarding the path in both directions. After a while, Amber was finally able to open the gates and got everyone out.

"Now, everyone," Om commanded, "follow Amber towards the lake and then outside the caves."

The entire group followed slowly, with no sign of other Kimpurusas. In their struggle, they had forgotten that the cave was designed using a number of mirrors, which were reflecting their activities outside.

One of the Kimpurusas noticed them and sounded the alarm. Om signaled for the group to hurry, and along with

Jabala, held the position.

Soon, Kimpurusas showed up in large numbers, and Om and Jabala were surrounded from both sides. They used all their powers to keep the Kimpurusas at bay. Om used his divine arrows to fire and recalled them quickly, then fired them back, causing confusion for the Kimpurusas. He fired a rope arrow between the legs of the Kimpurusas, and from other end, Jabala pulled it so quickly that many of them fell directly into the lake.

Jabala used his voulge to hold one front. "Time to jump in the lake and swim to the other end!" he whispered to Om. While Jabala was speaking with Om, one of the Kimpurusas overpowered him and caught him.

One of them put his claws near Jabala's throat. "Time to surrender."

Om was already pointing the arrow towards this Kimpurusa's face. Om threw his bow in one corner, but while doing that, he used his tiger claws and sent shockwaves that knocked down the Kimpurusas near Jabala. The Kimpurusas were astonished by this power, as only the elite among them could use it.

Hearing the shockwaves, the Kimpurusas' leader Karvara arrived with his elite group of soldiers. The Kimpurusas, Om, and Jabala were fighting more like guards than soldiers. The soldiers that came with the leader were taller, larger, and looked more powerful than the rest. They were clad in full-body armor. There was no chance for Om and Jabala to escape now.

The leader Karvara came forward. "Who gave you those tiger claws? Where did you get them?"

Om answered, "From one of the Kimpurusas at the Mountains of Rishis."

Karvara ordered his men, "Apprehend both of them!"

Om lifted his sword, ready to fight. Seeing this, the soldiers of Karvara quickly came forward and formed a line. On both sides, there were elite Kimpurusa soldiers with Karvara in between and Om with his sword. Jabala was standing next to Om, but without his voulge. There was no fight and Jabala told Om to stand down.

Karvara came towards Om and looked at the tiger claws. He spoke stiffly. "This was designed to be given to a person who wasn't a Kimpurusa, but would be as powerful as them and was worthy of it." He waved at the guards to take them away.

Om and Jabala were put in the same prison.

"Karvara, we are on a journey, a very important one to fulfill our obligations," Jabala tried to tell him.

Karvara didn't listen, but he could see that these men were honest and not afraid.

He had already taken the tiger claws from Om, so Karvara went straight to one of the makers. "Are they truly the ones made in our kingdom?"

The maker told Karvara, "Yes, they are Kimpurusa tiger claws, carved inside the kingdom."

Karvara was now satisfied and sought permission of his king to let these men go.

"I agree, Karvara. Guide them out of the kingdom."

Karvara came back to the prison and opened the doors. "Om, Jabala, the king will allow you to leave, and we will help you get outside the kingdom."

Om stood at the entrance while Jabala went to bring the others, waiting for them near the spring through which they had entered the lake. The entrance from the spring was sealed by the Kimpurusas who went with Jabala.

Once the group met Om at the entrance, all of them started their journey again. The Kimpurusa soldier left them with all the rations they would need for the rest of their journey. A few Kimpurusa soldiers followed them to the end of the kingdom, and towards Lake Manas.

CHAPTER 15

Manas: "Lake of the Mind"

Om and his team finally reached Lake Manas after days of traveling. Among the snow-capped mountains was the perfect blue water lake. Clouds descended down to touch the waters, and sunshine through these clouds turned them into puffs of gold. Such serene beauty none of them had experienced before.

Jabala told them how the name "Manas" came into being. "It is said that the lake is alive, and the water increases the power of the mind, so it's called 'lake of the mind,' or 'Manas'. Soma, the divine drink, is made using water from this lake, and the lake water can cure any disease."

Walking near a series of tall trees, they saw a boat with its boatman seated at the front. The man had long white hair in braids and wore a circlet of gold atop his head. He had dark, intense eyes, and his nose looked precisely like the beak of an eagle.

The man sat in his boat, completely ignoring them, as if they weren't there. He didn't even speak until Om handed him the tiny statue of the Kinnar queen, which he had carried carefully throughout the Kimpurusa land.

After taking possession of the queen's statue, he brightened and warmed up to them. "I am Hari. You may board the boat."

Om told him, "We want to go to the Gandharva Kingdom."

The boat was fairly commodious; Hari took his seat at the end and started rowing after everyone had settled inside. Soon, all they could hear was the rowing of the oars, the chirping of birds, and the sound of water. They were surrounded with enchanting views as far as they could see.

The beauty they had enjoyed at a distance from the lake was nothing compared to seeing it up close. The snow-covered mountains, the company of clouds, and being the only boat in the lake added to the tranquility.

A few thousand feet from the shore, the group was absorbed in the serenity of the moment, when a sudden silence inundated the area. Even the air stopped moving.

The group looked at each other in confusion. While they were still trying to discern what had happened, the boat started shaking, and the water started to rise all around it.

"The coward has abandoned us," Maghavan grunted in anger. Everyone turned around to see that the boatman was gone and had left his circlet behind. He was nowhere to be seen. Jabala had just risen from his seat to grab the oars when he froze in stunned disbelief.

A snake rose from the water—a creature bigger than any they had ever seen. The snake had seven heads, with a different-colored gem sparkling on each head. The snake had already wrapped its tail around one end of the boat. Its heads were facing the boat and Om's group.

"Where are you going, my friends?" it spoke. "Why are you in such a hurry? Did Hari forget to tell you that this is my home—the region ruled by the great Aga?" the snake said, feigning a concerned tone. "I am Aga, and no one crosses these waters without my permission." Its eyes gleamed with a malfeasant desire.

"Let me first finish you one by one, and then I will give you my permission to go further—further into the land of death," it said, pretending to count the number of people on the boat. "It's been a long time since I have tasted human meat. I am so tired of eating fish," the snake added with an impish grin.

Om and Sarvin took aim at the snake, but the arrows stopped right before it and dropped in the water.

"You puny creatures. You want to kill the great Aga with your tiny weapons!" It smiled and rattled the boat. "I admire your bravery, but, alas, you are at my mercy. Try as hard as you can. The only way out is through my stomach." The snake laughed again, louder this time.

Jabala told Aga who they were, their purpose, and that it was important for them to continue the journey. "Furthermore, I am a demi-god, and killing me or my men will call down the wrath of all demi-gods."

"It is always delightful meeting a demi-god," said the serpent, acting courteous. "I am wrath itself! And I bring wrath upon whoever crosses me." Aga, hissed angrily at Jabala's face.

Aga quickly lifted up Rabia and was about to eat her when Samva stopped him.

"Hey, mighty Aga, you are powerful. Have mercy and let us go for the noblest of reasons. We will make sure we come back to you once our quest is complete," said Samva.

The snake looked at him in amazement. "No, no, no… there can be no reason to prevent me from a human feast." The snake opened his mouth and swallowed Rabia.

Om moved everyone else behind him and started firing his divine weapons one by one at the giant serpent, but all the weapons failed to reach him. Every single one of them stopped before the snake and fell into the lake. The gems on the snake's head were saving it from all the weapons they had tried so far. Sarvin and others tried to help Om, but they didn't have any success. The snake kept on laughing at them.

Jabala was holding the oars tightly so that he could start rowing at the first chance he got. He prayed to the god of water, Varuna, but it seemed the gods were deaf to their pleas for protection from Aga.

"Revat, do you have anything that could help?" Om asked.

"I have nothing that could prevail upon this beast!"

Aga pounced at Om, but he quickly moved away from his grip. It spun the boat around with its tail, and before

Om could react, Amber was already the snake's second meal.

"Jabala, Sarvin, hold it off for a moment," Om ordered. He closed his eyes and thought of Rishi, seeking his advice.

Soon, he heard a voice say, "Tear the snake apart from within."

Om knew he could tear the snake from within, but as soon as he stopped fighting, the snake would realize his motives. Om thought of something, signaled to Jabala, and jumped into the lake.

Aga, sure that Om would attack from under the lake, followed him immediately. Om swam away from the boat. He had already told Jabala to row towards land once the snake was away.

Aga realized that he had been tricked. As soon as the boat turned, he struck it with his tail and split the boat in half.

Everyone was in the water, and started swimming towards the land. The snake wanted to follow them, but Om struck him from within the water and slashed the snake's belly open. The snake swam fiercely towards Om, and smashed its tail towards him.

Om had anticipated this. He pretended to be unconscious. Aga warily came closer and swallowed him, then turned back to the rest of the fleeing group.

Inside the snake, Om tried to use his sword, but the inside of the snake was thicker than he had thought. He used all his strength and stabbed the serpent with his tiger claws.

Aga's screams of pain and anger filled the air as the monster was ripped apart from head to tail.

Freed of the serpent, Om was unconscious, and had floated to the surface. Jabala quickly grabbed him and brought him to the shore.

Om opened his eyes. It was almost evening, and he was glad to see both Rabia and Amber alive and standing before him. Om again fell back into a deep sleep, and everyone else settled down to prepare something to eat.

While saving Om, Jabala had secretively collected all the seven gems, which now floated on the lake like lotus blossoms. Jabala kept this to himself, and didn't tell anyone of what he saw or had done when he went back to bring Om.

The next morning, Om woke up early with a ravenous hunger and ate whatever was left from the previous night. He went near the lake and wondered what they were going to do about the boat. He sat on a rock near the lake, examining all his weapons. An option was to swim across the lake, but they neither knew the distance they would have to swim, nor what other creatures the lake might be hiding in its belly.

Soon, everybody was up. They prepared to discuss their next assignment. The discussion started, with everyone having different opinions. Arin and Idha recommended avoiding the lake and instead going through the gatekeepers.

Jabala disapproved, saying, "Going through the gatekeepers will be like going through a long battle." He sat on a rock near the fire pit. Looking at their belongings, he said, "At this point, we are all tired and running out of time."

Om, standing quietly for some time, said, "Jabala is right. We have to find a way to cross the lake. We have to find a way to build a boat."

Amber was still trying to come to grips with what had happened the day before. "I think we should return." A silence fell over the group. "What if we reach near the waterfall, but we still don't make it?" he added, breaking the silence.

Om said, "Returning is not an option, not now and not ever. Amber, we will figure something out once we are near the falls." But he was unable to convince himself, and he was worried that he might be wrong.

Overwrought, he closed his eyes and concentrated on trying to reach Rishi through their telepathic connection.

Rishi told Om, "Going through the gatekeepers is not an option. They will fight until they have killed every last person in the group. Unlike the other three demi-god kingdoms, the gatekeepers' numbers are huge and will increase as soon as the message reaches the Gandharva capital. You have to find your way through the lake."

Finally, before ending the conversation, he said one last thing: "When you reach the palace, make sure to create a lot of chaos with all your weapons so that the king hears it and comes out of his chambers."

Om was now more sure of the path they needed to follow. He went back to the group to plan the building of a boat.

The only builder among them was Maghavan. "But I

have never built a boat so big as to carry all of us," he huffed. "I need all of you to start cutting down trees for the boat."

The group began their next big endeavor, and each one was assigned a task by Maghavan.

Half the day had gone by, and the group sat down to fill their empty stomachs.

"I can help you build a boat with a nominal payment," came a voice from nowhere. Om looked up to see Hari, the boatman, standing nearby.

Sarvin almost instantly had an arrow pointed at him, squarely in the face. "Who are you? Why did you leave us to die? Why didn't you tell us there was danger lurking in the depths of the lake?"

The boatman politely said, "Please, lower your weapons. I come in peace. The Gandharvas have always known that there is a way into the kingdom going through the lake. Aga, the seven-headed snake, and I were tasked to guard the lake."

He held his smile while everyone listened to him, disbelief clouding their faces, as he continued, "Anyone who was able to defeat the indomitable Aga and enter the kingdom must be truly blessed. As I see it, you have made it halfway by killing the serpent. I hope that someone among you is blessed by gods themselves. In my life, I have never seen anyone defeat Aga, as Aga was a form of deity."

Sarvin and others had lowered their weapons. Om asked Hari, "What do you need in return for the boat, and why are you helping us now?"

He answered, "Since I abandoned you at the lake, oblivious to the peril that lurked ahead, it is my turn to repay you. But I must also bring Aga back to life."

Om asked him again, "What do you want in return?"

The boatman said, "All I wish is that you return all the gems that were taken from Aga, as the stones are the only way I can bring Aga back to life."

"We don't have them," Om told him, but the boatman was adamant that someone among the group had taken them. Everyone looked at each other with confused gazes, not knowing what to make of the situation.

"We don't have what you want. Kindly go away unless you can help."

Everyone went back to cutting trees, and Hari stayed back near a rock. "Your boat will not make the falls. It is only I who can only make a special boat to withstand the falls," he warned.

A few days passed, and the boat was half ready. Hari returned every evening, and said the same thing: the boat wasn't going to help them.

One day, Arin put his sword to Hari's neck. "Go away. Return again, and you will be dead," said Arin.

Om came forward, holding his headband. "You can take my blue gem instead if you will give us your help."

Hari looked at the gem. "It's of no use to me, but I will help." He started with dismantling what they had built so far.

He was an artist, with a divine talent for building. In four days, the boat was ready. They had worked night and day to construct the boat, and they were exhausted. Hari told everyone, "Get a good night's sleep, and I will help you get past the falls tomorrow."

With a little more hope than before, the group retired for the day and went to sleep. The next morning would be a new adventure for them.

At Om's camp, everyone was up at daybreak, and they began pulling the boat on the lake. After almost mid-day, they were able to roll the boat over the logs and finally land it in the water. After loading their weapons and belongings, the journey to the Gandharva Kingdom began yet again.

It took another day for them to reach the falls.

Hari had stopped the boat right before the falls. "You should wait for sunset before we start for the falls. That way, the guards won't see you, and you will have a chance to at least make it to the palace."

On the other side, in the Malla Kingdom, Isvasa and Udadhir were preparing the kingdom for the upcoming battle. The king had given orders for all able men and women to undergo the training. The princess was not falling behind, and had already organized the palace guards and commanded their training. The palace guards would be the last defense, and she wanted them to be ready to protect the kingdom at all cost. She would often think of Om, but she knew that there was no way she could talk to him. Preoccupied with his concerns, Om had forgotten that he had not visited the princess since he'd left on this quest.

The king, along with Rishi, had organized massive yajnas throughout the kingdom. The nearby friendly kingdoms, Madhya and Kanika, were informed about the upcoming war and were told to gather as many able soldiers as possible. Isvasa was relying on his spies more than before to get continuous updates on the movements of the evil army.

At the same time, Udadhir had asked all his Ganas to assemble inside the Malla Kingdom and meet him near Sarsi, Isvasa's training grounds. The captains of all forts were also asked to train harder and tasked to strengthen their forts.

CHAPTER 16

The Mesmerizing Kingdom

After sunset, Hari steered the boat towards the falls. He asked everyone to hold on to something strong and brace themselves for the falls. The fall was quick, but it knocked many of them into the water. Before the commotion could alert the guards, the boatman swiftly moved the boat to an area concealed by the shadows of giant trees.

The group was separated once again, with Om, Jabala, Loka, and Hari on one side of the falls, and everyone else on the other side. It was decided that the following morning, Om would take up the charge on the palace guards and make enough noise to draw the king outside. They hoped not to encounter any Gandharvas at night. The group on the other side also hid among the trees.

All of them waited for Om to make his move the next day. During the night, Om told Jabala to escape with the rest of them, if he couldn't make it in the morning. In the meantime, they admired the beautiful surroundings while they set up a campsite.

The royal palace stood elegantly in the heart of the lake, created by the first waterfall. Further still, the lake turned into another waterfall, and emptied into another lake, and continued until it reached the bottom of the mountains. Each fall formed a small lake, and the lake was adorned with delicately designed palaces. The entire Gandharva Kingdom was an amalgam of breathtaking waterfalls, lakes, and palaces. A string of bridges connected each one of the palaces from both ends of the fall. Moonlight shone so bright on the royal palace that it gleamed like a precious white pearl in a celestial setting.

In the early morning, Om and Loka took cover near the bridge towards the palace. As the first light fell on the palace, Om fired two of his divine arrows at once towards the palace gates. The impact blew open the doors of the palace and flung a few of the guards in the lake. Behind him, Loka had turned into the black beast and roared at the top of his voice.

The blast and the thundering roar shook the whole kingdom. The palace guards blew the horn, and the troops began to run towards the palace with their weapons drawn. Om and Loka forced their way in towards the palace, fighting the guards. The guards held back Om and Loka both for a while.

Jabala was watching silently so far, and seeing Om struggle, he threw his weapon towards the palace. The impact of the weapon not only shook the palace, but also ravaged one of its pillars.

King Marut came out of his chamber and looked down at the chaos from his gallery. He saw Om and the beast fighting his soldiers, and ordered everyone to cease the fight.

As soon as Om saw the king, both he and Loka kneeled down to salute. Om raised his hand, holding the red gem given to him by Rishi.

"Guards, bring the stranger in!" called King Marut when he saw the gem.

Om was brought into the king's chambers, while Loka was held outside. Patiently waiting, he stood in the middle of a round and capacious room, with a ceiling as high as Himalayan trees. Statues of gods surrounded the room, clustering around the walls. King Marut entered, and without wasting any more time, Om explained the entire situation to the king and handed the gem to him.

King Marut had locked himself in the kingdom for a long time. After hearing what Om had to say, he admitted, "I myself am one of the reasons that the fate of humanity is in grave danger. If I'd wanted, the evil army would have perished in the ruins hundreds of years ago."

King Marut told Om, "It's brave of you and your team to travel this treacherous path. I'll let you know my decision. Please stay a few days as guests of the Gandharva Kingdom."

Om nodded and thanked the king.

"Guards, take Om to the royal guest quarters and cater to all his needs, as you would for other nobility."

Om inquired, "What about my friends?"

The king replied, "Your friends will be treated the

same as you."

Om and his friends were taken to the royal quarters in the same palace. Meanwhile, the king summoned his general. "Look into matters. Find out if Om was telling the truth about the evil army."

The general replied, "I know that the evil army is getting stronger and that they have conquered most of the Western Himalayan Kingdoms. I will find out details and let you know in a day."

The city of Gandharva existed in parallels of unreality—it had rainbows in the day, reflections of the moon in water at night, and illusions created by clever magicians. It was a heavenly experience for the group. From Om's chamber, he could see the falls and the glorious kingdom below him.

The next day, the general confirmed the threats about the evil army. "Your Highness, we might have five months at most before the evil army reaches Malla."

Om was summoned. "Om, I have decided to support Malla in the war against evil."

"Not only do you have to help, but you must command the entirety of the demi-gods' army, too," Om urged the king.

"I will do whatever is necessary."

"Of course, Your Highness. Then may we have permission to leave?"

The king had something else in his mind. "Om, I am told that you are a great warrior and have blessings from gods. I know that you still struggle to control the heavenly weapons, the gem, the sword, and the arrows. The heir to the Gandharva throne will teach you how to control your weapons. After the training, you will be skilled in wielding these weapons."

Om said, "You are correct, my king, but our return to Malla is of supreme importance."

"It will not take more than a few days for your training, and until then, you will be a guest of the kingdom." Om and the group had no other alternative than to delay their journey back to Malla.

The next morning, one of the guards escorted Om for training. He was left in the open on a terrace. Sauntering over the lush carpet of verdant green, he saw someone standing in one corner, all armored up. The person came close and lifted her mask.

The heir to the throne was a princess. She greeted Om. "I am Rati." The training started at once. Om was spellbound by the ways she taught him to control the powers of his weapons. The first day ended, and Om took leave to join his friends in the royal quarters.

The shadow hunters had already sent a message to Malla that they had safely arrived in Gandharva, and that the king was ready to help them fight the battle. Om's training continued for a few days. He had learned how to control his gem, and now could use it at will, rather than just relying on lucky accidents. He got better at using the divine powers of his arrows and sword.

Om was a diamond, cut by the rishis; the princess of Gandharva offered the final polish. In fifteen days, Om had mastered his skills and finished the last few lessons from the princess. His friends, deeply enthralled with the king's hospitality, had forgotten all the hardships they'd faced to reach the place.

At the same time, in Malla, Isvasa's spies were active all around the Himalayan Kingdoms, and they provided him with a constant flow of information about the evil army.

One fine day, Isvasa came to know that the evil army was planning to attack right after the monsoon, in the winter days. Isvasa called upon the council and met the king with them.

He updated everyone. The king declared, "You must send word to Om. Notify the people that we have declared war, and begin to prepare. All men must be given orders to train and ready for the approaching battle."

Isvasa assented. "Princess Abha, send the message to Om."

In the next few days, shadow hunters in Gandharva had received a message from Malla. On learning the content of the letter, Om went straight to King Marut. "You must call together all of the demi-gods and raise an army against evil. If we don't march soon enough, it will be too late to save Malla."

"I agreed to the battle, but it will still take time to assemble the army and reach Malla. Along with your team and a unit of Gandharva soldiers, go forth. In the meantime, I will assemble the army and march towards the kingdom. It will take the army almost two months to reach the Malla battlegrounds. Get ready for the journey."

Om gathered his group and was told to meet at one of

the small palaces under the main palace. They would continue their journey down from there.

King Marut ordered the general to fire the "light of faith," a light as bright as a blazing star. The light went straight into the skies.

All the demi-gods saw a light that they had not seen for hundreds of years and started assembling their troops.

Meanwhile, at the smaller palace where Om was all prepared to leave, the king told him, "I have a quicker way to reach Malla, but it can accommodate only fifty people."

The king led the way to an elegant boat moored for them. "This is a divine boat that floats above water and will take you to Malla in a few days. The boat will take you down the series of falls to the divine river, which, in turn, becomes Medhavi in Malla. My general will accompany you, along with my finest men. In a situation where we wouldn't arrive in time, the general could help you in any way possible to keep the enemy at bay," said King Marut.

While the general was about to board, Princess Rati arrived where everyone had gathered. She looked at the king. "Shouldn't I march ahead with the group, in place of the general? The general is needed to command the demi-god army, while I could be the one helping the humans until the arrival of the demi-gods."

King Marut agreed.

Om, along with his friends, the princess, and a few dozen Gandharva warriors, sailed towards the Malla lands.

It had been a few months since the group had

embarked on a journey that had been fraught with danger, and via the river. The return, however, took them merely five days to arrive back in Malla. It was almost dark when they anchored close to Nanda Mountain and used the way through the caves towards the palace.

Princess Abha, duly apprised of how things had unfolded at the Gandharva Kingdom and their advent, had informed the king as well. She waited at the other end of the cave, which opened into the palace to greet them. Quarters were readied for each of Om's men and the Gandharvas.

She greeted the Gandharva soldiers with grace. "Thank you for joining us. My servant will show you to your quarters."

The Malla princess, along with Om, escorted Princess Rati to her personal chambers. Om told Rati, "I will take you to the king's court in the morning, but for now, I'd like to take my leave."

Om hurried to meet his old friend, his horse, Meer, who greeted him with a nuzzle and an emphatic whinny of welcome.

Soon after, Om had an elaborate meal with his friends. "My friends, I am grateful for the bravery you have shown and the courage you displayed alongside me," said Om. "I have no right to ask any more from you, but if you agree to be a part of the battle, I would be glad to fight alongside you."

All of them agreed to fight alongside him.

One of Isvasa's men entered the dinner hall, looking

for Om. "Isvasa is expecting you in Sarsi after you have met with the king," he said, and left.

"Please accompany Isvasa's soldiers to the training camp in Sarsi. I will join you in two days' time," Om said to his team.

In the morning, Om accompanied the Gandharva princess to the king's court. Both of them were greeted warmly by the king and the queen. The king was already acquainted with what had happened at the Gandharva Kingdom, and by his estimates, he knew that they had to fight the evil army initially without the demi-gods, and hold them off for at least seven to eight days.

"This is the best estimate, but we don't know the worst," said King Neera. Isvasa's spies were updating the king frequently, and all the moves were planned based on their input. "Om, I will accompany you to Sarsi tomorrow, where we can plan our next moves."

Om spent the night with Abha; he had not seen her for months. Both of them told each other what they had done during his absence.

"I am worried about the battle," said Abha.

"Winning?" he teased.

"Worried about what it might take away from me. I think we should get married before the battle."

Om held her hand to comfort her. "No priest would marry you without the king's consent, and in this tense situation, the king won't give it."

But the princess was adamant. "It was hard for me to wait for you when you weren't around. Not anymore," insisted the princess. "I spent days watching the sun set, and then nights waiting for it to rise again," she continued without looking at him.

"But we can't marry without a priest. Another option is for Rishi to marry us, I suppose." He wrapped his arms around her waist and looked at her with the intense brown eyes she so loved. "Will you come with me to Medhya after my return from Sarsi?"

"Absolutely not. I'm coming with you to Sarsi. Nothing would have changed after our return from Sarsi, and there is no reason for us to delay the wedding," she said as she wriggled out of his grasp.

Both of them finally decided to meet Rishi that same night. They quickly dressed like commoners.

Meanwhile, the Gandharva Princess Rati couldn't sleep and was walking in the corridors. She saw some movement near the princess's chambers and went straight to it. Rati was nonplussed to see both Om and Abha dressed like commoners. "Why are you dressed like that?"

Om couldn't resist explaining the situation to his new friend. Rati stood silently as she listened to his dilemma.

She smiled at them and said, "As the princess of a demi-god kingdom, I have the authority to marry you both, and it would be a marriage blessed by the gods themselves."

Om and Abha looked at each other, pleased that they had confided their secret to Rati. "We accept," they both said.

In a rather quiet ceremony, with no one else present, Om and Princess Abha were married by Princess Rati. They were now husband and wife, but they still had to obtain the king's permission to make the marriage public. "Will you keep our matrimony a secret until the war is over? Then I will ask the king for his blessings," Om said to Rati.

The newlywed couple spent the rest of the night with each other. Enjoying the brief respite, they prayed for the war to be over soon.

The next morning, King Neera, Om, the Gandharva soldiers, and both princesses marched towards Sarsi. In Sarsi, they were greeted by Isvasa and Udadhir and taken directly to the captain's chambers. The king asked them about their strategy to hold the evil army off for the seven to eight days before the demi-gods could arrive.

Udadhir said, "All of my Gana soldiers have been assembled in Sarsi and are ready to fight. Even with all of Malla's army and Gana, it will be difficult holding them for long."

"We have to devise a plan that should be less confrontational and more strategic," said King Neera.

"We would still need more men," noted Udadhir.

Isvasa agreed with Udadhir and said, "Kanika and Madhya would help, but they are already required to hold the fort when Anga attacks from the east. Madhya will be used to shelter the citizens who cannot fight."

Om told them, "I have a plan, and it will require traveling to my village, Medhya, soon. I think we should persuade the rishis to fight with us."

The king replied, "Rishis only protect or help a kingdom prosper through their prayers. Since rishis never

fight for any kingdom, why would they fight on our side?"
He looked at Om as he waited for a response.

Om explained, "We have to convince the rishis that
the fight is not for a kingdom; the fight is to survive
against evil. I know people who can help me convince the
rishis, and I may have to travel to the Mountains of
Rishis," said Om.

It was decided that Om would travel to the Mountains
of Rishis and persuade the rishis to side with them—as
best as he could.

Om was going home after such a long time; he wanted
to continue the journey alone. But when he looked at
Abha, the determination in her eyes made it evident that
she wouldn't give him a choice in the matter. Along with
Meer and Loka by their sides, they began the journey
towards Medhya.

King Neera headed back to Ogana, but the others
remained behind to strategize on the next moves. Om
reached his hometown, and the two were welcomed by
his family eagerly waiting for his return. After talking for
hours, they finally sat down to have a warm meal with
family and friends.

Leaving Abha and Loka to rest, he rode to meet his
guru, Rishi Rig Muni. Rishi already knew the purpose of
his visit, and conveyed the same feeling as King Neera.

"None of the rishis will fight for you," said Rishi.

Om refused to give in. "I want to meet all my gurus
who trained me at the Mountains of Rishis."

"There has been a grand yajna organized in the
Madhya Kingdom, and all of them are already there."

Om took Rishi's blessings and left. Without any delay, both Om and Abha rode towards the town in the Madhya Kingdom where the yajna had been organized.

In a few days' time, they arrived near the border city of Bagha. It was the yearly yajna that was organized, and the locale was famous for the worship and devotion people showed. There were a lot of prayers organized, but the most remarkable one was in the Shiva temple.

Om met all his teachers, but he was unable to convince any of them. Empty-handed, Om returned to Rishi Rig Muni's hut. "I am going to fight and defend my land, whether the rishis will fight or not."

In the evening, he went back home and prepared for the journey back to Sarsi next day. At night, Om quietly lay down near the window, disappointed that he had failed in his purpose.

Abha walked up to him and lightly brushed her fingers to smooth the crease on his forehead. "I am going out for a walk with your mother, and I will return soon," she said.

Om didn't realize when the princess returned, and he slept restlessly the whole night. He saw in a dream that the whole kingdom was on fire, and the bodies of Malla's soldiers were lying everywhere. All the forts in the border areas of the kingdom were captured and burned to ruins.

He woke up terrified and covered in sweat. Without waking anyone, he left immediately to see Rishi Rig Muni.

Rishi was meditating in a corner of his hut, but he woke up once he felt Om's presence. They talked at length, and Rishi saw that Om was doubtful whether they could defeat the demons.

Rishi explained, "It is not defeat that is tormenting you, but the well-being of your family and friends. My dear, the passage of the soul from this body has been scripted by the divine. Whatever we do, destiny will reign. Worry not, and let's prepare for the battle. I will come with you. If other rishis cannot fight, so be it. But they can't stop me from fighting," said Rishi.

Om, along with Rishi and Abha, reached Sarsi. It seemed that the plan to control the demonic army before the arrival of demi-gods had been finalized. Everyone was waiting for Om and Abha to return to make a final decision.

Princess Rati was an exceptional war-strategist; she was the one who had come up with the strategy for the first few battles to begin with.

As per the plan, the western forts would be emptied to allow the enemy to enter without a fight. The battleground would be between the forts of Nav and Voana. Both forts were not more than a few dozen yojanas apart, and were the only way to the capital city. All the other ways were too difficult and would take months for the evil army to reach the capital.

"The evil armies are not here to sneak their way to the capital. They are here to destroy everything in their path," said Rati. "We will have a small skirmish at the landing docks by the first battalion, near the eastern and southern forts, and then the soldiers will be advised to fall back quickly to the battlegrounds in the middle of the forts."

Uncertain whether the strategy would work, Om said, "Emptying the forts doesn't sound like a good idea. These forts can hold the evil army longer. This way, we give them straight access to the final holds before the capital."

With a valiant grin on her face, Rati continued, "Forts will only appear empty, and the underground channels will house all the soldiers. Once the evil army had crossed the fort, the soldiers from the western and southern forts will follow them. From the weapons perspective, Ganas have already prepared long range heavy metal arrows, catapults, and projectiles. The Ganas carry a few flying chariots, their own specialty."

Revat, the Ayurveda expert, had worked night and day and had come up with his own series of projectiles to be fired at the enemy. All of these projectiles were the result of his interminable experiments, the effect of which would be seen in the battle.

Satisfied with the plan, everyone started training. Soldiers trained heavily, preparing all day and all night. The plans to control the evil army near the middle battlegrounds were being worked on. Every day, the armies would do a round of exercises, fire projectiles, and mark the distances that they traveled.

Isvasa was tasked with escorting all the elderly, women and children who could not fight in the war to the Madhya Kingdom. He had finished all the arrangements, and the people were being transferred. It was a boost to the soldiers to know that their families were safe somewhere and that they could give all they had to this war.

The war was near, and it was supposed to bring tension and chaos, but the Sarsi and the middle forts seemed calm. Samva's hawk and Isvasa's spies were keeping a close eye on the evil armies' movements and gave regular updates. Prayers and yajnas were carried out all over the Malla Kingdom. The capital, Ogana, was fortified with all sorts of weapons and would serve as the fallback should the middle forts fall to the enemies.

King Neera and the palace guards had assembled near the middle forts. Trenches were created all along the two forts and filled with oil. Abha had stationed her shadow hunters throughout the forts. They were the ones who could hunt and kill in the dark without making a sound. Every one of the captains waited patiently for the war to begin. Every person spent time practicing their weapons' skills.

Om was now far more competent with his weapons, but that didn't stop him from practicing.

The hawk had passed the message that the evil army was now more or less five days from the docks. Time had come to put the plan into action.

Rati explained the plan once more to everyone. The first battalion of soldiers to intercept and fight at the landing docks were prepared, and given orders for the march. These five days would be the hardest for all the captains. Kanika would have to hold near the southern shores and then march on the signal. Kanika and Madhya were also tasked to control Anga if they tried to march towards Malla. Two more days for the dock, the first battalion was close to the southern shores, from whence the evil army would arrive.

CHAPTER 17
Change in Plans

Om woke up gasping for air in the middle of the night, with horrifying nightmares about the battalion that had marched towards the southern and eastern forts.

Two days had passed since the first battalion had marched. Knowing that something wasn't right, he went to see Udadhir. "I fear the first battalion's strategy may not work. We must help save our men."

Udadhir knew that it was against the strategy they had discussed, but he also knew that Om might be right and that these men were marching towards their own destruction. He agreed, and they devised a plan to take advantage of the flying chariots and reach the first battalion faster. Rati was in charge of the whole strategy, and was chosen as the supreme leader for the battle. They had to move without permission from anyone, and had to return before anyone noticed their absence.

Om got up in a hurry to gather the others.

"Om, wait." Udadhir hastily stopped him. "We have to go alone. Anyone who accompanies us on this mission will be in serious trouble."

Om agreed with his suggestion, and the two of them left silently in the dark of the night to find the first battalion. No one else was informed, but Loka stealthily accompanied them. They rode at great speed to meet the first battalion. Neither knew what their next move was or what they would do after meeting the battalion.

In almost half a day, they approached an area where they saw several vultures circling overhead. On arriving, they found nothing but the remains of their brutally massacred men. The entire first battalion, even their horses, lay dead. There were fires still burning, and it seemed that the battle had just ended.

Neither of them understood how a battalion of two thousand soldiers had died so quickly. All around them was a strange blue fire. Not a single enemy soldier was dead.

Udadhir knew the blue fires were mystical. "I believe this is not the work of an army, but may be of a group of demons who have control over the mysterious blue fire." The two mounted the chariot, preparing to leave. "During the Gana war, we saw a few demons who could control blue fire and destroy anything in their path ruthlessly," Udadhir added.

They were a day's ride from the approximate location where the evil army would have camped after slaughtering the first battalion.

"I want to continue and look for the evil army base inside Malla."

"We should return," Udadhir countered.

"But we should check if the fort soldiers hiding in the dungeons are safe," Om said.

Udadhir nodded. "I will accompany you to the fort, but after that, I will return to the capital."

They went to Sarit, the western fort, to check on the soldiers.

The fort captains had abandoned the forts exactly in the way they had been told. All the fort captains were given orders to take shelter, along with all soldiers, inside underground passages and dungeons. They were ordered to keep a close eye on the movement of enemy soldiers and to assemble after the final battalion of enemy soldiers had marched. Once any of the fort soldiers confirmed that every last enemy soldier had marched towards the main battlegrounds, the fort captain was responsible for conveying the message to adjoining forts.

Om and Udadhir entered the fort, and after waiting for a long time, one of the soldiers approached them and took them to the underground passage, where they met the captain of the fort.

Om asked the captain about the enemy's movements. "Do you know how the first battalion was killed?"

"I had no idea about the massacre of the first battalion, but I know everything about the enemy's movements. My soldiers have destroyed all the bridges, as per the orders. It will take more time now for the evil army to make progress through the river. There are very few enemy boats compared to the number of soldiers. It's taking even longer to transport heavy artillery. It will still take the evil army a few days to cross the river and enter Malla. So far, my men have counted one thousand battalions of two thousand soldiers each. There are Paksi men, Raksas, Pisachs, and demons that none have seen before. One of them was almost thirty feet tall and had a bull-like face, and his eyes and hands were burning with blue fire," said the captain.

This certainly confirmed Udadhir and Om's theory that the demons were responsible for the destruction of the first battalion.

"Furthermore, the evil army is already constructing temporary bridges to cross the Uttara river," the captain updated.

"But how did the evil army get to know about the first battalion?" Om asked himself out loud.

The captain replied, "There might be enemy spies in the middle forts."

"I am now almost convinced that there had to be someone from the group of the captains passing information to the enemy."

Udadhir shook his head. "Impossible. I know all in the inner circle of captains very well. The captains do talk with their close aides, and it might be one of them who is spying for the evil army."

"There should be someone leading the fort armies from behind when the enemy's army reaches the battleground," Om said in a muted tone.

Udadhir replied in the same hushed tone, "I am not

very certain of how skilled and capable the fort captains are, but Isvasa is highly confident about their abilities."

Skeptical, Om said, "I will return to the middle forts and then join the fort army from behind."

Udadhir said, "None of the captains will agree on this, as you are one of the main commanders."

"I won't budge an inch, but this isn't the place to decide."

Om and Udadhir started their journey back to Sarsi to update the army captains about the first encounter.

The captains had gathered to discuss the battle strategies and the movements of the enemy's army. Om and Udadhir updated everyone at Sarsi about what had happened with the first battalion. The room went silent; everyone was worried, since nobody knew how many of such demons the evil army would unleash.

Rati was enraged that they had left without informing anyone. When she came to know about the fate that had befallen the first battalion, her rage subsided into sorrow.

Om told Rati, "We must change the strategy and confront the enemy once more before the main battleground. This will test our strength—"

Rati refused almost before he had finished his sentence, and said, "I will not squander men's lives in impracticable expeditions. The best strategy is to stick to the main battleground and hold the evil army until the demi-gods arrive."

Unable to reason with her, Om suggested, "I will take my team and lead the fort armies from behind."

Rati objected to this as well and was about to speak

when Isvasa interrupted her and said, "The fort captains are capable enough for an attack once they are given the signal."

"You didn't see how the first battalion was slaughtered, with not a single enemy soldier dead? If the same happens to our fort armies that are to charge at the enemy from behind, it will weaken the morale of all the soldiers," Om said. He shook his head as if to clear his mind of the terrifying memory, and added, "The soldiers are fighting because they know that they are on the right side, but there is a limit to their endurance."

Rati, slightly agitated by then, rose from her seat and looked Om straight in the eyes. Her lips curled in a smile, but her eyes were unmistakably hardened. She said to him politely, "You haven't fought a single battle in your life yet. Thus, you cannot possibly know whether you are making the right decision." Rati looked around at everyone else. "And your opinions?"

Everybody opposed Om's departure. Even Isvasa and Udadhir supported Rati. Isvasa told Om, "You are a hero to the army, and your departure now would send the wrong message."

At that moment, Princess Abha entered the hall with Rishi Rig Muni. By the look on his face, it seemed that without being present, he knew everything that had been discussed in the room. He took a seat close to Om's. "Everyone, calm down. The decision made by Om is worth pursuing."

Om looked at Abha and thanked her silently.

Rishi went on. "I am here to fight with the armies, and

I will fill in for Om's position. Rati, find out how much more time it will take for the demi-gods to arrive, so that we will know how much time we have to defend the battleground."

Om announced, "My team and I will leave in a day, and travel through the western mountains to avoid direct contact with the evil army."

Om was glad, and along with Abha, went to meet his team. He explained all that had happened to the men in the first battalion. "There are enemy spies moving around the kingdom, and I intend to benefit from them."

"I'm interested. But how do you plan to accomplish such a thing?" Abha asked.

He could see the curiosity gleaming in her eyes. Smiling, Om explained, "I will use the spy to spread false rumors of an attack on the evil army from western mountains."

"The enemy captain might hear the rumor and send one of his best to fight, and it might be the blue-fire demon," said Om.

The princess wasn't convinced. "Even if the evil army knew about an attack from western mountains, why would they send the same demon again?" she asked.

"For some reason, the evil army is not yet fighting with its main battalions, but they are instead using their best fighters, the blue-fire demons, for skirmishes. One of the reasons could be that they are waiting for all of their army to assemble," Om said, justifying his strategy.

He told her, "It's worth a try, as we'd be using the western mountain passes to reach the most western forts anyways."

Both reached Om's quarters to meet his friends, already waiting for them. Om told everyone about his decision and his quest towards the western mountains to lead the fort armies.

"What I am planning to do is not sanctioned by Rati and the captains. I must thank you all, because you have all helped me a lot, and it is all right if you do not want to join me."

The group was already upset with him for not letting them in on his little crusade to find the first battalion. They stared at him with eyes like daggers. Om stopped talking and tapped his head with an apologetic smile. Everyone laughed and agreed to join him at once.

Om told Maghavan, sitting across from him, "Order your fifth battalion to be ready for a drill."

Maghavan enquired, "Will the army join us?"

"This is only a drill. I was given the command of the fifth battalion once I became the king's adviser. The fifth battalion is the fiercest among all Malla battalions," Om replied.

Om stopped Amber when everyone was leaving and told him about the spy. "I have one day to find the spy and plant the information that there will be an attack from the western mountains. Let the spy know that the soldiers are already waiting at the mountains and that more battalions are on their way. I have already asked the fifth battalion to be ready for drill, and I will ask them to move west," said Om. "This will give the impression that the march is happening for real."

Amber knew that the leaks would be happening in the busy taverns where the soldiers drank in the evening. He figured out three such taverns. *If nothing happens in these three, then it won't happen anywhere else,* he thought.

Amber went inside one of the taverns; he knew that every spy would carry something to identify themselves to the army they were spying for. The only way to check was to steal their bag and place them back before anyone would notice.

There were too many people, and Amber relied on his face-reading skills to identify the ones that could be spies. He finished checking the bags of all the people he had cornered in his mind. After checking two taverns, he was about to enter the third one. He saw a dozen people walking towards the first tavern and instinctively decided to check them, too. He followed them and entered the first tavern. After several tries, Amber stole a pouch from the dozen people he had followed into the tavern.

The pouch that appeared least significant had a ring with the Paksi seal on it. Unfortunately, it was one of the captains' subordinates for the tenth battalion. He knew whom to convey the message to now.

Acting drunk, he started talking to another drunken soldier next to him and talked about the movement of many battalions to round up the evil army from behind. The spy had already heard from his captain about men ready to march west, but he wasn't sure.

After hearing Amber, he knew that something was to happen through the western mountains. After a while, Amber left and waited outside in the dark alley. Soon after

Amber left, the spy gathered his belongings and started to leave. He walked out of the tavern, and Amber followed.

The spy entered a small hut and hastily scribbled a few words on a piece of cloth. He tied it to a bird's leg and let it go. Amber was certain that his work was done and thought to inform Om in the morning.

Om, meanwhile, had spent the whole time with Abha. They talked about the war and whether they would have a future if the war turned in their favor. They were married now, and hoped that even if something unfortunate happened, they would meet beyond this life. They were destined to be together in this life and all the others.

For the rest of the night, they didn't talk much about the war, but instead, about a world where there would be no war. Om knew that this war had to end in such a way that peace prevailed in all the Himalayan lands.

The night passed by, and Om woke up at the sound of a knock on the door. He opened the door to find Amber waiting patiently. They stood outside, and Amber told him about his move the day before.

Om asked Amber to inform everyone that they would march before sunrise the next day, then went back inside. After the morning meal, they went to meet Rishi again. Most of the day went to preparations. Om asked Udadhir for two of the incredible Gana chariots, and he was also given two Gana soldiers who could ride them.

Udadhir was unhappy that he couldn't join forces with Om, but Om reminded him that staying back was in the best interests of the armies. Udadhir was the only commander among Ganas and the only one who had the experience to fight the same evil army as the one from a hundred years back.

The spy, on the other hand, saw Om and his friends marching ahead with the fifth battalion. He sent another message to the evil army about this march. After reaching the outskirts of the kingdom, Om asked the fifth battalion to return not in formation, but in small groups. With only his group and two Gana soldiers, Om reached the foothills of the western mountains within two days.

There were tall trees that surrounded almost all of the mountains. The team crossed to the other side of the mountains, and Om asked them to equip the mountains with structures, to be battle-ready, in the same way as they had discussed and practiced during their journey. The other side of the mountain foothills formed a curve, giving an edge to anyone fighting from above the mountains. The dense foliage of the giant trees was an added advantage. The hawk kept an eye from above, and they came to know that the evil army camp was not more than a day away from the foothills.

At the evil army camp, everyone was still waiting for the Raksas King Amura to arrive. The Raksas king was giving his final offerings to Lord Shiva. Meanwhile, the Paksi King Darad heard about the attack from the western mountains and ordered two thousand each of the Raksas and Pisach soldiers to march towards the location their spy had provided; with them was a blue-fire demon. At the western mountains, Om's team was prepared for the encounter.

The team had taken position at various intervals, completely surrounding the foothills from three sides, sitting high above in the mountains. Anyone approaching the mountains would be an easy target. Om had brought back chariot pieces that were burnt by the blue fire. Revat had already identified which materials would be burnt by the blue fire and what would ignite it even more.

Om's team laid several traps in the middle of the mountain, right above the foothills. The plan was to wait until the army approached the middle so that they would be surrounded by Om's forces.

The evil army arrived when the sun was at its peak. Om spotted the blue fire demon. It was tall and had the face of a bull with hands, mouth, and eyes all covered in blue fire.

Om and Sarvin covered the extreme ends of the foothills. The evil army reached closer to the foothills, and soldiers checked everywhere, but they couldn't find any sign of a single man. One of the captains among the evil army battalion sounded the horn to get back to the main army base.

When they were about to turn, Om signaled Sarvin to fire. Both fired their arrows at the same time, and huge boulders started tumbling down towards the evil army. The blue fire demon sent fireballs towards the falling rocks. The rocks burst as soon as the fire struck them, but the smaller portions ignited and fell onto the evil army's soldiers. Revat had splashed some kind of a liquid all around the rocks, and he had asked the team to pour some in the rock cavities as well. The liquid turned these rocks into explosives, making them ignite and burst at the same time. The rocks killed many of the Raksas soldiers, but the Pisachs flew and saved themselves. The demon started randomly firing at the mountain above, towards the tall, dense trees.

Om fired an arrow, hitting the demon's right hand. The maddened demon sent fireballs towards his own army, killing many of the Pisach and Raksas soldiers. Om did this a few times, and the demon went insane with rage. Panic rose among the evil army soldiers, and they ran, taking shelter among smaller rocks.

The chaos only angered the demon further, and he opened his mouth wide. A stream of blue fire swept around from one end of the foothill to the other.

Revat had expected this and had asked the team to sprinkle the area with a liquid he had prepared to extinguish the blue fire. Many of the tall trees at the front burnt down within moments, but most others survived, the liquid dampening the blue fire.

The time had come to end this little battle, and Om and his team sent out flaming arrows and hit numerous wooden structures they had placed randomly at the foothills earlier. The wooden structures exploded into flames, releasing a special smoke. The evil army went into a frenzy and started slaughtering each other. The smoke, however, had much less impact on the blue-fire demon; it was merely killing anyone coming near it.

Om used his arrows to prevent the demon from burning the Pisach soldiers when they were attacking him. Many of the Pisachs came near the blue-fire demons and entered his eyes, giving him excruciating pain. The demon managed to kill the Pisachs, but not before it lost both eyes. The demon bellowed with rage, opened his mouth, and burnt every single one of the Pisachs and the Raksas soldiers left. Now the fight was between Om's team and the blind demon. Om and Sarvin had silently entered the foothills from two sides. They fired rope arrows to the demon's feet. The arrows cut through its legs, and pitched the beast on the ground. The demon was already in pain, and this was no easier on him. Before he could burn the ropes, Om fired two divine arrows that penetrated his palms and pinned them to its chest. The roar of the demon filled the air with doom. It couldn't move at all.

Om went closer and stood on its chest, sending another arrow inside its mouth, which hit the ground behind the demon's head. Another arrow to the head, and the demon was on its way to the underworld. The small battle in the western mountains was over, and Rabia sent news to the main battlegrounds of their success.

"Let Rati know who the spy was," Om commanded. "When the evil army comes to know, they might send more soldiers. We can't keep fighting, as we have to regroup with the fort armies. The plan is to burn the foothills in such a way that the evil army will not recognize their soldiers. They will think that the fight is equally matched and everything had been destroyed. Not finding any traces of our army, they will return eventually."

CHAPTER 18
The First Battle

The evil army was eagerly waiting for the Raksas King Amura to join them, making preparations when they heard of his arrival. The Raksas king's arrival after a long yajna was so joyous that no one remembered the lost battalion at the western mountains.

Paksi King Darad wanted to check on the battalion, but he was too confident to do so, assuming that the human army had perished at the hands of the blue-fire demon.

Amura had returned after decades of meditation, and had pleased many powerful gods. He now had powers— but no one knew for sure. Nobody knew what he was capable of. It was often said that he couldn't be defeated by anyone, either living or dead.

The Raksas king received a glorious welcome from King Darad, the Pisach King Picasa, and the entire evil army. He rode a monstrous bull whose mouth dripped

269

with fresh blood.

The Raksas king addressed the evil army. "We have won the underground and taken the whole of western lands. And now we have to win the eastern and the mountains!"

The army roared with approval.

"Once we are done, we will march towards the celestial kingdom and dethrone the tyrants who call themselves gods. Soon, my brothers, we will conquer and rule the heavens, the earth, and the underworld. I have powers that no gods possess, and no one living or dead can kill me. I am indestructible, and so are you. My armies are unmatched. Let's win the mountains and the remaining lands. After that, we will join forces to take down Mount Meru, the home of gods!"

Hearing this, everyone in the evil army cheered. The bull stamped its foot, and fissures cracked the ground and spread out like ice, shattering a few yojanas ahead and behind. The uproar of the demons echoed across the entire kingdom.

"Now, my armies, march towards the capital city of Ogana!"

The men in the main battlegrounds of Malla waited patiently for their enemy to arrive.

Om had already reached Fort Uttara and had started working with the captain of the fort. They started the preparations for the march towards the capital. Other forts were informed to assemble all armies at the southern town of Cavila, a few days' ride from the main battleground.

In less than a day, the Uttara fort's army was ready, and the very next day, they marched towards Cavila. In a few more days, the town was awash with armies arriving from all the forts. Most of these armies consisted of chariots and cavalry, improving their mobility.

As soon as all of the fort armies had arrived, their captains were invited to Om's chambers. The plan of attack came together, and the captains received orders to march to the main battleground first thing in the morning. Om and his battalion from Fort Uttara would lead the entire army to the battleground. With the fort's armies, he would command hundreds of thousands of soldiers—a force as huge as the army holding the defenses at the battleground.

A moment after the captains had left, Samva came running into Om's chambers, breathless and drenched in sweat. Half-conscious, he yelled, "Everything has been destroyed!" and fainted.

Once Samva regained consciousness, Om and his team heard one of the most terrifying stories of their lives. "The evil army and its infernal assemblage of demons stormed the battleground," panted Samva. "Slaughtering men, the demons relished the carnage as they butchered and burned the Malla army one by one. The first battle has been lost—in favor of the evil army. Fort Nav and Fort Voana, their camps, and the defenses—all destroyed, burned to the ground. The rest of us have retreated to Ogana for the final stand."

A silence took over, reverberating with grief and rage.

Om finally said, "I am worried for the lives of my friends and soldiers. I'm astonished at how swiftly the evil army has finished the battle when there were numerous great warriors at the battleground. I thought we were not more than two days behind. Losing a strong defensive unit in two days isn't possible."

Without another word, Om ran to one of the Gana chariots.

"Om, stop!" Jabala tried to intercede. "Don't act in haste."

But Om wasn't going to listen to anyone. "Head towards the battleground!" he ordered the charioteer.

Watching Om leave, with Loka and Jabala beside him, Maghavan, Rabia, and Idha followed them—soon accompanied by Revat, Samva, Amber, Sarvin, and Arin.

In the early morning, Om's team arrived at the battleground. A haze of smoke was still lingering in the air, with soldiers' bodies lying everywhere. The camp devastated, forts still burned in the distance.

"We should rush to the capital city," Om said.

Jabala stopped him again. "Not yet. The capital will need reinforcements, and we should march with the fort armies waiting for us at Cavila," said Jabala.

"Lead the army. I will ride alone for now."

Jabala countered, "That isn't the right decision. At this very moment, the army needs you more than ever."

"I need to see who all have survived the battle, and whether my beloved is still alive."

"Most of them did," came the voice of Rishi from somewhere behind. Rishi was bleeding, and his staff was broken into two halves. Om rushed to hold Rishi and slowly helped him lie down.

"Now, now, don't worry. I will survive."

"What happened?" they implored.

"Once all the artillery and the external defenses were down, Udadhir and I held off the evil army until all the captains and soldiers retreated to the city," said Rishi. "Much of the army survived and must be preparing at the capital for the last stand."

"I wish I hadn't left the capital," said Om.

Rishi held up a hand. "It was for a good reason."

"But what exactly happened at the battlegrounds?" Om wanted to know. "It was too extensive and heavily fortified to be destroyed in two days. We had the finest captains and warriors. How is it even possible?"

"Blue-fire demons," came the reply from the Rishi.

"I thought we killed the one in the western mountains," said Amber.

"There was a troop of blue-fire demons, each as strong as the others. Fire demons came from all directions and brought down all the initial defenses, then our camps' and forts' artillery," he explained.

"Our projectiles hit many of the demons and the evil army, but caused very little harm to them. The evil army was beyond our range, and the projectiles had no significant impact on blue-fire demons. By the evening, all the defenses were destroyed. The captains met at night at Rati's chambers, and everyone agreed that the only real alternative now was hand-to-hand combat." He paused for a moment to catch his breath.

"We didn't know how to combat the blue-fire demons. Revat had already made a shield that would withstand the blue fire. But without Revat at the battlefield, we didn't have enough of those shields. The soldiers with special shields were the only ones tasked to tackle the blue-fire demons, along with Rati.

"The following morning, Rati marched to the battleground along with all the captains and the army. The morale of most of the army wasn't high from the previous days' fight, but seeing all the captains and their fellow soldiers stand for each other was a consequential boost for them. The armies were divided into three: Ganas were led by Udadhir; Rati led the Gandharva battalion and soldiers with special shields to fight blue-fire demons; finally, Isvasa led the rest of the men. To our surprise, the enemy had changed its disposition. The blue-fire demons were called back and sent to their base camp, behind the main evil army battalions."

He continued while everyone listened to him with undivided attention, "A strategy was quickly developed, and plans were put in place. Rati's battalion, along with Isvasa's, fought the Pisachs and the Paksi army. Rati fought Picasa, and Isvasa battled the Paksi King Darad. Udadhir and his Gana army fought with Raksas, and Udadhir himself fought with the Raksas King Amura. The fierce Ganas fought several Raksas at once. They had a long overdue revenge to exact. Rati and Isvasa were already overpowering the evil armies they were engaged with.

"The fight was in our favor until mid-day. After noon,

new battalions of the evil army replaced the old. The fresh blood renewed the powers of the evil army, and they kept switching throughout the day.

"The evil army kept bringing fresh blood in the battle, and they wanted to let us believe that their number was far greater than ours to demoralize our soldiers. The fight with Amura was worse than others. Udadhir had prepared for this for a hundred years. He was the perfect opponent for the Raksas king, and Udadhir's techniques had Amura struggling to withdraw his weapons.

"After a few blows from Udadhir, the Raksas king began to use all kinds of mystical powers he had gained during his long meditation. He used a bow given by Lord Brahma himself. He shot the arrows in the air, heavenly red fire trailing after them; they rent the ground like meteors. The Raksas king didn't even care if the fire killed his own men. The vicious fire claimed the lives of many of our soldiers. I intervened and used my staff, creating a blanket of power over our soldiers, and it saved us for a while.

"The blanket didn't last for long, and the powers died down after a while. On seeing this, Udadhir threw a violent blow on the Raksas king's chariot. The chariot collapsed and broke Amura's concentration, putting an end to the heavenly fire. Udadhir pulled his bow, firing a continuous stream of arrows at the Raksas king before a new chariot could be brought to him.

"The fight with Pisachs had worsened, and Rati had lost most of her Gandharva soldiers. Isvasa slowly merged the fight with evil men, and with Rati, was fighting Pisachs and the Paksi men. The demi-gods' armies, which were still a few days away, received all updates from Princess Abha's guards. I joined Udadhir to fight the Raksas king."

Om and his friends were now sitting on the ground, listening to Rishi silently.

"With every weapon or blow we used, Amura became stronger. It was like he was using our powers to magnify his own. I noticed this after a while. The more power we used, the more swiftly the Raksas king would adapt and use them on us. Until now, Princess Abha had not joined the battle; she was still managing the remaining defenses in case we had to fall back. Looking at her army suffering heavy blows, she decided to join the fight.

"She led her own personal guards, along with the shadow hunters. The shadow hunters' ways of fighting were very unorthodox. No one among the enemy or our soldiers could recognize them. Most of the shadow hunters wore Paksi uniforms, and they easily killed and wounded many of the evil soldiers. The arrival of Princess Abha, and watching her fight, inspired the soldiers. Every single one of our soldiers rallied behind her. She fought like a tigress—merciless against the evil army. Whether Pisachs or Raksas or Paksi men, everyone feared her. I had never seen a more talented noble warrior in my entire life.

"But King Amura was getting stronger. Udadhir and I combined our forces, keeping him from inflicting any major damage. At the sight, both Picasa and Darad moved back from the battlefield. I didn't notice at the time, but this was a very strategic change.

"After some time, the fight strategy slowly shifted, and the Pisachs started surrounding Rati and Isvasa's battalions. The Pisachs formed an inner circle, followed by Paksi men on the outside. This was mostly to single out Princess Abha so that the next level of the fight could happen only with her and no support from other captains.

"After a while, I saw Princess Abha fighting both Picasa and Darad at once. The evil kings were not able to overpower her, and they struggled to gain an edge over her. It seemed that their evil strategy wasn't working. To come out of this circle and to outwit their evil strategy, the princess turned towards the Paksi king. She attacked Darad and his chariot at once. The impact from the weapons knocked over King Darad's chariot, and he fell on the ground. The princess spurred her horse and furiously rode towards Darad, to finish him once and for all.

"Picasa watched Darad writhing in agony, his foot trapped under the chariot. To shield Darad, Picasa created an illusion that only the princess and I could see.

"In the illusion, the princess suddenly saw her entire army lying dead before her. Baffled, she looked around for an explanation, and she saw me holding your body, Om, in my arms. I could see her, and my mirror image holding you. I ran towards her, but she kept looking at your image and crying for help. I saw her riding towards my image at full speed—and she missed the real me. The next thing I saw was that coward King Picasa, firing an arrow towards the princess. Her horse took the brunt of the impact—the arrow pierced it and then struck her leg. Both fell down, and the illusion faded. The princess was gravely injured."

Om looked at Rishi with anguish. "Is she all right?"

Rishi nodded. "The arrow was poisonous, but she was fine once she was taken back to the camp. She is recovering well at the capital city."

Rishi paused for a while. "I had to use one of my fiercest weapons to save her. The weapon's power helped cast aside the evil shadow, but the sound of it made everyone deaf. I saw that our soldiers were also affected, but there was little I could do. Udadhir, Rati, and a few Ganas were not affected, and they rode towards the princess. I told Rati to take the princess back to the capital and that we should retreat. This might have been a bad judgment on my behalf, but seeing the amount of blood she had lost, I didn't see any alternative. Rati agreed.

"Everyone started to leave and take their positions. I stopped Udadhir and told him that I would eventually use the same weapon again, and this time, he should make sure that most of our soldiers were behind me, and start retreating towards the capital.

"It took a while for everyone to regain their senses. Udadhir had already managed to bring Isvasa back to normal and started slowly moving the soldiers behind me, while remaining stealthy. Isvasa was ferocious, and didn't look happy at all to retreat. I rode towards him, destroying as many evil army chariots and soldiers on my way as I could.

"After a brief discussion, he concurred that we

couldn't stand the ground more than a day, until the demi-gods arrived. Exactly as I had asked Udadhir, I told him to move as many soldiers as he could behind me, and asked them to put wet cloths in their ears.

"As soon as they were all behind me, I used my powers again, until I could see my army getting far away from the evil. This time, I used all my powers at once, and I wreaked havoc on the evil army. Nonetheless, commanding such powers twice had made me weak, and I was vulnerable to their attacks.

"The last thing I remember was seeing our men far behind. Then an unexpected blow broke my staff into pieces. The blow killed my horse and struck my chest. I fell to the ground. Next I remember is seeing you here." He closed his eyes briefly in a wince.

All of them looked at each other, trying to decide what to do next. Amber, meanwhile, had gathered something for them to eat.

After a while, Samva's hawk signaled that someone from afar was coming towards them, and coming very fast.

Om used his looking glasses and saw Udadhir riding. From the distance, all he could tell was that Udadhir looked unwell, injured in some serious way. As Udadhir came closer, they saw that the left side of his body was half-burned.

Before Om could ask him anything, Udadhir said, "I am glad I found everyone and that Rishi is unharmed. I'm sorry, Rishi, that I had to leave you behind, but I had to do so to save your life."

"What about your wounds, Udadhir?" Om worried.

"He will be all right in a few days," Revat convinced him.

"All this was done by Amura, who became immune to Rishi's powers the second time he used them," Udadhir told them.

Udadhir continued, "I saw Rishi fall, and I rushed my chariot towards him. The Raksas king followed on his bull chariot, but fell behind us," said Udadhir. "I picked Rishi up and started riding towards the capital as fast as I could.

"After a few yojanas, I saw the most horrifying thing— Amura flew behind us on his dark, monstrous, black bird, Changadur, riding faster than I was. I couldn't have saved Rishi from him if I had continued towards the capital, so I took the chariot towards the dense forest.

"It was impossible for the Raksas king to follow me there, but he rode over the forest. Amura used all kinds of weapons and rained fire on us, destroying everything below him.

"When the jungles grew denser, I left Rishi under one of the trees with his weapons and marched ahead. Amura was still following me, but he hadn't realized that Rishi wasn't with me. I had to make sure to lose the Raksas king before the jungle ended and then return for Rishi.

"Near one of the hills, I had reached a wild beast trap set by the locals. Before I could devise a plan to get rid of Amura, he fired an arrow that shattered my chariot. I fell off, but somehow managed not to fall into the pit. The chariot fell in and burned to cinders. The Raksas king saw this and returned, thinking that his task was done."

Om and his group now had to devise their next move. It would still take a few days for both Rishi and Udadhir to heal, and time was running out. As Om worked on his plans, the captains from the capital had already regrouped. At the capital, they needed the outer walls to stand at least until the demi-gods arrived.

Rati was still their leader, and she had devised a strategy. "No more defense! Hereafter, all our moves will be, and have to be, offensive and unforgiving!"

All captains except Isvasa were against her. "The strategy will backfire and cause more harm to us than to the evil army!" they protested.

"But we're going to lose the outer defenses much sooner than we have expected. If instead of defending the fort, we attack the enemy and use fort artillery to protect our troops, we have a better chance to survive."

Meanwhile, Princess Abha was also recovering from her wounds and was preparing herself for the next battle. The only thing that she longed for was Om holding her in his arms.

The demi-gods were three days behind the capital, and the evil army was planning to attack the next day.

Back at Om's camp, Jabala was sent back to gather the fort armies and meet them there. Om and the others devised a strategy to help the capital city.

CHAPTER 19
At the Capital

It rained fire on the capital the next day. The front walls suffered the greatest damage. The blue-fire demons summoned waves of flame that pierced through the second boundary wall towards the capital and landed inside the city. The flames burned several buildings and consumed anything in their path; chaos and panic ran rampant. Under Isvasa's command, the capital's artillery was firing back as hard as possible. They had taken down one of the chariot battalions and destabilized the evil army, forcing it to pull back all of its other battalions. The evil army was now fighting with only the blue-fire demons. The artillery had less of an effect on the demons, but it was enough to slow them down. The only way to end the enemy was through hand-to-hand combat.

Meanwhile, Rati prepared to march on the demons outside the gates. The predatory gleam in her eyes, the conviction in her speech, and her stolidly calm demeanor were no less than a divine source of encouragement for her troops. Thousands of cavalrymen lined up behind her and slowly moved towards the gate.

King Neera, also in armor, was in charge of the palace guards, the last defensive line of Malla. The king was supposed to fight the final battle, in case the evil army crossed the walls and reached the palace. The queen and other royals had refused to take shelter and were helping the armies in whatever form they could. The queen remained in Abha's chambers and watched the fight from a distance. Prayers echoed throughout the palace and the main temple.

The main gates of the capital were opened, and Rati's army assembled outside in formation. The front three rows were units with special shields to tackle the blue fire. Their horses were also covered in the shields, crossing their flanks and from top to bottom. Countless streams of sapphire flames fell on the city, but the capital artillery was giving a befitting reply.

Rati called, "Metal arrow chariots, behind me!" The heavy metallic bows on the chariots would release arrows with strong, thick ropes tied to them. Rati wanted to use them to bring down the vicious fire-spitting demons. Her soldiers slowly moved forward in the same formation. Their eyes were focused, their muscles tensed, but a hint of fear still lingered in their hearts.

Rati's unit slowly gained pace and moved faster. The blue-fire demons noticed their movement and concentrated their fire on them. The fire walled them off. Each time the soldiers advanced, the demons would shoot out their bursts. Sometimes the impact created large pits, deep enough to swallow a horse. The demons had restricted Rati's movement, and her army wasn't close enough to use the metal arrows.

Waving the flags from her chariot, Rati signaled Isvasa to concentrate arrows on the section of demons she pointed out. The artillery targeted demons on one side, allowing Rati and her men to advance towards them. They were now close enough to fire the metal arrows.

The use of metal arrows, along with Rati's strategy, helped the men bring down a number of blue-fire demons. From Om's earlier message, Rati knew how to give the final blow to the demons, and she used it to take down a few. The number of blue-fire demons was still tremendous. It would take her days to end them all by this strategy—if no one else intervened.

The Raksas king saw this and ordered his archers to open fire on Rati's army. The hail of arrows slowed their movement and made them switch back to a defensive position. Enemy archers were too far for the capital artillery to reach them. Rati's soldiers suffered many casualties.

Following the volley of arrows, the Raksas king deployed his battalions of Raksas mounted on bulls. The men of the Paksi and Pisachs were still waiting for their orders. The Raksas troops marched towards Rati's men— all riding on bulls of different shapes and sizes, each one more ghastly than the last. They wore dark colors, with skulls and bones tied all around their body. They were carrying all sorts of axes, javelins, and maces. They moved, making a thunder-like noise, and roared with their ugly mouths opened wide. Some even wore headbands made from slain bulls and bears. It looked like they had ascended directly from the underworld. Together, they moved like a shroud of death, blanketing everything it touched.

The blue-fire demons changed their targets back to the city, blasting it. The outer city walls were half-destroyed and wouldn't survive the onslaught much longer. Isvasa and his men moved to the second wall and took their positions. Rati's unit marched forward to counter the incoming army of Raksas.

The hooves of the horses on one end and the bulls on other stirred clouds of dust. When the two armies clashed, no one could even see who they were fighting with. Isvasa couldn't figure out how to use his archers on the wall— all he saw was dust, and all he heard was the clashing of swords.

After a while, the dust settled. By then, Rati had lost close to half of her men. The other half were still in the fight, but were struggling. Rati knew that she couldn't hold on for long. The demi-gods had to show up soon, or they would lose.

With a deafening explosion, the outer front walls crumbled. The artillery on the walls, as well as the ones between the outer and inner walls, fell in waves. The remaining half of Rati's army, Isvasa's artillery, and archers were all that remained. Seeing this, King Neera moved his palace guards near the second walls from the palace and prepared for an attack.

Rati had no other choice. She decided to retreat. As soon as she was about to signal for one of her soldiers to blow the horn, she heard the sound of drums thundering from the south. Om had arrived with the fort's armies, and they had prepared their position for attack.

Hearing the drums reverberating in the air, Rati's army started fighting again, with even more courage and valor. Om and his team were in the front, along with the fort captains.

Om moved forward and spoke in a booming voice. "I know you are afraid, and I don't blame any of you. The enemy we are fighting is straight from the underworld, and they are unlike anything we have ever fought before. What I know is that they can be killed; they can be defeated. Our ancestors fought them and defeated them. I, along with my friends, have fought many of these and killed them.

"I also know that they fear us in the same way we fear them. All we need to do is make them fear us more. How you do that is up to you. How I sowed fear was stabbing the heart of their biggest giant and killing it at one blow. Don't be afraid—be fierce. Don't fight to protect; fight to take lives. Don't merely take lives; kill in such a way that you instill fear. Keep in mind that we are not fighting only to protect our kingdom and its people, but to protect our entire civilization. The gods are on our side, and together, we have to send these creatures back to where they came from. Fight with me until the end, and we will have our victory. *For our gods and our people, let's march!*"

Om's army descended on the evil army like a storm.

The evil army was forced to deploy everything it had. Now the fight was on two fronts, north and south, with the evil army trapped in between. No one alive in the evil army had seen Om fight before. The way Om advanced through the evil army, viciously slaughtering the enemy in his path, brought fear to them.

Loka followed Om close behind, and even his roar was enough to send shivers among the evil soldiers. Om used his tiger claws, sword, the gem, and his divine arrows the best ways he could. Everyone in the evil army who came in Om's path fell, fatally injured, or returned to their realm of evil. Whether Raksas, Pisachs, or men, no one from the evil army came close to attacking Om.

Another battalion of the fort army, commanded by Jabala, took down the entire artillery division of the evil army. Om unleashed the thunder from his sword and burned down the first three lines of the chariot battalion of the evil army. Seeing the destruction, Amura and Picasa both rode towards Om. The Paksi King Darad marched north to fight Rati and bring down the second wall sooner.

Om knew that soldiers on the northern front were still very low in number, and needed their help. The only solution was to fight their way towards the north and merge the armies. But fighting the Raksas and Pisach kings would slow them down. He signaled Jabala to attack the Raksas king. Jabala, along with Sarvin and Arin, attacked the Raksas king's forces before they could reach Om.

Om circled the Pisach king and held him up with the

powers from his gem. The Pisach king struggled, but he escaped his grasp. As soon as the Pisach king came out of the gem's hold, Om fired one of his divine arrows. Before the Pisach king realized what was happening, the impact blasted him far away from the battleground.

Om quickly moved with all his fort armies to join forces up north with Rati. Rati was glad to see him, and welcomed him with a bright smile on her face.

The fight in the north was over as soon as Om joined. Surveying the events, the Paksi king sounded the horn to end the day's fight. Isvasa did the same. The battle for that day was over, and the armies marched towards their respective directions.

Some stayed behind to identify and bring the bodies of their soldiers. Om, Rati, and others returned to the capital. They had won the battle for the day. All the captains were instructed to meet in the king's chamber as soon as they arrived.

Om, however, went straight to meet Abha. Abha was in her chambers and was still recovering. On seeing Om, her joy knew no bounds.

"You are here!" she breathed in amazement.

"Leave us in privacy, please," Om asked all the caretakers.

They departed. Om embraced and kissed her—the two leaving aside all their worries and escaping into each other for a while. He wanted to spend some time with his wife now—as only a handful of people knew.

"Your wound," Om expressed with regret. He looked at Abha's wounded leg. "I vow to hunt down whoever gave you this wound."

The princess replied with an infectious smile. "In a few days' time, I'll take care of that myself."

Om smiled at her and nodded in agreement. He told her about his journey to unite the fort armies and the great win they had had. Abha calmly looked at Om's face while he narrated the events of his journey. She always loved the way Om told his stories.

Back in the king's chambers, all the captains and council members had assembled to hear King Neera speak. "Rati and Isvasa, do you think you can hold off the enemy for a few more days in this fight?"

Rati replied, "The demi-gods will be here in a day; all we need is to survive another day."

"The evil army will return with their deadliest weapons after their defeat in today's battle," Isvasa told them.

"I agree," King Neera asserted. "You don't merely have to hold the evil army off for a day, but do it such that we can avoid losing our men."

Rati and Isvasa nodded at each other and began discussing the plan for the next day.

As they were speaking, Udadhir joined the conversation. His hands were now almost healed, and he seemed ready for battle. "The evil army hasn't brought in their worst soldiers yet. The Kumbhas have not arrived."

"Whatever we do, first, we have to tackle the blue-fire demons. Otherwise, there will be no second wall to hold, and that would put the whole city and our people in danger," said Isvasa. "If the blue-fire demons are taken care of and we are able to hold the inner walls, in the current situation, we can fight with the demons for another week."

Everyone agreed with Isvasa, but no one could arrive at a concrete strategy to deal with the blue-fire demons. King Neera asked, "How did these demons get such powers?"

"My spies have seen them eating bizarre, gleaming violet flowers," said Udadhir. "Our ancestors told us about these flowers. These could be the source of power for the giants."

"My King," Isvasa interrupted, "if such a thing exists, it should be destroyed. I will assign someone to find and destroy every last trace of these flowers."

"I will do it," came a voice from behind. It was Jabala. "Om's team shall fulfill the task. I will discuss it with the team and complete the task tonight." After what the team had achieved so far, Jabala's proposal was accepted unopposed.

King Neera continued with his counsel and captains, discussing the plan for the next day. After some time, fully satisfied, the king adjourned the meeting and asked everyone to take rest and prepare for the next day. Everyone left the king's court—some in hope, some in prayer, and some in dismay.

Jabala hurried to Princess Abha's chambers, where Om and the rest of the team had already gathered to discuss the proposal set forth by him in the king's chamber.

"How do you want to do this?" Om prompted.

Jabala inhaled. "I have to enter the enemy's base without being noticed. That means only a handful of people can accompany me."

"Being shadow hunters, Idha and Rabia seem like the right candidates for the task. They could enter the enemy base camp with much ease and without being spotted. Take Amber with you as well. He is the finest of thieves," Om suggested.

Jabala asked, "Idha, will you accompany me, and take a few more shadow hunters?"

Their council of war adjourned and each went their separate ways for the night.

Om was still with the princess. "How are you feeling? Are you worried about tomorrow?" asked Abha.

"No, I'm not."

"You aren't?"

"I only want to spend the moment with you."

"There is more on your mind. Be honest."

"The future is looking more and more bleak. I hope that the good will win and that the evil army will be destroyed, but I don't know if I will be able to make it to the end. My father told me that wars are always won with sacrifices. I'm willing to give my life to protect everyone I love."

"And I merely hope you don't have to."

Meanwhile, Jabala was with the shadow hunters, preparing for the task ahead. The shadow hunters were trained to enter any place without being seen. They could become anyone, and even the person they became wouldn't recognize them. They were fierce warriors, who could slay in silence. They were all but thieves—making Amber the best person to locate the flowers. Amber wasn't as great a warrior as the shadow hunters, but he was definitely the finest thief in the entire Himalayan region—something to be proud of in the given situation.

Dressed as Paksi soldiers, Jabala, Idha, Amber, Rabia, and two other of the princess's bodyguards reached the evil army camps through a secret underground passage from the palace. It wasn't hard to locate the camps of the blue-fire demons, as their tents were the tallest and heavily guarded by Paksi soldiers.

The group separated in different directions, but remained close enough to keep an eye on each other. They silently went through the camp, but they couldn't locate the flowers.

In the end, they regrouped in a dark corner outside the camp to decide what to do next.

Amber got an idea and signaled Samva's hawk. Amber had learned how to pass instructions to the hawk and read its reactions, but unlike Samva, he couldn't see through the hawk's eyes. "Locate anything glowing in large numbers, and let us know by circling the area above it," he said in barely a whisper.

The hawk's vision was very strong. She could easily see behind walls, and soon began circling the location of the tents where the flowers were hidden.

The only problem was that the tents were surrounded by Raksas. There was also no possibility of destroying them without being noticed. The Raksas had an excellent sense of smell and would sense their presence before they could even get close to the tent.

Before Amber could propose anything else, Idha looked at Jabala and fired a special arrow towards the tent.

The tent burst into flames. "Everyone, leave!" Idha whispered. "I'll stay in case the fire extinguishes before burning all the flowers."

Jabala, Amber, and others quickly moved towards the palace and waited at the underground entrance for Idha.

A panic coursed through the evil army. The Raksas rushed forward, carrying pots brimming with water to smother the fire. But the fire was not an ordinary fire— the flowers inside the tent burned with the same blue flame as that burning inside the blue-fire demons. There was no stopping it.

Idha finally moved towards the entrance, and everyone safely returned to the palace.

"The flowers have been destroyed once and for all," Jabala informed Isvasa and Rati.

It was past the middle of the night. Apart from the guards at the inner walls, every one of the soldiers slumbered, prepared to fight yet another day.

Om was still talking to the princess, but soon he noticed that she had fallen asleep already. He tucked her in a blanket and walked towards the terrace to see the city outside. The silence of the city worried him, as if something dreadful was going to happen. He sat on a chair, looked at the city below, and soon fell asleep.

Om was awakened by a thunderous bang, as if something mighty had fallen from the sky. There was still time before sunrise, yet the enemy was bombarding the walls!

No one expected the fight to begin this early. The evil army had cautiously sneaked close enough before the attack, while the Malla army was still asleep, unsuspecting of the enemy's ploy.

Boulders and giant trees struck the front gates, bashing them apart.

The Kumbhas had arrived, and their strength seemed limitless. Their roars shook the city, the guttural sound of rage curdling the blood of every citizen. Backed by the blue-fire demons, they uprooted rocks and trees to target the walls.

Burning the flowers hadn't been enough to stop them. The rest of the evil army stood behind the Kumbhas and the blue-fire demons. They knew that the walls wouldn't last until sunrise, and they were prepared to march towards the capital with everything they had.

The captains quickly assembled, drafted a strategy, and Rati presented it to King Neera. "For the first time, we must use the palace guards' elephant battalion. The king's elephant battalion is the finest in the land. We have saved it for last."

"The elephant battalion fought with Raksas during my father's reign. I know they can give a fitting reply to the Kumbhas," affirmed the king. "Rati, you will lead the main capital army. Udadhir, you will lead the fort armies. The elephant battalion will be under Isvasa's command, and I along with the palace guards will be the last defense."

Om, along with his friends, commanded his very own

battalion, "the fifth," along with the princess's battalion, "the shadow hunters." The plan was to lead the fight with the elephants in front. They would endure most of the blows from Kumbhas and blue-fire demons. Rati was tasked again to fight the blue-fire demons once they were close enough, with the same strategy. Udadhir and Om were to fight with the rest of the evil army.

Om rode quickly to Udadhir, whispered in his ear, and came back to stand in front of his battalion. "Jabala, I need you to command the archers and artillery unit left in the city and the inner walls," Om commanded.

It was now sunrise. The front gates had collapsed, and there was no use in repairing them. The inner walls still had given the Malla soldiers enough time to assemble. The elephants marched ahead and the armies followed close behind in an eagle formation. The strategy was working. Even the raining fire didn't cause any significant damage to the elephants; they were as steady as before. After the elephant battalion was close enough, Om and his men cut through the side and marched towards the evil army.

This time, Raksas King Amura and his army marched towards Om. Midway through, Amura slowed his chariot. He saw Om's battalion leaving the battleground instead of directly coming towards them. Om's battalion was moving further left, and even the Malla soldiers, still behind the elephant battalion, were confused.

Udadhir's face lit up with an impish smile. Only he knew what was happening, and patiently he waited for the others to find out.

After Om and his men had moved completely to the left, Amura realized what was happening. He saw hundreds of rishis standing against him, ready to face him and his armies. They stood beside Om's battalion, willing to unleash mayhem and inflict death upon the enemy.

All the rishis from the mountains had come to the fight and were now charging towards the Raksas king's battalion. Amura had made a pact with them long ago that rishis wouldn't fight on either side in any battle. But for the rishis that the pact had been broken the moment Amura had wounded Om's guru: Rishi Rig Muni.

Only Om had known about the arrival of the rishis. Earlier that day, moments after the day's strategy was approved by King Neera and everyone was leaving to prepare for battle, a servant boy came running, looking for Om. Gasping for air, he said, "Rishi Rig Muni wants to meet with you urgently!"

Om dismissed the boy and at once went to see Rishi. "I have now received word from the rishis that they have decided to join the battle, and will arrive at any moment."

With the enemy at the gates, there was no time to inform everyone and build a new strategy. They decided to follow the same strategy, with the difference that Om's battalion would be joined by the rishis. This was what Om had told Udadhir when he walked towards him earlier.

Meanwhile, taking advantage of the enemy's distraction, Rati's army parted from behind the elephant battalion and marched towards the blue-fire demons. Udadhir marched towards the Pisachs, exactly as Om had requested him to do. Om's army circled back and marched towards the Paksi King Darad. Om was going to avenge the wounds Darad had caused his wife.

CHAPTER 20
Arrival of the Demi-gods

The gods from the heavens above watched with foreboding, and from his palace, so did King Neera. He patiently waited, praying for the war to be over.

King Amura was both surprised and worried to see the rishis; they were regarded as some of the most powerful beings in the world. However, he reassured himself that were there only a few hundred rishis, and with the Raksas' limitless powers and brutal army, the rishis wouldn't survive.

Rati's battalion used the metal arrows to bring down blue-fire demons, fighting like wild beasts. Isvasa's elephant battalion sparred brutally with the Kumbhas. From the area right outside the fallen walls, Jabala was providing all the artillery firepower he could. He'd also mobilized his archers outside the walls to cover the width of the battlegrounds. The archers had all kinds of firepower specifically crafted under Revat's supervision, using his special techniques. Udadhir was last to leave the eagle formation on the battleground. He marched towards the Pisachs with full force.

At the other end, the Darad, unaware of Om's move, was marching behind the Pisach battalion. His eyes following Darad, Om commanded, "Begin a full march towards the Paksis!"

Darad realized what was happening after hearing the beat of drums from Om's battalion. "Stop! March towards Om!"

The view from the palace would have sent shivers down anyone's body. The evil army was growing larger by the day, as if new recruits were joining them from the underworld. From the palace, the king saw his elephant battalion clash directly with the Kumbhas. It seemed as if giants from this land were fighting giants from the underworld.

Not far away from the Kumbhas, Rati's army tackled successive fiery explosions, still moving forward and taking down one blue-fire demon at a time. The rishis had already engaged the Raksas. Udadhir's army moved into formation right before fighting with the Pisachs. They formed the lotus formation, where the large outer lotus had small lotus formations within. The lotus had heavily armored soldiers with shields outside and archers inside.

Om marched towards the Paksis in a trident formation, with himself in the front of the middle line, and Amber and Arin in the other two. Loka rode right beside Om, and Samva's hawk kept an eye from above.

Seeing Om's formation, Darad stayed behind and asked the best of his cavalry to ride in between the tridents. "And now, archers, fire at will!" he commanded.

The elephants in King Neera's battalion were strong and heavily armored, with soldiers sitting on the mounted platforms. The Kumbhas, on other hand, were lightly armored, but were stronger and larger than the elephants. Each Kumbha could easily take down a couple of elephants at once, but the soldiers with barbed javelins were making the fight even.

Each clash of a Kumbha with an elephant shook the earth beneath them. Their falls shook the battlefield. Slowly, the Kumbhas gained the upper hand. Isvasa, leading the elephant battalion, was using all his skills to attack in formation. After a few clashes, the Kumbhas soon dispersed from formation, and the fight fell to individual Kumbhas. The only good sign for Isvasa was that the elephant battalion was far larger in number than the Kumbhas. He kept changing his strategies to tackle these beasts from another world.

Rati moved in from one corner and was able to take down many blue-fire demons one by one. Soon after that, it became tougher, as all the remaining blue-fire demons now concentrated their fire on her battalion. Even the ones that were focused on the capital now turned to Rati's battalion.

The demons aimed at the chariots, burning many to the ground. Rati quickly moved some of her soldiers with the special shields to protect the remaining chariots from the blue fire. She also assembled her cavalry in front to engage in a close combat. The fight continued, Rati's soldiers sustaining heavy damage. In this part of the battle, too, the evil army seemed to have the upper hand.

Udadhir's fight with Pisachs was holding fine until the Pisachs figured out how to penetrate their formation. They would come down on the lotus formations from above, take a few archers with them in the air, and then savagely hurl them to the ground later. The archers, trying everything they could, fired unique arrows that would shock the whole body of the evil spirits and brought them to the ground.

Udadhir quickly explained to his soldiers, "Fire from small openings in the lotus formation and prevent the Pisachs from penetrating!"

Udadhir had fought with Pisachs before, and was using his experience to tackle them. He used his aerial chariot to rise above the Pisachs and shot them from above without being noticed. The men stood firmly against the Pisachs and gave them a befitting fight.

The rishis were indeed the finest of all currently fighting on the battleground. Their fight with Raksas was a spectacle to watch for the gods and the king alike. Each one of them fought thousands of Raksas, and yet they were winning with ease. The rishis used every kind of mystical weapon they had—thunder shocks, fire arrows, wind, and lightning—to wipe out as many Raksas as they could, not even sparing the bulls that the evil creatures rode.

The Raksas King Amura was fighting from a distance and using his mystical powers too, but he had not yet used his heavenly weapons in this entire battle. The Raksas king would choose and pick from the rishis he wanted to fight, and chose the fiercest among them. The rishis easily managed to kill Raksas soldiers, but making the Raksas king lose even a hair was difficult. Each strike on the Raksas king was making him stronger—it was impossible to control him. He was giving his evil army its only hope; the rishis seemed to have the upper hand here for now.

All the Paksis' finest couldn't do much to Om and his battalion. Loka had turned into the fierce beast, and he moved like a storm, hitting, breaking and killing all evil soldiers in his path. Om was fighting like an ordinary soldier, saving his mystical weapons for more difficult opponents. This far into the fight, half of the Paksi men were either heavily injured or dead at the hands of Om's battalion. The battalion was one-tenth of the Paksi army, yet making them run for their lives.

The shadow hunters were an addition to Om's battalion, and their fighting skills were unlike any other. They moved swiftly, killed silently, and would move on to the next soldier before the first one fell to the ground. The fight continued, and Om kept pushing towards Darad.

Half the day had passed since the battle started in the morning. Om's battalion had killed the remaining half of the Paksi army, and Om was not far away from the Paksi king. As Om advanced, Darad scattered his troops, and rode towards Amura. Om, along with Loka, followed Darad and left the current battle in Arin's able hands.

In the middle of his pursuit, he heard Rati's anguished

scream. Om hurried in her direction. One of the blue-fire demons was dragging her by the foot. None of the Malla soldiers were able to help her. Om commanded Loka to attack the demon, and within moments, Loka was on top of the demon, his claws mercilessly digging through the demon's flesh. Rati lay on the ground beside them, now unconscious.

Om rode as fast as he could towards Rati. He was so concentrated on Rati that he saw nothing else. While Om aimed at one of the blue-fire demons, a sudden burst of fire struck his horse from the side, and threw him into the air. Thrown clear, he still managed to fire his arrow and hit the demon.

Om quickly got up to aim another arrow at a blue-fire demon who had lifted his feet to crush Rati. Before Om could fire, he saw the demon's body tear asunder, spattering to pieces. The Yaksa that tossed the blue-fire demon in the air moved closer to Rati and lifted her up.

The demi-gods had arrived!

The Yaksas fought with the blue-fire demons, and the Gandharvas, Kimpurusas, and Kinnars joined the battle soon after. The battle shifted in Malla's favor. The Kinnars had joined Isvasa's elephant battalion to fight the Kumbhas; Gandharvas joined hands with Udadhir to attack Pisachs, and Kimpurusas charged towards the Raksas. The demi-gods fought valiantly. Their divine strength consumed the enemy ranks in thousands.

The Yaksas could take any form and size, which they did. Sometimes they rose above the blue-fire demons, and threw them in the air or crushed them. Sometimes they would become small enough to fly into the demon's mouth and then explode them from within. The blue-fire demons had never fought with a force so strong before and were struggling to keep up. They were fighting back, but the Yaksas were far superior and fended off their every move with ease. They became a rock or a tree to protect any of the men fighting alongside them.

The Yaksa who was carrying Rati back to the palace was surprised to see her awake. "Let me down, please, so I can rejoin the fight!"

Now Rati's men were fighting blue-fire demons alongside the Yaksas and were overjoyed to see her back in the fight.

The blue-fire demons saw men fighting hand in hand with demi-gods and decided to change their strategy. Each one of the blue-fire demons moved into an arc formation, attacking their opponents with more fire power.

The Kimpurusas were death personified. Children and followers of the war god himself, they were unconquerable. Their teeth were strong enough to shear through the bone, and their claws could slice a man in half with a single swing. The Kimpurusas fought alongside the rishis. Running towards a Raksas, they lifted it up in the air, and tore it apart with their claws.

Some of them didn't even spare the bulls on which Raksas were riding. They would hold the bulls by their horns and would lift them up and crush them on the ground. The roar from the Kimpurusas as they moved in the battlefield, their exceptional war tactics, and their beastly looks ignited fear in the hearts of the Raksas.

Amura tried to use all kinds of mystical powers and his heavenly weapons to bring the fight back in his favor. One of the Kimpurusas came close to Amura and shredded his chariot with his claws before Amura wounded him with his axe. A few Kimpurusas worked with the rishis and shielded them from the Raksas who dared to come close. This helped the rishis use their powers on other Raksas freely rather than fight with them in hand-to-hand combat, which they weren't good at.

The Kinnars, half-men and half-horse, had the abilities of men and the strength and speed of several horses. They were shorter compared to Kumbhas and elephants, but one blow from them made the monstrous Kumbhas fall. The Kinnars fought alongside the elephants and used them as shields to get close to Kumbhas, then knock them down. They held a long shield in their left hand and a long fine spear in their right hand. The Kinnars protected Malla soldiers. If they fell from an elephant or if an elephant died, they lifted the soldiers and carried them to a safe place nearby. The elephants and the Kinnars fought side by side, tackling the Kumbhas. The Kinnars' brisk movements and their swift kills confused the Kumbhas and drove them insane. They ran blindly across the battlefield and struck or wounded each other. The evil army found itself in chaos.

The Gandharvas were no doubt the most superior among the demi-gods. Their mystical and divine powers were equivalent to the gods themselves. Some Gandharvas even had powers to use their shadows to fight for them. They muddled the Pisachs, who struggled to respond to them. With illusions, the Gandharvas knocked down a number of Pisachs in a hit-and-catch game. They would suddenly appear in front of a Pisach, smite it hard, and before it could recover, another Gandharva would tie it with a divine rope. There was no way one could untie the knots of the divine rope. The rope sucked the Pisach back and dragged it to the underworld.

The brave men alongside Udadhir fought with the divine rope arrows of the Gandharvas. The Gandharvas were also caretakers of Soma, the divine drink, and shared it with their fellow Malla soldiers.

So far, the Pisach King Picasa had watched the fight from a distance. Watching the Pisachs suffer, he finally joined the fight himself, and used all of his illusions. The illusions didn't work much on Gandharvas, but they did slow down the battle a bit.

Om was immensely delighted to see the demi-gods finally join them in this war against evil. He rode back towards the Paksi king. Every soldier in the evil army to cross Om's path tasted his true powers. Even the demi-gods were surprised to watch the way he fought.

When Darad saw Om closing in, he rode his chariot near Amura. But the Raksas king was already occupied in his fight with rishis and Kimpurusas. He had not used most of his evil mystical weapons so far, as he was saving them for the demi-gods. Seeing demi-gods walk towards him, he was more than willing to finally use his arsenal on them.

Om saw Darad move closer to Amura, and he understood that the battle would now be very difficult. He knew of the powers that the Raksas king possessed. He also knew that the frequent use of his weapons would make the Raksas king more immune to them. Om wanted to play his own tricks and avoid confronting Amura for now. He knew that he could use his companion Loka, but he alone wouldn't be enough to hold off Amura for long. His decision had to happen very soon, as the sunset was near.

Om was determined to avenge the wounds that Darad had caused his loving wife. He started fighting the Pisachs, then whispered something to one of the Gandharvas. The Gandharva immediately left the battle and delivered Om's message to the Kimpurusa captain.

The Gandharva quickly signaled Om, and in no time, Om rode towards Darad. Before Amura could comprehend it, two of Om's arrows struck his chariot. Then the Raksas king saw the Kimpurusas captain tear apart his chariot, and with help of his finest men, they threw him and his chariot away bodily.

Next, the Kimpurusas struck the land so powerfully that the surface cracked. A deep trench now separated Darad's chariot from other Raksas. The shock shattered the Paksi king's chariot and hurled him to the ground. Before he could get up, he saw Om standing next to him. The Kimpurusa soldiers surrounded Om and acted as barriers to prevent anyone from the Raksas army from getting near Om and him.

Already annoyed by the series of events, Amura

summoned his big black bird, Changadur. Soon, he was up in the air, on the back of this atrocious beast. He reached Om and circled him from above. While the Kimpurusas protected Om from the Raksas army on the ground, they couldn't do anything to the Raksas king in the sky.

Om and Darad were immersed in a brutal combat, but Om held his own powers back. At that moment, Amura shot an arrow towards Om. Om saw the arrow and created a shielding halo by using his gem's powers. The halo blocked any further attacks on Om and his men from above.

The use of his gem interrupted his concentration for a moment. Darad pierced Om's arm with his sword. A stream of blood ran from Om's upper arm and dripped to the ground from his fingers. Amura attacked again, and fighting both at once was getting difficult for Om.

Meanwhile, Udadhir watched Om's strategy closely. When he saw the Raksas king attack him from the top, he flew up in his chariot and fired his arrow. Udadhir struck his arrow so deep in the big black bird's eye that it shrieked in agony and began flying in circles. Amura couldn't focus on the fight.

Om bashed Darad with his ivory shield and severed his left arm with his sword. Darad dropped his sword and fell to his knees in searing pain. Om lifted Darad's sword and killed him with it. The Paksi king was dead.

Before Amura could continue the fight, one of the captains of his army signaled the end of the battle for the day. Everyone returned to their respective bases, and the evil army prepared to cremate the Paksi King Darad that night.

There was a celebration all over the city of Ogana. They'd seen the demi-gods fighting alongside them and had witnessed the fall of one of the three evil kings. The Malla army knew they could win this fight with Om as their leader and demi-gods fighting by their side.

Om, on the other hand, was very calm. He somehow knew that this was only the beginning. The death of the Paksi king would make both the remaining evil kings more furious and vicious. He knew that the next day, the evil army would unleash everything they had. Only the gods knew what they were still hiding, but he was sure they would soon find out. He believed that the evil army was saving the best for the demi-gods, and now that they had arrived, brutality awaited them.

King Neera called for another meeting with the captains. After the meeting was over, Om went straight to meet Rishi. On learning all that had happened in the battlefield, a look of worry crowded his eyes. "Tomorrow will be the day of the evil army, and the men and demi-gods should be prepared for the worst," said Rishi.

A few moments later, a soldier knocked at the door. "Om, the king awaits you. King Neera is with the Gandharva King Marut, in his chambers."

Om hurried to see them.

King Marut was delighted to meet Om again. Smiling at him, he said, "What you did out there was not only brave but unparalleled. It was a morale boost to your men and sent a message to the demi-gods as well. If a man can work wonders, why can't we? Every one of the demi-gods will think this tonight."

Both of the kings thanked Om for his bravery and devotion to this great cause. The three discussed the next day's strategy at length, and all that had occurred in the battles so far.

King Neera asked Om, "How long do you think the war will last, now that all the Himalayan Kingdoms have united against the enemy?"

Telling them what Rishi had told him, Om replied, "The evil army is still strong, and we have to be cautious tomorrow."

Om left the king's chambers a few moments later and went to the princess's chambers. That night was darker, with no moon, and looked evil. While the soldiers in Malla rejoiced, the soldiers in the evil army cremated one of their kings.

Om slipped in bed beside Abha and held her close to his heart. Still awake, she whispered, "You couldn't even wait for me to get better!"

CHAPTER 21
The Heavens Stood Still

In the morning, before sunrise, the evil army assembled and their artillery opened fire. This time, there were no drums beating—nothing to indicate any movement outside the city walls when the first fireball landed on the capital. The city guards alerted the army of Malla, and the soldiers assembled, waiting for their leaders to join.

The size of the evil army still seemed the same as the day the fight had started. There was a rumor that fresh blood had joined them last night. The Malla soldiers' celebration from last night had faded in their minds. Now everyone was looking at yet another day of battle.

The battalions assembled in the same formation as they'd fought the previous day. The leaders rode forward from the capital and joined their battalion. Om was with his battalion in the far west, with no demi-gods in his forces. The rest of the battalions had a combination of men and demi-gods. The Gandharvas were with Udadhir and his battalion to fight Pisachs. The Kimpurusas were with rishis to fight Raksas. The Kinnars were with Isvasa and his battalion to fight Kumbhas. Finally, Yaksas joined Rati and her men to fight the blue-fire demons. Om's plan was to enter the fight after its start and make his way towards Amura to fight him directly.

The evil army looked fiercer and more cold-blooded than before, their bodies painted black and the ashes of their fallen soldiers on their faces. They seemed to have swallowed any kind of fear of death and looked like messengers of death themselves. Both sides waited for the final orders, while the artillery on both sides kept firing at each other at will.

While Om was waiting to move towards Amura, he heard from Samva that a large army was marching towards them from the far west. In a few days, they would join the evil army at the battleground. Om knew that any addition to that army would tip the scales on their side. He didn't want to inform any of his captains or soldiers. The previous day's victory had spurred a wave of fervor and spirit throughout the army, and this wasn't the time to lower morale.

"Jabala, Revat, lead my troops towards the Uttara River, and prevent the enemy's reinforcements from crossing by all means! My battalion and shadow hunters, follow Jabala," he ordered.

It would take a few days for them to reach the Uttara River, so he made yet another plan. He asked one of the Ganas to ride a flying chariot, carrying them to the river.

This way, they could keep an eye on any movement in the area.

The horns sounded, and the battle began. Om gave the command of artillery from Jabala to Maghavan.

After the sound of the horns, the Malla soldiers marched, and so did the evil army. Different battalions marched at different speeds and different formations, and the giants on both sides shook the land beneath them. The dust rose high, and for now, the people in the city could only hear the sound of hooves and war cries of their soldiers. Soon, the armies collided, and one could hear the elephants trumpeting, horses squealing, giants roaring, shields smashing, and swords clashing. Moments after the fight started, everyone other than Om's battalion was either fighting or watching the fight.

At that very moment, almost all of Om's battalion marched unnoticed towards the Uttara River. Jabala and Revat rode on the flying chariot ahead of the battalion with a Gana soldier. The Gandharva king was on the ground, but stayed behind and didn't enter the battlegrounds. King Neera accompanied him, with his palace guards lined up behind them. They stood right inside the fallen city gates, waiting for intelligence from the battlefield.

The gods in heaven watched the fight patiently. The turn of events that this battle would produce would shape the very future of heaven. The gods knew that if the Raksas King Amura won this fight, his next war would be with them.

Om looked at Loka as if telling him to be ready for the

move. Rishi had told Om the evil army would fight to kill, and that's what Om saw. The evil army killed without mercy, their kills even more brutal. It was clear now that to defeat the entire army would take days, and the only way to save lives was to put an end to the evil army's leaders. Amura used all his mystic powers and armory to attack rishis, and injured many of them. It was time for Om to march and fight the Raksas king before he injured any more of the rishis.

The Raksas king had an arsenal of arrows gifted from different gods. It was hard to compete with him from a distance. Om wanted to fight with him up close. He marched towards Amura with the few men left in his battalion. The battalion fought to make a path for Om to reach the Raksas king faster.

After a while, Amura saw Om's group nearing. He changed his chariot's direction and concentrated his fire on Om. Om's battalion rode in an arrow formation with Loka in the front and Om right in the middle. Loka's mystical powers protected the formation from any attacks from Amura.

Amura fired two arrows at once towards Om's formation. Loka jumped, grabbed one of them, and broke it into two. The other arrow hit the rightmost wing of the formation and killed a dozen of the soldiers. The soldiers from the rear quickly moved up and filled the void. The battalion now rode even faster towards Amura, fiercely fighting their way. The Raksas king fired another arrow, but this time, it landed right in front of the battalion. A bright red light came out from the ground, and Om's soldiers felt themselves burning.

All of his men screamed in pain. Om concentrated, using the sapphire in his headband to protect his men. The blue light from the gem eased the pain, and the soldiers continued their ride further towards Amura. The light from the gem was now protecting the whole formation, shielding them from strikes by the Raksas king, but it was becoming weaker and weaker with each arrow fired at it.

After a while, Om couldn't use the powers of his gem anymore. Before anyone could get hurt, he changed his formation. Loka transformed into the formidable beast, and this time, Om rode on its back with his sword held high. The battalion now formed an arc, and all together, they fired a volley of arrows at Amura. This gave enough time for Om to reach Amura and attack.

Om jumped off Loka's back at the exact moment as Loka lunged ahead and rammed into Amura's chariot. The impact knocked the chariot over. Amura fell to the ground. The infuriated bulls that surrounded and attacked Loka lay dead before him within moments. Om ran towards the Raksas king. His plan was to climb the fallen chariot, jump right on top of Amura, and end him. Before Om could move ahead, Amura shot an arrow at the exact same place he had shot the bright red-light arrow.

This was no ordinary arrow. As it struck, it deafened everyone, and a sudden tremor shook the whole kingdom. The land split and moved in opposite directions, a deep trench grew deeper and deeper. The gods above could now see the red molten rocks of the underworld. When the land finally stopped moving, a death-like silence reigned.

Soon, an army of Nagas clambered out of the torn earth, from deep inside the underworld. Their number kept on increasing, and soon, the Malla army was surrounded by hundreds of thousands of them. No one, including the gods, had ever imagined that the Raksas king would draw on the army of Nagas from the underworld.

The dwellers of the celestial realm stopped to look at this turn of events, hoping that it wouldn't change the course of the war. A chill settled among the demi-gods, especially Gandharvas, who had fought the Nagas once before. Around a hundred years ago, with the help of the previous Malla king, King Marut was able to defeat and send them back to the underworld. No one had ever seen Nagas since then.

The Gandharvas and Kimpurusas moved forward to attack the Nagas. The move weakened Udadhir's fight with the Pisach and the rishis' fight with Raksas. Noticing the sudden change in tactics, Om ordered Loka and his battalion to fight with the Raksas, and he rode towards Udadhir to help his battalion.

The presence of the Nagas encouraged the already bloodthirsty evil army, and now the slightest fear they had of demi-gods was also gone. The Nagas had been locked in the underworld for a century now and had mastered weapons never seen before on this land. Even the Gandharvas and Kimpurusas found it difficult to hold back the Nagas. They were greater in number and were stronger than before. The Nagas were easily fighting the best of demi-gods. The weapons of Gandharvas and claws of Kimpurusas had no grievous impact on the Nagas.

The tide had been turned in favor of the enemy, and now the Malla soldiers were being run down like men facing a herd of wild bulls. It seemed that Malla soldiers had lost their way and even fighting within the finest formations wasn't barring the enemy from killing and advancing. King Marut saw this inhuman carnage and joined the fight, along with his guards, helping Udadhir tackle the Pisach. He avoided Nagas for now.

He'd fought with Nagas before, and he wasn't eager to face them again. The Gandharva king had distanced himself from the gods after an event in the past that destroyed the marriage of one of his daughters to one of the gods. He had sworn, from that day, that no one from his kingdom would ever seek help from the gods. The gods also had shown him that, unless he prayed to them, no one from heaven would help him.

The Malla king also joined the battle, along with his palace guards, taking down a slew of Raksas at once. The last defense of the city was now in the battle, and there was no one left to protect the city of Ogana. Half the day had passed. A large number of Malla soldiers lay dead, along with many demi-gods. It looked like the fight would not last more than a day or two, and would definitely not end in favor of the Malla Kingdom.

The sun was almost dipping down to the horizon, and the Nagas now fought not only demi-gods, but also men.

The men of Malla had no idea how to contend with the Nagas; they were easy prey.

The gods debated whether to help the men and demi-gods. Some of the gods, annoyed by the atrocities that the evil army had committed before entering the Malla Kingdom, stood in favor.

One of the war god's sons, Adi, spoke up. "At this speed, the war will end by sunset. No one in the evil army will cease the fight unless the gods do something."

His father, the war god, empathized with the men, but he was not willing to interfere in this war.

"After years of prayer, Lord Brahma granted the Raksas king his wish, that none among the gods would ever fight him. If we do, we will call upon the wrath of Brahma," said the war god. "If the evil army wins and brings the war to us, then we shall fight them."

Dissatisfied with his father's response, Adi left the courtroom and watched the course of the war from his chambers. He was a god who couldn't see the men who worshiped him being crushed like ants.

All the leaders from the side of Malla were failing to unite the army to fight like before. The arrival of Nagas had truly shifted the balance. Amura was now enjoying the fight, and was attacking only for the pleasure of killing. Om, along with Loka, had moved to help Rati, and by now, he had killed half a dozen blue-fire demons alone. He kept moving through the battlefield on Loka's back, helping the battalions that he thought needed extra hands.

The Gandharva king stood by his captain, Sakra, and watched his men die.

"My lord, you must pray to the gods, put aside your personal grievances and pray to protect your people. This bitterness, my lord, has cost the lives of our men," said the captain.

"Whatever choice you make, the Gandharva battalions will fight till their last blood."

The king replied, "I have seen my son die in my arms, and now I see many of my own soldiers suffering the same fate." He looked up at the sky and prayed to the war god, asking for his help.

Lord Adi rushed to his father's chambers. "Father! Father!"

The war god told him, "Only deal with the Nagas, and in no way engage with the Raksas."

Lord Adi was waiting for this. Seeking the blessing of his father, he left the celestial realm. Adi called for his ride Garuda, an eagle-faced heavenly beast. His ride was the fiercest beast the gods had ever created, and Adi had mastered it on his own when he was a child. The beast had the face of an eagle, the body of a lion, and a pair of wings. It had the strength of more than a thousand elephants, and it was faster than any of the divine wagons.

Everyone on land saw the clouds suddenly burst with an ear-shattering roar, and with the brightest white light, Adi appeared on the battleground, right in the middle of a group of Nagas. His appearance shook the whole battleground and raised a heavy cloud around him. Brilliance emanated from his trident, as well as from the eyes of the glorious beast he rode.

No one but the Gandharva King Marut could see

anything other than the bright white light. King Marut bowed to him. Lord Adi pointed his trident towards the Nagas, and the light emitting from it blinded them. The Nagas shrieked in agony and fear, running around wildly in anguish, trying to escape the pain.

Garuda, the divine ride, slayer of serpents, massacred the Nagas, taking pride in tearing apart each one it could. Holding the trident in one hand, Adi threw his dagger at one end of the trench, from where the Nagas had entered the battleground.

In this piercing brightness, the Nagas could now only see a soothing light from the dagger, which had created an illusion that none of them could resist. All of them started running towards it to rid themselves of the misery and pain. On the way, each one of them fell back into the trench from where they had emerged. Moments later, each one of the Nagas was either killed or had been pulled back to the underworld. Before returning, Lord Adi fired a bolt that sealed the trench, using his trident, and he cursed the Nagas to suffer the unbearable miseries of hellfire for infinity.

It was a spectacle none had witnessed before. A few of the Gandharvas were the only ones who had seen a god in their lifetime. This called for the end of the battle for the day. The armies moved back to their camps.

Jabala, on the other hand, had reached the river to witness an army as huge as the one they were fighting back at the capital on the other side. The evil army on this side was preparing to cross the river, and by their movement, Jabala judged they would start crossing first thing in the morning.

The leaders of the Malla army assembled in the king's court and talked about their strategy for the next day. The Gandharva King Marut started the discussion. "Amura may still have powers no one knows. We don't know what other secrets, like the Nagas, the evil king is hiding. Amura is a devout Brahma worshipper. The Nagas were one thing, but everyone knows that the gods won't come down to help us against him."

"The strategy that we choose has to be to end the lives of the two evil kings," said King Marut.

The plan was to create two teams; each would fight one of the evil kings. All the others would help those two teams reach the evil kings. The strategy was agreed to by all the captains, and everyone left to rest for the night.

Meanwhile, at Uttara River, Jabala, Revat, and the Gana soldier were the only ones looking at the fresh troops ready to join the evil army. Watching the enemy closely, they discussed what their next step should be. The fifth battalion and shadow hunters were still behind. Their strength wasn't enough to engage an army this large.

"I've taken a barrel of my special oils from one of the forts on my way. This oil can light even in water and cause heavy damage, but we have only one barrel," said Revat.

While they were evaluating the situation, Jabala noticed a lot of movement on the other side of the river. "It appears that the evil army is preparing to cross now!"

If they wanted to stop them, they had to act quickly. The first set of boats was loaded with evil army soldiers and was ready to cross. The boats were not enough in number, and they had to take many turns to cross all of the evil army.

Revat looked at Jabala. "You need to lay the oil from the barrel on the side of the river where the boats land and then light it once they are ready to disembark."

Jabala and Revat rolled the barrel to the riverbank on their side of the river and poured the oil, while the Gana soldier kept lookout.

At that moment, Jabala had a lightning inspiration. "I still have the gems I stole from the seven-headed serpent Aga from Lake Manas. By arranging the gems in their original order and chanting a very specific verse, the serpent could come to life! I learned the verse from my guru when I returned from the demi-gods' land!"

Moving behind the bushes, he stepped into the river, arranged the stones, chanted the verse, and quickly stepped back. The serpent would be obedient to anyone who had brought it to life and would obey their commands, something Jabala had known even before stealing the gems.

The glorious seven-headed serpent appeared within the river. Aga had come to life. It graciously bowed to its master, waiting for his command. Jabala told him, "Destroy every single boat that crosses the river or is currently at the other side of the river!"

He came back to where Revat was standing, and saw Revat looking at him with questioning eyes. Revat said bluntly, "The boatman was right," and kept quiet.

Jabala told Revat, "I knew the snake would be useful in the war rather than sitting in a lake that hardly anyone crosses."

After Jabala left, Aga went straight for the boats on the other side. It emerged from one side of the array of boats and kept rising up until almost all of its body was outside the river. It then plunged on the boats lined up one after the other, destroying almost all of them. Splinters of wood shot in all directions. Most boats fell apart. Destroyed or sunk, all remaining were heavily damaged.

One of the boats managed to escape to the other side, where Jabala waited with his fiery arrows. The evil army soldiers that fell into the river from the boats were now a meal for a snake that had not eaten for months. The remaining soldiers fled to their camps and started firing their artillery at the snake. The gems on the snake's head protected it from all the incoming shots, and it kept on filling its stomach.

At the capital, the strategy was to divide the fight into two fronts. Om laid out his strategy. "I will lead the team that will attack Amura." He had the Kimpurusa captain and his finest men with him. "Amber, Idha, you are with me as well."

One of the rishis, Rishi Dinkar, came forward to help Om. "Meet the rishi whose training has led me to master the weapons I wield," greeted Om.

"On the other hand, to fight with the Pisach King Picasa, I want Udadhir to take command; bring with you the finest of Yaksas and Gandharvas," he continued.

"The remaining battalions, shield both the teams until they reach their opponents. Once the fight begins, form a barrier around the teams and do not allow external forces to interfere."

The Gandharva King Marut had fought both Amura and Picasa in the past, and shared whatever experience he had with both Om and Udadhir.

The special teams stayed behind the next day, when the fight began.

Rishi Dinkar went to Udadhir and gave him an arrow. "Use it on Picasa when you get a clean shot. Use it wisely and aim it precisely. If missed, it could cause greater harm than good," said Rishi Dinkar.

The evil army wasn't worried. They knew that the Nagas had weakened their enemy, and that a huge army was on its way to join them.

That morning, Amura informed them that not only would he use all the heavenly weapons that he had but he would also summon other forces from the underworld if needed. The Raksas king did use one of his mystical weapons at the beginning of the fight. The weapon impacted hundreds of Kimpurusas and created an illusion because of which they saw their fellow soldiers as enemies and started fighting them.

Om knew it was time to move. Both of the teams marched towards their opponents at great speed. Udadhir used his flying chariot, and didn't face any difficulty in reaching the Pisach king. Om, however, broke through a ferocious wave of the Raksas. He chose to enter the battle from the rear to avoid a confrontation with the Raksas king too soon. He was closing in on Amura so that he and others could fire their arrows.

Amura was the most heinous soul on the land and had mystical powers beyond imagination. He already knew Om's strategy and was watching his moves. Udadhir and his team started fighting Picasa, and quickly surrounded him. The rest of the battalion made every effort to shield them from other Pisach soldiers. Meanwhile, Amura was patiently waiting for the right moment. As soon as Om came close enough, he drew one of his godly arrows.

Rishi Dinkar saw Amura, his bowstring taut, and threw his double-sided axe. The axe hit the arrow and cleft it in half. The arrow fell to the ground, and with a clap of thunder, a massive hole appeared in the ground. The axe ricocheted off the arrow and buried itself in Amura's chariot, lodging on top of it. Before Amura could aim again, both Om and Sarvin fired quick arrows in succession. The arrows caused little damage to the Raksas king or his chariot, but gave enough time for Idha to make her move.

She swiftly climbed on top of the chariot, grabbed the rishi's axe, and struck Amura with it. The impact threw both of them off their feet. They fell on the ground in opposite directions, but Idha had already stolen Amura's quiver, which held his divine weapons.

Picasa, on other hand, used all kinds of illusions, but had little or no effect on the demi-gods. Soon, he struggled to defend himself from the demi-gods and Udadhir. Even when the Pisach king tried to escape, the Yaksas followed him, and Gandharvas would not let another Pisach help him. Udadhir continued firing all his arrows from his flying chariot, quite undisturbed.

Picasa was getting annoyed by the combined efforts of the demi-gods against him. Blinded by wrath, he lifted up in the air and opened his mouth wide, unleashing violent gusts of whirling wind in all directions. The heavy wind shook Udadhir's enormous chariot. No one saw what happened, but soon, the Yaksas fighting him started to choke. The Gandharvas couldn't rescue them, but continued to maintain the barrier and defend them from the Pisachs outside.

None of the arrows that Udadhir fired reached Picasa. Udadhir tried to move his chariot near him, but the force of the wind wouldn't allow him to come anywhere close. He realized that if he didn't do anything, soon there would be no Yaksas left to help him. He thought of firing Rishi Dinkar's arrow, but realized the arrow might not even reach Picasa.

Udadhir went to the Gandharvas in his team. "Could your rope arrows be used to tie Yaksas, take them somewhere else, and bring them back? This would save them from the mystical power, and if they return, we can be more cautious," said Udadhir.

One of the Gandharvas told him, "The arrows will only take them to the underworld, and it cannot bring them back. The destination was crafted while making these special arrows in the forges."

One of the Gandharvas then came forward and handed Udadhir a mystical shiny rope. "This rope could be used to bring them back, but there is no guarantee."

"I am willing to take the risk."

"I will show you how to use it," said the Gandharva soldier. The team moved fast. They tied Udadhir at one end of the mystical returning rope and Yaksas at the other. Next, they fired a rope arrow at each of the Yaksas—one that sucked its victim to the underworld. Each unearthly arrow snared its prey and teleported them to the gates of hell.

Meanwhile, on the other side, Idha held Amura's quiver of arrows with her. Amura stood on the other side of the shattered chariot. Anger burned deep within his eyes.

"Loka, now!" Om ordered. Before Loka could jump, the Raksas king was lifted up by his big black bird, Changadur.

Up in the air, Amura closed his eyes. The next moment, all the arrows from the quiver were in his hands. With no delay, he fired one at Om's team, and they found themselves trapped inside a vast metal cage, surrounded by numerous ghastly birds, similar to the one Amura was flying on.

The team knew in their heads that this was an illusion, but then the birds began attacking them. Some of them started to bleed from the wounds. The unholy creatures could fly in and out of the cage, as if it had no restrictions on them. They entered the cage to attack, and slipped out quickly to dodge attacks from Om's team.

Om stuck his sword in the ground and prayed to the heavens. "Come close!" He touched the gem on his forehead. Lightning struck his sword from above, and the gem's power protected Om's men.

When the thunder ceased, all the birds lay dead and the cage was gone. The illusion had ended, but Amura fired another arrow at them. This time, Loka dived to destroy it, but took the hit himself. Loka was thrown apart, and he fell on the ground, unconscious.

Furious, Om fired one of his divine arrows straight at the Raksas king's bird. The arrow hit one eye of the bird and penetrated the other from within. The bird lost its balance and fell down. So did the Raksas king.

Om rushed towards Loka with faint hope, but it was too late. Loka was already dead.

At Udadhir's end, the fight was now in his favor. He was still holding the rope at his end, along with a Gandharva soldier. Picasa was distracted after all the Yaksas disappeared, and the Gandharvas seized this opportunity to attack him. He was now on the ground, taking attacks from all directions. The Gandharvas surrounded him, leaving him no escape.

With no means to escape the enemy, Picasa used his deadliest weapons. He waved his hand up above, and soon the clouds thundered and rained an army of infernal spirits, like thick black smoke in the air. The spirits started circling the Gandharvas and attacking them. The Gandharvas' retorts were of no use.

One of the Gandharva lay on the ground struggling as spirits swallowed it. It sent a chill among the Gandharvas and anyone else who saw this from the ground.

Udadhir didn't get a signal from the Gandharva soldier

with whom he was holding the rope. The Yaksas that were sent to the gates of the underworld felt the heat coming towards them. The gates slowly opened. Powerless before the unbearable heat, they screamed in pain.

The Gandharva soldier screamed, "Pull!"

Both of them pulled, and suddenly all of the Yaksas lay on the ground in front of him, horrified, thrashing and flailing their hands in all directions.

Udadhir noticed that the Pisach King Picasa was using his mind to give orders to the spirits and that he wasn't watching anything else. This was the right time for Udadhir to use the arrow given to him by Rishi Dinkar. Udadhir aimed and fired at Picasa.

The arrow struck him in the back. He screamed in excruciating pain, the arrow burning him. The arrow had the power of the fire from the underworld, which was the only power that could burn the Pisach king. Udadhir wasn't sure if this would end Picasa, so he took one rope arrow and fired it at him. The arrow dragged Picasa to the gates of the underworld, bringing an end to his tyranny. He writhed in pain, and all he could do was lie there as the flames consumed him.

The fight between Amura and Om's team continued. They fired different, powerful weapons at each other. Amura was stronger than Om and all of his team combined, and he was wreaking havoc on them. When the Pisach king burned and screamed, Amura paused and looked at him in astonishment. This was the right time for Om to strike. Om, along with Rishi Dinkar and Sarvin, fired all of their weapons at the Raksas king. Amura was hit and fell to the ground. Before he could get up, the Kimpurusa captain ran and lifted him up in air.

He threw him to the spot where Idha had arranged Rishi Rig Muni's broken staff. As soon as the Raksas king fell inside the circle, the stick encircled him with a blue light. Amura was trapped inside and struggled to come out. Rishi Dinkar and all other rishis came forward and used their powers to form another halo around the blue light.

The night when Rishi Rig Muni and Om were discussing the war, Rishi had told Om everything about the Raksas king. Om already knew that Amura could only be killed by Lord Shiva himself, but he could be contained by a weapon provided by Shiva. Lord Shiva had never killed his disciples, however evil they were. So the only way was to use one of his weapons. Rishi's staff was given to him as a blessing by Lord Shiva, and it was the only weapon that was powerful enough to contain the strengths of the Raksas king. Rishi had already told Om how and when to use the weapon.

The circle of lights around Amura was strong enough to hold him for now, but Om wasn't sure it would prevent him from gaining more power and coming out of it eventually. Om, however, had another plan for him. This time, too, it was Rishi Rig Muni's ideas that guided him.

The Kimpurusas were given the command to carry the Raksas king to the lands of demi-gods and bury him inside Lake Manas. The waters of Lake Manas would prevent Amura from regaining power and would keep him contained for eternity. Om suggested the Kimpurusas should build the highest level of security around the waters where they would bury the Raksas king.

With the Raksas king captured and the Pisach king in hell, the evil army was scattered, and they ran for their lives. The armies of Malla returned to Ogana. All the dead were cremated peacefully that night. It was decided that the next day, the armies of Malla would spread across the kingdom, making sure none of the evil soldiers had taken shelter within the kingdom's walls.

At the Uttara River, the snake Aga didn't allow a single soul to cross the water. Jabala was glad that his idea had worked, but he didn't know how to move the giant back to Lake Manas. Early the next morning, Jabala woke up to see that the rest of the evil armies on the far side of the river had vanished. He ordered the snake to be on the lookout and left for the capital along with Revat and all the men who had joined them later.

Jabala had to learn from King Marut how to take the snake back to where it came from. At the capital, everyone was celebrating the victory. Om looked at the enemy's base from the princess's chambers. The evil army had disappeared, and their camps had burned to ashes.

"Thank you for everything that you have done for me and the kingdom," said Abha. Om smiled back at her and the two said a prayer for all the souls who fought in the war.

The next morning, all the captains assembled in the king's chambers to discuss the future of the kingdom. The fort captains were ordered to return to their respective forts with their soldiers and to work on repairing them. They were also assigned to repair and build new bridges on all the rivers. The city walls were to be reconstructed, and a Gana architect had agreed to stay back and make them stronger. The demi-gods were ready to leave for their journey back home.

The Gandharva King Marut, along with Princess Rati, thanked Om and his team for all that they had done in this battle. King Marut held out both his hands to thank him.

"Before we leave," said the king, "I want to say to you that your skill, resilience, and courage were an ever-present source of encouragement for every virtuous soul on the battlefield, and you inspired everyone in this war against evil."

He embraced Om fondly and said, "You have conquered the hearts of both men and demi-gods alike. If you ever need our help, our gates will always be open. This is all I can say to prove how proud and thankful I am."

Om, at loss for words after King Marut's speech, smiled and embraced him back to express his gratitude, then asked them for a final favor.

King Marut thought he might ask him for his permission to marry his daughter, Rati, as she already liked Om. To his disappointment, Om asked something he would never have dreamt of. "I would like you to give Udadhir back the kingdom of Ganas from the Pisachs and crown him king. He is the only one who has prepared for this fight for more than a hundred years," he said.

The demi-god's captain, Udadhir, agreed when this proposal was put forward.

A troop was arranged for Udadhir to rebuild the Gana Kingdom back to its original beauty. Udadhir looked at Om with hope and gratitude in his eyes and a peaceful smile on his lips.

He moved forward. "I must thank you all for bestowing your faith in me."

Everyone wanted to leave, but King Neera of Malla entreated them, "Please wait for two more days for my daughter's wedding ceremony."

Om looked at the Malla king with surprise, his face lighting up.

King Neera announced, "Princess Abha will marry Om in a grand ceremony tomorrow!"

All of Om's friends congratulated him as Om bowed in front of the king. When he rose, he saw the princess standing next to the Malla king. The journey that Om began had finally come to an end. Peace had finally been restored to the Himalayan Kingdoms... for now.

Who Were the Demi-gods?

Gandharvas were descendants of the sun god and respected by all the other demi-gods. The closest to the gods themselves, they served as messengers to the living. They possessed great powers. Though they looked like very tall men, they could take any form—animals, birds, men, or women. The Gandharvas were crafters of many mighty divine weapons, and creators of a celestial drink called "Soma," a drink that gave strength even to gods. The land of Gandharvas was ruled by their King Marut, along with Princess Rati.

Kimpurusas were half-lion and half-human, with the head and claws of a lion but the body and limbs of a human. The descendants of the god of war, they were the fiercest warriors and killers on the battlefield, with strength comparable to hordes of elephants. A Kimpurusa could shatter a mountain with their bare hands. Their leader was Karvara, a powerful captain.

Kinnars were half-horse and half-human, with the upper torso of a man and the body and legs of a horse. They rode at great speed, and were formidable warriors on the battlefield. They carried a spear in one hand and a shield in the other, and were said to be the most disciplined soldiers. The land of the Kinnars was ruled by their able Queen Kinnari.

Yaksas were spirits who could take any form, living or not. They could be in mountains, trees, or even rivers. Their power was such that they could bend the laws of nature at will. They were also guardians of nature and of the heavenly stones and gems.

Ganas were architects of gods and impressive builders. They were descendants of Indra, god of thunder, and Varuna, god of water. They could build cities in a week. They had built many of the gods' cities and structures, with their own kingdom being the most beautiful kingdom of all. It was said that Ogana, the capital city of Malla, was built by Ganas. Udadhir was their mightiest soldier and captain.

Who Were the Demonic Forces?

Raksas were the most powerful of all the demonic forces. They looked like wild beasts, with long, thick hair covering their entire body. Their King Amura was the strongest of all living beings, and had mastered wielding heavenly weapons. It was also rumored that he could not be killed by any living creature. Not only did he have an army of different demonic forces, but he also had allies in the underworld who would fight for him.

Pisachs were more ghosts that living beings. They were flesh-eating demons. Dark as the night, with bulging veins and protruding red eyes, they were the ugliest of demons, and could control other ghosts and wandering spirits. They spoke their own language, Paisaci. They were ruled by the powerful King Picasa.

The Paksis Kingdom included men who allied with the Raksas. Theirs was the largest kingdom in the Himalayas. King Darad ruled over Paksi, with the help of Raksas, and had captured a vast territory of land. The king considered himself as powerful as the gods themselves, and treated everyone beneath him with contempt.